By Gig Goodloe

MURDER
at the
GOLDEN BEAR
Nightclub

Llumina
Press

Requests for permission to make copies of any part of this work should be mailed to Permissions Department, Llumina Press, 7580 NW 5th Street #16535 Plantation, FL 33318.

ISBN: 978-1-62550-374-9

Dedicated to my two sons Dugan and Travis;

"With enough dedication, perseverance
and fortitude anything is possible."

"Believe in yourself"

***

Thanks to Sandi Graham for moral and technical support.

INTRODUCTION

THE GOLDEN BEAR; the iconic nightclub and restaurant originally established on Main St. in Huntington Beach, California in 1923 was re-opened at its present location at 306 Pacific Coast Highway in June of 1929. Since its opening *the Golden Bear* has presented virtually every top name in the music industry from jazz to folk, to country, swing, big bands, R and B and rock and roll. *The Golden Bear* has always been an intimate club located across from the Huntington Beach pier where the current popular recording stars could fine-tune their performances in a quaint, friendly atmosphere before they venture into the unforgivingly hip chaos of Hollywood and the Sunset Strip.

The Golden Bear is Orange County's premier venue for the brightest stars in the entertainment industry that have graced the well-worn boards of *the Bear's* venerable and iconic stage over its long and illustrious history.

Renowned for its world class cuisine including steak, seafood, and signature Italian pasta dishes, a fabulous array of mixed drinks from a well- staffed bar, and an impressive selection of domestic and imported beer and wine, all served by a friendly and enthusiastic squad of tanned and toned beach bunnies. *The Golden Bear* is a romantic getaway on the shores of the beautiful blue Pacific, reminiscent of those nostalgic days of yester-year and heady days of 'The Golden Era of Entertainment.'

The Golden Bear holds a special place in the hearts of all the wonderful entertainers who have graced the stage over the years, as well as those who have experienced the warmth and nostalgic romance that the venerable and iconic nightclub has presented to its life-long friends and family for generations. There will never be another nightclub with the spirit, energy, and soul one experiences within the *Golden Bear*. There will never be another *Golden Bear.*

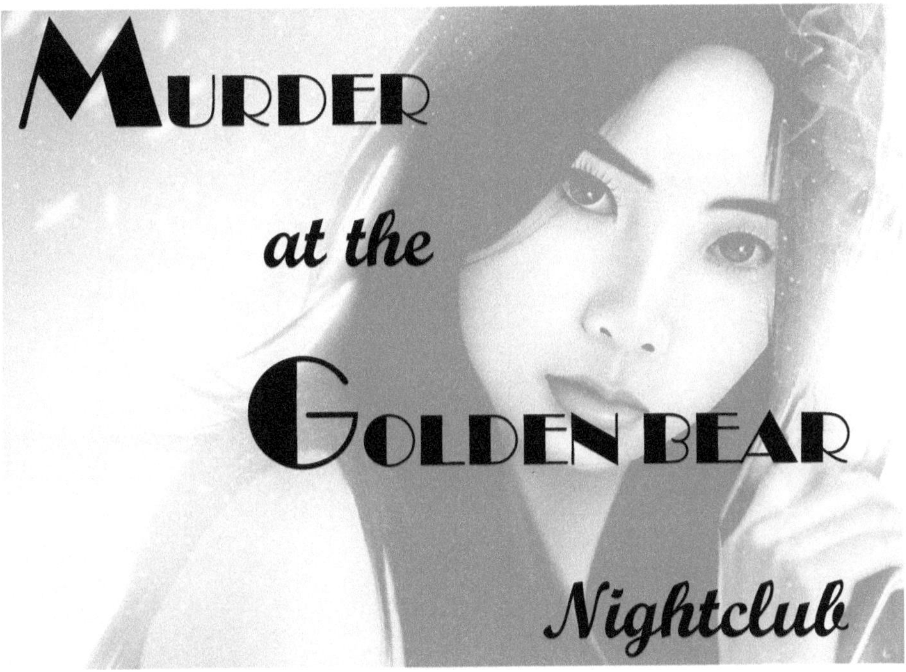
MURDER
at the
GOLDEN BEAR
Nightclub

Chapter One

Day 1

The glistening wake disappeared into the purple silhouette of Catalina Island against golden radiance of setting sun. I took the last boat of the day from Avalon with an ETA on Balboa Island at dusk. It had been a long time since I had crossed the channel and re-entered the brown grunge of mainland haze. I had no desire to submerge myself within the quagmire of back-street slime-balls that squirm along the mean underbelly of L.A.'s neon streets. I was not eagerly anticipating the exhilaration of the chase, or the thrill of the kill.

I had become comfortable, content, and perhaps even complacent with my current situation. Once I had organized the operational flow with the appropriate checks and balances in place, and arranged all the ducks into an efficiently functioning row, the Casino now runs smoothly with the minimum of oversight or micro-management required. "Ease of operation" was my keystone modus operandi.

Rita Rigney, the younger of the two island princesses and I enjoy a familiar intimate relationship that seems free of jealousy, resentment or rejection, in an exotic location that is 'pert near paradise' as the tourist travel brochures proudly proclaim. I didn't want to go. I knew that I shouldn't go. But as before, I'm going just the same. And as before, I some-how knew that the late night call from an old friend was about to change my life once again.

The lingering shafts of setting sun began to surrender to the long shadows of dusk and the twinkling lights of Balboa Island. Balboa

Island is the enriched enclave of the beautifully tanned people, with their million dollar mansions and ridiculously ostentatious mega yachts nestled within luxurious forest of gleaming white masts, a mere stones-throw across a narrow channel from Newport Beach.

Balboa Island provides a secluded upscale beach community to the well-healed, without the crowded, trendy, and pretentious bullshit of Malibu or Marina Del Rey. Many movie people call Balboa their home. The Duke, John Wayne raises his family here. Howard Duff and Ida Lupino live here, as well as 'rat pack' party girl Angie Dickenson and B-movie blonde bomb shell sexpot Mamie van Doren. Mamie even owns a high-end European antique boutique in Newport's downtown Shopping Center.

Precious Goodlay waited seductively on the pier like a fashion model on a cover shoot. Tall, toned and tanned with gorgeously long legs that go all the way up to a magnificent protrusion of all-girl ass and beautifully rounded hips, deliciously contained within mint green short shorts, with firm abs, and proud and perky breasts that seemed intent on escaping over confinement of miniscule pink tank top. The longest, blondest long blonde hair and biggest, bluest big blue eyes you can imagine, and the biggest brightest smile of a mythical Norwegian goddess. Precious Goodlay, my secretary- extraordinaire', was the quintessential prototype for the original Barbie Doll.

I grabbed my valise and crossed the gangway to the small pier where I gathered her in with warm embrace and passionate kisses that must have given the impression to the uninformed that we were long lost lovers.

She looked me up and down, then down and up with obvious approval. "Wow Travis, judging by that deep-water tan, those few extra muscles, the sun-streaked tousle of hair, and that shit-eating grin on your face, I'd say some promiscuous little island girl is taking very good care of you." She was right of course, Precious Goodlay is very perceptive.

We casually strolled through the small but bright and energetic little carnival that is a permanent attraction here on the island. The centerpiece of which is the whirling calliope driven carousel that goes up and down and round and round. There were brightly painted ponies, elephants and giraffes, and lions, tigers, and bears, oh my! There were hot dogs, cotton candy and popcorn. Dart throws, dime tosses and little bowls of gold fish. There were pyramids of led milk bottles to be toppled by powerful softball throws, and stuffed animal prizes of every size and color. Just about everything one would find along the coast at Venice Beach, Pacific Ocean Park, or the Long Beach Pike.....only smaller, cleaner, and with fewer weirdoes.

We exited the carnival through a lush botanical garden onto a wide pebbled path and across a short bridge, through a security gate and onto the pristine immaculately manicured estate of *the Pacific Bay Luxury Apartments*.....palm trees, swimming pools, movie stars.

The lobby paid homage to South Beach Miami with its bright décor of turquoise, pink and white. Lots of terra cotta tile, potted palms and pink flamingos. Precious pushed the penthouse button in the elevator and we began a smooth quiet ascent to the tenth floor.

Once the elevator cleared the lobby the remainder of the ascending journey was an astonishing rise clinging to the exterior of the gleaming white tower that afforded a spectacular view of the sparkling sandy shore and the rambunctious blue pacific from Pacific Palisades to the north all the way to Dana Point to the south, and of course, resting serenely upon the misty horizon, Santa Catalina. I miss her already.

The elevator came to a smooth quiet stop and the penthouse light on the elevator panel illuminated. She inserted her perforated card into the key pad slot, punched-in a series of numbers and the elevator doors silently parted. We stepped into a spacious and elegantly decorated suite in the same turquoise, pink and white as was the lobby far, far below. There were very high ceilings, spritely spinning fans, magnificent paintings and impressive life-size statuary. The pacific side of the immense room was floor to ceiling sheets of thick plate glass that opened onto a veranda that extended along the front of the penthouse and around to a kidney shaped pool and surrounding deck enclosed within glass-panel wind shears.

On the interior wall, opposite the wall of glass, was an immense, colorful mural of an underwater seascape painted by a talented entrepreneurial young artist that signed his impressive work with the name 'Wayland.' He has quickly become famous for his "Wayland Walls" that festoon blank walls of tall buildings throughout southern California and Hawaii with magnificent renditions of breeching whales, leaping dolphins and flying fish. Just such a mural covers the tall southern side of the *Pacific Bay Luxury Apartments* as well.

"Make us a drink while I dress for dinner," she said, strolling off and disappearing somewhere within her immense gleaming palace of pink and green. I found the bar with little difficulty and prepared twin vodka martinis. I strolled out onto the veranda and gazed out into the dark void of Pacific Ocean and the twinkling lights of Avalon.

Precious joined me on the veranda only half dressed in half- slip, half-bra, and the top half of her gorgeous breasts proudly poised and sporting deep, dark, delicious Coppertone tan. She took a sip of her crystalline concoction, leaned softly on the veranda rail, and looked deep into my eyes.

"Travis, I don't want to flog a dead horse, and I'm not talking about your questionable sexual exploits," she said with a giggle. "But I must express to you my strong feelings against your participation in this investigation. It's an open murder case currently being strenuously investigated by HBPD. You know very well that they do not appreciate clod-hopping private dicks schlepping around in an active investigation. Besides Travis, while the deep-water tan and the extra toned- up pounds are impressive, sexy, and look fantastic on you, I feel that your senses have dulled, your reflexes have slowed, and you have become complacent, calm, and therefore instinctively compromised. Those are traits that have never been apparent with you before and could result in getting you killed. Casino manager is a good fit for you at this time in your life. Why fuck it up? Let one of the young guns handle this. That is for which they have been trained and tested in the field. I know Papa Nikos will be tremendously relieved now that you are on the case, but once he has been sufficiently reassured, please bring in the young bloods to do the hard slogging and heavy lifting. Relegate your participation to logistics coordination and morale support."

She put her drink down and moved close to me. She cradled my face softly in her hands, pressed firmly against me and looked deep into my eyes. "Let's face it lover boy, we're getting too old for this shit. It's a young guns game now. Life is too short and we're not getting any younger. For shit sakes Travis, you're lucky you made it this far. Be satisfied, relax and enjoy life. "

She had the bright shiny T-Bird whipping north along Coast Highway. It was a two-seat sports car with a hard-top convertible including port holes, continental kit, white side-wall tires and spinner hubcaps. It was robin's egg blue with blue and white Naga-hide interior stripped from the wild Naga-beast stalking the teaming jungles of Motor City. Visions of Ed "Kooky" Burns and Cricket Muldoon snapping our fingers to the T.V. theme for *"77 Sunset Strip."*

"Travis, I know you're bound and determined to get involved with this case and try to help-out Papa Nikos, but I must remind you that this is a current on-going investigation by HBPD and the Orange County Sherriff's Department. I have no doubt that it will expand into Hollywood, the Strip, and LAPD. Are you sure you want to open that can of worms? Do you really think you're still up-to-the-task? You've been living the cushy champagne and caviar playboy lifestyle of Avalon Casino Manager and resident Island 'bon vivant'. I can tell by the deep salt-water tan, sun-streaked hair and a few extra pounds of toned muscle that some enthusiastic and forgiving young island girl, or knowing you as I do, a bevy of young island girls are taking very good care of you. Why worry, be happy."

We passed *The Golden Bear* on the right and the pier on the left. We continued north down the mesa and the long stretch of road with Tin Can beach on the left and the wetlands estuary on the right. At the top of the hill beyond the estuary was the palm covered paradise where Raven and I enjoyed an enchanting summer between the wars. Probably the best summer of my life. After crossing Warner Avenue into the shoreline enclave of ramshackle beach bungalows known as Sunset Beach she pulled into the parking lot of *Sam's Seafood*, the iconic eatery tucked between the hamlet of Surfside and the narrow canal that separates it from the eccentrically quaint and bohemian island of scattered and battered bungalows and eclectic flotilla of fishing a sailing boats, that would eventually become '*Huntington Harbor*; Miami Beach of the west' with its endless white forest of gleaming yacht masts and multi-million dollar mansions. "All I ask is that once you have calmed Papa Nikos, you convince him to allow the young guns at the agency to take over. That's what they're trained for after all."

Sam's Seafood had subtle lighting, plush comfortable booths and a quiet, romantic atmosphere. I ordered a vodka martini, a Mahi Tai for Precious, and oysters on the half shell for hors d'oeuvres'. We got caught-up on old news over drinks and oysters.

When *Sam*'s famous sea food platter arrived I allowed for introductory indulgence before explaining the late night call from a very distressed George Nikos 'Papa' Pappadopolis. "Papa Nikos, long time proprietor of the iconic *Golden Bear Night Club and Restaurant*, was an old friend from the days between the wars when I flew smuggled booze and black market small arms from Catalina to the mainland. His phone call was a hysterical and confusing jumble of scattered outbursts. Papa Nikos was extremely distraught and begging me to come help. I couldn't turn him down."

"The limited amount of useful information I was able to discern, was that the body of an upscale call- girl had been discovered in the dumpster in the alley behind *the Golden Bear*. HBPD is aggressively investigating it as a homicide. Papa Nikos is scared to death and doesn't know where to turn or what to do."

Precious listened intently while indulging in crab and lobster fest. She asked several pertinent questions for which I had no answers at present. We concluded our meal and had the little blue T-bird headed south on Coast Highway back toward *the Golden Bear*. We *passed Mother's Biker Bar and Grill* on the right, just beyond *Woody's market*, and the *New England Live Lobster House* on the left. We crossed Warner Avenue, retraced our path between the wetland estuary and Tin Can beach, then up the mesa and the flat stretch of road along the bluffs teaming with churning oil wells and tall derricks.

She drove passed the pier, made a u turn at Third Street and parked at the curb in front of *the Bear*. The marque out front proudly announced tonight's entertainment to be Teri 'Cupcake' O'Hara, risqué, adult comedy recording artist, singing her current album favorites, such as; " Get off the table Mable, that quarter is for a beer ", "He likes to nibble on my cupcakes," and "Bounce your boobies", with opening act Alan Sherman of "Camp Granada" fame. Tomorrow night to be mob favorite, crooner Vic Damone, with special guest comedian Shecky Green, and the following night to be Julie London with newcomer comedian Bob Newhart.

Precious popped the trunk lid so that I could retrieve my valise. We held each other close and kissed long and hard. She said that she would be in the office early tomorrow to meet with her niece Precocious, secretary trainee and also Barbie Doll delicious, to begin assembling the personnel required to take-over the investigation once I had calmed Papa Nikos. Before she left, Precious felt compelled to make one last pitch to persuade me to return to my island paradise before I get myself killed. (I get it; dually noted already.)

I watched as she pulled from the curb and make a u turn at the pier. She blew me a kiss as she went by heading south back toward Balboa. Seems like I've experienced that same heavenly apparition somewhere in my lecherous past; a mysterious blonde bombshell driving a baby blue T-bird? (Makes you wanna' go hmmmm?)

I gathered my bag and walked up to the ticket window. "Orale' Niño'!,Que' paso baby?" I recognized that haunting little hottie's voice...........a naughty nurse from my sordid past. It was Anita Menage', Puerto Rican and French Creole sexpot that arrived on the west coast by way of New Orleans, New York and Miami. Nita is a red hot chili pepper. Spicy and feisty, a spontaneously combustible little fire cracker.

I first met Nita many moons ago when she was a young dental hygienist fresh out of dental school. She would introduce herself as 'Nurse Nita, oral specialist.' A few years later she acquired an RN certification and when asked what she did, she would extend her hand just below waist level and mockingly squeeze as if testing the firmness of ripe fruit. "I'm Nurse Nita, Herniator for the FBI."

She rushed into my arms in the lobby adjacent to the ticket office and smothered me with passionate kisses. Warm breath, smoldering kisses, the freshness of all-girl parts pressed firmly against the awakening of all-boy parts. Yes, I remember Anita Menage'. I remember a scorching spit-fire. She's singed into my mind as from a searing branding iron.

"Who's the Scandinavian Barbie Doll in the baby blue T-bird? Trophy- wife? Arm candy? Or just a deliciously deceptive decoy?" she asked coyly with a wicked little smile. "She's my niece," I replied with my own wicked little smile. Nita batted her long lovely lashes and put an index finger to her now pouty lip. "Niece, nurse, delicious deception, I thought I was the only one?" "You are my dear, the only one of many," I replied.

Just then Devin, the floor manager, appeared from the main room, "Dugan my friend, good to see you again." Devin had short curly hair and a Gilbert Roland pencil mustache. He wore some kind if white puffy pirate shirt with a bolero waist jacket and toreador pants. The Patten-leather ballerina inspired slippers flamboyantly completed the 'gay caballero' persona he was so flagrantly trying to achieve. I think he thought that he was Sal Mineo, only taller. (I predict that Devin will

8

fall victim to the predominantly male affliction peculiar to the genital region, causation to be repetitious, enthusiastic gyrations of the pelvic area within the confines of tight sweaty toreador dance pants. This irritating affliction shall be known as 'Disco Balls'..........Whatever those are?)

Devin smiled and went into the ticket office to retrieve the cash drawer. Nita put her arms around my neck and whispered, "wait for me Niño'. I have to close-out my cash drawer, and then we can go for a drink and get caught up." Devin emerged with the cash drawer in hand. He and Nita went through the main room and the café doors that led backstage.

I leaned against the door frame and watched the conclusion of the show. The sign above the door said the room capacity was 157. I estimated there were several more than that being comfortably accommodated, two shows a night, every night.

The Golden Bear was an intimate little club that proudly presented top rate entertainment, renowned cuisine, an impressive array of exotic mixed drinks and an extensive list of fine wines and beer. All served happily by tanned, comely little waitresses with big smiles, big breasts, and big ambitions.

Entry to *the Golden Bear* was through the lobby door into an entry vestibule where tickets were taken, I.D.'s were checked for the questionably-young, and unobtrusive pat-downs for the questionably moral. There was a hat and coat check kiosk in the corner and a fire door that opened into the parking lot. The show room consisted of general seating at intimate candle lit tables on the main floor, surrounded against the walls by private alcoves on raised platforms with wrought iron bannisters. The stage was against the back wall, with a small dance floor, and café doors that led back-stage to the talent dressing rooms, the kitchen, the bar, and Papa Nikos' office. Exiting the showroom was through double doors that opened onto the sidewalk out front.

A rowdy crowd of oil-field Okies were causing a ruckus in the corner over a gentleman and his niece, or cousin, or financially arranged date. I whipped- out my Popeil pocket P.I. pin light and gave Lumpy Klopshinski, the diplomat of the head-bashing bounce staff, a quick flash, then over to the hub-bub in the corner. Lumpy was a big blonde college kid with a happy disposition and a big smile that resembled a '56 Buick's front grill. If 'Lumpy' was unsuccessful in defusing the situation, then he would simply point-out the backstage bouncer Tommy Manson, scowling stage right, or over to Big Dick Buttkiss, (no relation to the Chicago Bears Hall of Fame Line-backer), at the double door exit. Big Dick was a six-foot- five, three-hundred pound leather clad long-haired bearded biker. Big Dick was a real crowd pleaser. Tommy Manson on the other hand was small, wiry, and kinda' scary looking. He had a menacing, almost hypnotic stare and a maniacal grin that sent shivers down your spine. He was scruffy and scrappy and when he spoke, you got a definite sense that there was something wrong with that boy.

Having been ineffectual in calming the drunken dust bowl bunk-buddies, the mercenary head-bashers were summoned. The entire group was unceremoniously moved toward the vestibule doorway where I currently lingered holding up the door frame. I backed-off to the far corner next to the coat check kiosk to allow unobstructed access to the parking lot fire door. The crowd moved along in mass until the first idiot backed through the vestibule entry decided to grab the door frame and bring the whole parade to a screeching halt. The tight quarters made for a lot of pushing and shoving but very little progress. I walked up behind the big idiot that was clogging the flow and gave him a swift kick to his future inbreds. He released his grip on the door frame, re-gripped his screaming relatives, fell back into my waiting headlock and got dragged across the vestibule floor to the parking lot fire door. I kicked the bar across the door and it flew open. The whole bunch spilled out onto the parking lot on top of me in a big dog pile. Not realizing that I was still out there with that pack of pissed-off drunken shit-kickers, the bouncers slammed the door behind us. (Oh this could get real shitty for me real quick.)

I tried to laugh it off as if I were just swept up with the rest of the rowdy bunch that got tossed. "Well that was pretty fuckin' rude," I said as I dusted myself off and attempted to casually walk away. "I think my girlfriend is still in there." I attempted to get around the corner of the building and in the front door before they realized who I was............ didn't work-out too well.

The big clod-hopper that I had cold-cocked throttled and tossed, grabbed the back of my collar. I delivered the evening's second kick-start to his ancestral marble bag. He face planted onto the pavement like a swollen sack of throbbing cocoanuts. A crouching leg-sweep took the second redneck down hard on the back of his head with the mushy sound of a dropped watermelon.

I caught the next in-coming dip-stick by his throat. I was firmly centered so his forward momentum made it easy for me to lift him off the ground as he rushed forward and then body-slam him hard down onto the trunk lid of a parked car. I throttled him with my left and jack hammered his face with my right. Suddenly the car started and began to pull away. We slid off the back, his head bouncing off the rear bumper before a double dribble slam dunk onto the asphalt. The rest were on me like a pack of rabid jackals.

Suddenly the ear-shattering roar of screaming engine and the smoke-billowing squeal of raging tires ripped through the air. The red and white convertible raced across the parking lot scattering the frantic miscreants with an end-swapping skidding half-circle amid a huge billowing cloud of burning rubber. "Jump in Niño'!" I performed a flawless high-jump over the door that Olympic champion and *Wheaties* cereal box cover boy Bob Richards would be proud of, and stuck the landing firmly into the bucket seat.

She mashed the go peddle, the tack red lined, the engine screamed, she dumped the clutch and the rip-snorting red and white streak scratched out a layer of asphalt, screamed across the parking lot and leapt off the curb onto Coast Highway heading north at high speed. She ripped through the gears like she was 'Big Daddy Don Garlits'.

She glanced over to me with wide eyes and a wider grin. She threw her head back with the wind whipping her long mane of dark hair and laughed out loud. She had a wicked little twinkle in her eye. She loved this kinda' shit………..it was all part of her charm.

Two down-shifts, a quick right turn at 10th street, a block and a half on the right at the only street light on the block, she turned into the driveway next to a quaint little clad board beach bungalow. I got out and opened the barn doors of the single car garage. Lurking behind the garage, in silhouette against the pale yellow moon, the great steel mosquito relentlessly probes the very core of mother earth. Up and down, up and down, the great beast eternally sucks the marrow from the bones of our long ago fallen ancestors. We closed the garage doors then walked along the side of the cottage to the front porch.

A small covered porch extended across the front of the little house and was lovingly embraced by a massive Hibiscus that over time had grown into an impressively intertwined tree that engulfed the porch roof entirely and spilled forth over all roof edges with glorious displays of huge red flutes with bright yellow stamen. The sweet fragrance was enchanting. Inside, the comforting aroma of fresh mown grass wafted mystically from thick woven grass mats that covered the living room floor wall to wall. It was a neat and clean two bedroom beach bungalow typical for the neighborhood of retired long-time beach people, hard- working middle class oil field workers, a spattering of college kids, and a rising tide of unambitious bushy-haired surfers and beach bums.

"Come into the bathroom Niño'. Let me examine that hard-body for wounds." I stared into the mirror at a knuckled-up tough guy that seemed to have lost some of the spark that he once possessed. He no longer craved the excitement of the chase or the thrill of the kill. He looked tired and rough around the edges. "Oh my Mijo'! Oh Mijo' my!" she exclaimed while removing my clothing. She placed her hands softly on my chest, then gently, slowly caressed my entire body top to bottom, front to back and back to front. "Damn Niño', somebody has been taking very good care of you baby. I'm impressed. Bulging muscles in all the right places, full-body salt-water tan, and meticulous man-scaping. Hot damn Niño', I guess I can't really justify calling you Niño' anymore can I? I don't see any serious wounds. You have minor abrasions on your left cheek bone, both knees and both palms. I've seen a lot worse on you before Macho Man. Jump in the shower baby, and then come to mama. Nita love you long time G.I.", she purred.

Chapter Two

Day 2

I awoke to the familiar sound of gently breaking waves rushing up the smooth sandy beach and the receding hiss as they retreat back to the sea. I found my B.V.D.s on the floor on my way into the kitchen and managed to find all the necessary internal parts for the coffee pot in the dish rack as well as the coffee in a clearly marked canister. I assembled the internal parts, added the aromatic ingredients, enough water to brew a soothing morning concoction, and placed it on the stove.

I lit a cigarette, opened the front door and the screen, and stepped out onto the porch. There was still a chill in the air but the morning haze had cleared and the golden radiance of sunrise announced the beginnings of a glorious day. As I stood leaning against the corner post gazing out to sea with Catalina barely visible upon the grey horizon, I became aware of hushed giggling behind me. I turned to see the first bus load of pre-pubescent bubbly bouncy little nymphets on their way to summer vacation's sandy romps and adolescent adventures. I retreated through the screen door with a smile and a shameful stirring within B.V.D.'s. I fondly remember summer days of my well spent youth plying the early morning surf for that perfect wave and the afternoon's new arrivals of fresh young sand bunnies quivering with anticipation of amorous adventures with the local beach boys. Life was a beach and totally bitchin' dude.

The last burst of boiling java leapt into the glass cap on the pot then quietly settled. Nita, wrapped in thin white silk robe, joined me on the porch for the morning's first pick-me-up, then joined me in the shower for another.................and then another.

We strolled the few palm covered blocks to main street then turned toward the pier for half a block, to my old haunt, ' *The Sugar Shack.*' *The Sugar Shack* was owned by the Williams family and operated by the five spirited and vivacious young daughters. The surf board rack out front was as full as the bike rack or the one for fishing poles. The floor was constantly covered in a thin layer of beach sand, and you could always count on a delicious breakfast, lunch, or dinner served by an effervescent and lovely youngster with a bright and beautiful smile. The girls wore red, white, or blue horizontal striped knit tops and white shorts, white sneakers and sailor's cap. I received group hugs and kisses and got caught-up on the past and current status of all the sisters; older sister prego, another getting married. Two graduations; one college, one high school, and the youngest competing in the up-coming Huntington Beach surf championships. 'They all were coming to visit me in Catalina.'

The hot buzz around town was of course the dead girl found in the dumpster behind *the Bear*. The news spread faster than a case of the clap in a cow- town cat- house.

Nita and I finished our breakfast, bid aloha to the girls, and made our way down Main Street toward the *Golden Bear*. She was to open the ticket window and begin taking phone reservations for tonight's headliner and mob favorite, crooner Vic Damone and his opening act comic Shecky Green.

Presumably a few wise guys in the audience tonight, but otherwise a well behaved upscale crowd. There will be chaotic energy out front, the paparazzi swarming in flash bulb frenzy with each limo arrival, in stark contrast to the romance, elegance, and glamour within.

We crossed to the south side of the street and as we passed Dewey Weber's Surfboard shop, we heard a voice from above. "Hey Nita, where did you snag that hard body stud muffin you're with?" We looked up to the second floor window of the *'Wild Oats'* building, where the lovely Mona Loud leaned out with a big smile and bigger tits, offering a warm welcome to an old friend.

Mona Loud is a tall statuesque redhead with a long set of shapely gams, a pouty taut butt, and a perky pair of stunning sweater puppets that she proudly displays in an impressive collection of designer gowns. Mona was married to a high-flying Manhattan Beach real estate entrepreneur who was killed several years ago in a tragic private plane crash in the desert near Palm Springs.

After being sued by the heirs of the client in the plane's passenger seat, and having all the creditors call in their loans after her husband's death, Mona was left with a much depleted bank account and this second floor row of apartments above Main Street. She provides a home for wayward women and an upscale exclusive social club and escort service for well-healed L.A and Orange County Business moguls and power brokers.

I kept a corner apartment at Mona's for the occasional sojourn to the area, and it doubled as a safe-house for me or the young bloods at the agency who may be working a case in the southern beach areas. Nita kissed me on the cheek and headed for *the Bear*. She blew me another kiss as she disappeared around the corner of the building.

Mona pushed the buzzer upstairs and the deadbolt on the ornate glass door downstairs at the sidewalk entrance clicked open. I climbed the wide enclosed stairway to the center of a large foyer with plush wall to wall carpet and decorated with rich Victorian parlor furnishings. Long velvet couches and overstuffed chairs, Tiffany lamps, chandeliers and wall sconces. To the right of the foyer landing was the bar and lounge that offered a magnificent view of the wide white beach, the entire length of the pier, the deep blue Pacific and of course, ever beckoning from the distant horizon, Catalina.

The clients were greeted in the foyer by their lovely and charming escorts for the evening, and then the date would progress into the lounge where the party goers gathered and the festivities would begin. At some point the financially arranged romance would adjourn to attend the opening of the opera, charity ball, the theatre, or perhaps other top-drawer social functions. Short term romances would move their respective courtships to one of the two available rooms adjoining the foyer overlooking Main Street.

Between the lounge entry and the two short term romance rooms overlooking Main Street is the door to my room. It is a comfortable size corner studio with private bath and large closet area. Two windows looked out over the same white beach, the pier, and the blue pacific as does the lounge window. The other two windows overlook Main Street, and on the far side of the center stairwell are the two rooms currently occupied by the Agrande' sisters, Alana and Swallow. (I don't think Swallow was named after the little birds that come back to Capistrano..... But I digress.) Next to their rooms was the hall entry that led to a large Kitchen and dining area, with the bath at the end of the hall. Across the hall was Mona's private residence; a large, one- bedroom apartment with private bath. It was a neat and clean well- run set-up. Mona had a deal with the Sheraton Hotel, south on Coast highway, where lodging accommodations would be provided for her escorts and their dates post opera, or theatre, or charity ball. Mona operated the classiest, high-end, high-priced escort service in Orange County.

Mona's agency rivaled anything Brentwood, Bel Air, or Beverly Hills had to offer. Her portfolio included cover girls, fashion models, and motion picture actresses. Mona's girls were well educated, articulate, and spectacular arm-candy or trophy dates for any mega-wealthy record producer, movie mogul, or 'Fortune 500' corporate CEO. Did I mention that every one of Mona's girls were drop-dead gorgeous?

Mona waited at the top of the stairs with a welcoming smile and silhouette cast through pink negligee from the windows behind her, leaving little to the imagination. Didn't matter, I couldn't have imagined her any more stunning or alluring than she actually was.

I reached the top of the stairs where we embraced and kissed long and hard. Or maybe that better describes what I was erecting in the southern regions of my equatorial fun-zone, which she acknowledged with a wink and a smile. "Oh my, Travis, still the same randy horn-dog we've come to know and love I see or I feel, as it were," she said with a boisterous joyful laugh. "Come with me I have a surprise for you in the lounge." She took my hand and led me into the lounge where Alana and Swallow waited with anticipation in front of the large picture window which cast soft light through baby-doll peignoirs', creating spectacular silhouettes of their own. They leapt upon me and smothered me with giggly hugs and kisses. They seemed genuinely happy to see me again. The feeling was mutual.

The Agrande' sisters were like night and day. They couldn't have been more different. Swallow had Mediterranean features; olive skin, large brown eyes and long dark hair. All her girl parts were stunning and spectacular, unyieldingly firm, pouty and proudly protruding from all the right places.

Alana on the other hand, was fair skinned, had big blue eyes and strawberry blonde hair. Her parts were spectacular as well, only soft, rounded, delicate and petite. The Agrande' sisters and I have enjoyed some wonderfully erotic escapades in the past, individually and as a grope..........I mean group.

We spent a fair portion of the morning over coffee, getting caught-up on old news and current events. I eventually ventured cautiously to ask a few questions about the Asian girl found in the dumpster, which was clearly visible from where we now sat.

The sisters were visibly upset and understandably nervous about their safety. Mona said that they hadn't heard anything new or different than anyone else in town knew. "HBPD is keeping a tight lid on this. They're keeping the investigation close-to-the-vest and vigorously intimidating everyone they've interrogated thus far to keep their mouths shut to the newspaper reporters or anyone else snooping around where they don't belong." Mona went on to say that the atmosphere in town had changed. There was a palpable tension in town and the attitude of the entire police force became touchy, defensive, and seemed to have closed ranks so to speak.

I thanked Mona for the information and for her insight. She always had her finger on the pulse of the city, as well as a number of her high echelon clients found between the sheets and within the pages of her little black book. Politicians, police officials, bankers, financiers, corporate CEO's and gangland mobsters; lots of interesting pillow talk between these hallowed walls, many naked bodies running up and down the halls. Great pinnacles of power and she had them by the balls. Mona is a great source of the juiciest, most scandalous of information, and a great lay too.

I gazed out of the picture window that seemed to be sealed with a sheet of thin plastic that produced a mirror-like reflection on the outside, yet provided an unobstructed view from within. Mona informed me that it was one of her brainiac clients that worked for the *'DuPont'* Corporation who developed the thin plastic material she calls *'Mylar'*. She apparently is also responsible for something called *'Postems'* and *'Velcro'*. (Whatever those are?) I watched from on high as Papa Nikos arrived in his weird little French Simca Sport Coupe' automobile, and entered through the rear door of *the Bear.*

Mona handed me a key to the front door downstairs and one to my corner studio. Where she had concealed those keys within transparent wardrobe remains a mystery. I kissed Mona and the Agrande' sisters adieu, descended the stairs to the sidewalk out front, walked around the corner and down the alley to the *Bear.*

I found Papa Nikos in his office sorting through an enormous pile of paper work on his desk. He smiled wide and I could see a sense of relief in his eyes. He came from behind the desk, gave me a big bear hug and a kiss on both cheeks. "Oh Travis, my friend I am so glad that you have finally arrived. I feel much better now that you are here. I have been unable to concentrate on anything, as you can tell by the deplorable condition of my desk."

Papa Nikos is a happy-go-lucky little Greek in his early sixties, with a salt and pepper thick head of hair and a big bushy mustache to match. He has a twinkle in his eye, a big wide smile and an even bigger heart. His door is always open and he offers a helping hand for anyone in need. He is a happy little guy with a great demeanor and a wonderful outlook on life. I envy his contentment.

Daughter Caroline arrived and rushed to give me a big hug and kiss. Caroline is a beautiful dark Greek goddess with the same sparkle in her eyes as her dad. She is in her early thirties and perhaps a few pounds overweight. But she is a tall beauty that carries it very well in all the right places. She reminds me of a gypsy enchantress.

Caroline is in charge of the kitchen, the bar, waitresses, cooks and bar tenders. Papa Nikos booked talent, paid the bills, managed the ticket reservation office and security staff. It was a smooth operation and Papa Nikos made a concerted effort to keep everybody happy, from the staff to the talent, vendors and first and foremost the guests. An evening at *the Golden Bear* is enchanting, exciting, and always entertaining. The food is great, the booze top-notch, as is the entertainment and everyone always has an unforgettable night at *the Bear*, be you guest, talent or staff.

I gingerly began to ask a few questions regarding the ongoing investigation for which I was originally summoned. Neither Papa Nikos nor Caroline had any more information than did anyone else in town. I sensed that it made him uncomfortable to talk about, so I suggested that he give me the grand tour of his recent renovations and upgrades.

Across the large backstage area from Papa's office and next to the employee's bathroom was an innocuous broom closet door with a curious sliding peep-hole. He unlocked the door and we stepped onto a small stairwell landing. To the left the stairs went up to the attic. To the right they went down to the basement. Upstairs we came to another door with peep-hole. Through that door was Papa's book-making operation. There was a long table in the middle of the room lined with a bank of telephones and enough chairs to accommodate a dozen operators. The walls were covered in black boards and under the black boards were numerous wire service ticker-tape machines. Papa explained, to keep everybody happy, that he subscribes to L.A. Jewish mob boss Mickey Cohen's *Continental Wire service* for instantaneous sports results from the east coast venues, and buys his booze from L.A.'s Italian mob boss Jack Dragna's Chicago affiliated outfit. Most of Papa's action however came from the local west coast pony tracks like *Hollywood Park, Los Alamitos, Santa Anita* and *Del Mar.*

The room was empty, the phones were silent, the black boards wiped clean, and the ticker–tape machines sat quiet. Papa Nikos had shut down the bookie operation, as well as the intimate, invitation only gambling venue located in the basement. The subterranean gaming room was nearly as spacious as the night club above, carpeted in deep plush pile, furnished with over-stuffed soft leather, and decorated with lush, yet tasteful appointments. There were roulette wheels, baccarat, craps, and poker tables, as well as an impressive array of shiny, glimmering slot machines that lined the dark mahogany walls. The ornately carved mahogany bar was well stocked with fine wines and distilled liquors from around the civilized world.

I had to smile when I looked across the room and saw the arched brick façade camouflaged by the potted palm against the wall. In the old days when I flew smuggled Canadian Whiskey from Catalina across the channel, off-load onto a stake bed truck at *Meadow Lark airport*, then drive through the oil fields in the dark to the heavy equipment repair garage on the corner of 3rd Street and PCH and unload into the basement. They service the undercarriage, exhaust, and suspension systems on drilling rigs and other heavy equipment by way of a pit in the floor with access from the basement. On the back wall of the basement was an arched brick façade camouflaged by an innocuous potted palm identical to the one in the basement gambling parlor of the *Bear.* When slid to the side along the wall on tracks in the floor, the façade opens into a long tunnel under the vacant lot adjoining the equipment repair garage and *the Golden Bear.* From the garage basement the illicit cargo was then stored in the tunnel until it's extraction for use on the *Golden Bear* side. It was a pretty sweet set-up, but we were under constant pressure from the dis-jointed L.A. mafia thugs, either by not-so-subtle intimidation to buy bootleg hooch from them, or by way of out- right brute force truck hijacking in the darkness of the oil fields between *Meadow Lark airp*ort and *the Golden Bear*. Fortunately for us the current crop of mono-browed knuckle dragging troglodytes they sent to do the job got their asses handed to them every time they showed up and never got a drop of any cargo I ever shot-gunned.

Papa Nikos unlocked the façade and slid it open. He obviously was still utilizing the tunnel to store his inventory. Cases of hard liquor were stacked along the wall on one side and fine wines along the other. The brick tunnel made for an excellent wine cellar as well as an emergency escape route for the basement gamers should the local vice squad decide to raid the joint. I naturally assumed that there was plenty of graft going to the right badges to avoid such occurrences.

We returned upstairs amidst the hustle and bustle of the fruits, vegetables and the bakery trucks daily deliveries. Papa Nikos was anxious to show me the improvements he made in the show room. He renovated the room including new state of the art equipment in the sound and lighting booth at the front of the room above the ticket office. He was most proud of the new raised dining areas along the walls and across the front of the room, separated from the main floor dining by way of raised flooring, black wrought iron banisters and subtle lighting appointments.

Nita opened the door and leaned out of the ticket office to inform Papa Nikos that a Mr. Mickey Cohen, *'Haberdasher to the Hollywood Stars'*, was on the phone. Papa gave me a curious smile and excused himself to take the call in the privacy of his office. Nita propped open the front entry door as well as the fire exit door to the parking lot allowing the fresh sea breeze to blow through the building removing the stale odor of alcohol, cigarette smoke, and cheap perfume. She followed with a casual stroll about the main room spraying an industrial size container of an aerosol propellant called 'After You've Gone.'

We stepped out onto the sidewalk in front. I lit a cigarette for each of us, leaned back against the building and enjoyed the warm afternoon sun and the calm ocean breeze. It was a bright, beautiful day and Catalina beckoned from clear horizon. It appeared close enough that you could swim to it.

"You miss the island don't you Niño'? You're the last person that I would expect to get home sick after all the territory you've covered so far in your far-flung adventurous existence." Before I could formulate a clever response, Precious Goodlay pulled to the curb in her robin's-egg blue T-bird with top removed; the T-birds, not hers. "Can I give you a lift Sailor?" she asked coyly with a sly smile. I looked at Nita as if asking permission. "What are looking at me for Macho Man?" she asked with a big smile. "Hell man, Barbie Doll is waiting and she's so freakin' gorgeous I'd do her."

We were headed north up Coast Highway through Seal Beach and past the '*Glider Inn*' where Raven and I first met and became close friends that enchanting summer that now seems so long ago. We went past *Tiny Naylor's* restaurant on the right at Main Street and continued up the road to *the Edgewater Hotel* where Precious made a hard left toward the bridge leading to the seashore hamlets of Naples and Belmont shore and then another behind the hotel and in front of the boat marina. We followed the palm lined drive as it wound along the marina and eventually pulled into the parking lot at *The Captain's Table Surf and Turf*.

The interior décor was dark teak turn of the century nautical motif' adorned with lots of thick rope, wooden pulleys, turnbuckles, ship's lanterns, and a lovely crew of stunning little 'Swashbucklerettes.' A cute, perky little pirate in low-cut white peasant blouse, short black pleated skirt, wide belt with big square buckle and over-the-knee stiletto heeled lace-up boots, showed us to a plush leather booth at the big windows overlooking the wide glittering boat marina. She took our drink order and was away.

Precious looked deep into my eyes; "You're probably wondering why I'm here? Well so am I," she began, to the tune of Frank Zappa's

"Mothers of Invention and Suzy Cream Cheese" fame............ (What- ever that is?). "Precocious and I spent the entire day yesterday calling various municipal, county, and state agencies pretending to be important associates of an array of impressive sounding federal acronyms. After a series of Emmy Award winning performances, we managed, not only to dazzle them with brilliance, but baffle them with bullshit as well."

"We've managed to sift through the reams of information, read between the lines and separate shampoo from real poo. I believe we've come up with some fairly reliable information that the boys with the badges are not likely to be divulging any time soon."

"The Asian girl found in the dumpster behind *the Golden Bear* has been tentatively identified as twenty-nine year old China Lei. China Lei was a former *Bunny Club* waitress, men's magazine model, and aspiring actress. She appeared mostly in cameo and promotional appearances associated with Hef's *Bunny Clubs* or Men's entertainment magazine. She was married for a short time to political satirist and comedian Mort Stahl, who is a favorite of Hef's and plays the *Bunny Club* circuit in the major cities across the country."

"There hasn't been a lot of information as of late, except that she most likely had associations with several high-echelon escort agencies whose clients were among the wealthiest and most powerful people in the world. That's why you're not likely to get much information forthcoming from the investigating authorities. You can imagine the pressure they're receiving from higher-ups, and who knows who else, to keep the lid on in order to protect those within that client list."

Our vivacious little buccaneer arrived with our drinks and took our lunch order. Precious sipped her champagne and gazed at me over rim of crystal flute, with a curious sly grin. Her eyes twinkled mischievously. "Do you still have your Platinum Charter Member *Bunny Club* Key?" she asked. I smiled back at her, over rim of vodka martini, with a mischievous twinkle in my eyes and a sly grin of my own. She laughed out loud. "Of course you do, you womanizing pervert. How silly of me to even ask. I'll make reservations for tomorrow night, if your available............dick head."

The swashbuckling pixy princess returned with a platter filled with assorted sea food delicacies. There was shrimp, crab and lobster, as well as the 'fisherman's catch of the day,' bass, halibut and cod, baked, broiled and deep fried. The entre' was accompanied by an impressive array of sauces, dressings, citrus squeezes and melted butters. With sissy lobster bibs properly in place, conversation ceased and silent gluttonous indulgence commenced.

When lunch had concluded we hopped aboard the robin's egg blue convertible and headed back toward the *Golden Bear*. In route, Precious once again openly questioned my stagnating abilities and diminishing reflexes. I once again assured her that when the bell rings I'll come out swinging just as I always have. There was no reason to call out the cadets until I have something to go on. Otherwise they're just going to be underfoot and in the way. "Maybe we'll develop a solid lead at the *Bunny Club* tomorrow night."

She pulled to the curb in front of the *Golden Bear*. She said she would call me in the morning and leave a message at *the Bear* regarding our reservation. I gave her a quick kiss goodbye, got out and watched as she drove away, made a u turn at the pier and blew me a kiss as she whizzed by on her way back to *the Pacific Bay Luxury apartments*.

Papa Nikos met me at the front door. He said that he had a full house tonight and was short on personnel. He asked if I could help out, to which I readily agreed. I checked with Nita in the ticket booth as she was about to take a break and dash home to change for tonight's shows. The band's equipment truck had arrived and the roadies were busily off-loading and setting- up on stage. They park in the vacant lot between the *Bear* and the equipment repair shop on the corner, and un-load through the side door stage left. Tonight was Vic Damone and a small orchestra with special guest comedian Shecky Greene; two shows, seven-thirty and ten-thirty p.m.

I exited the rear door, walked the short distance down the alley and rounded the corner of the building. I put the key in the lock, opened the door and climbed the stairs to the foyer. I noticed the pungent aroma of vinegar and Babbo. There was no one in the party lounge so I continued on to my corner apartment. Once inside I flopped on the couch and drifted off to the soothing sounds of gentle waves lapping softly upon sandy shore, and warm thoughts of lovely Rita.

Late in the afternoon, with the setting sun just above Catalina, I put in a call to Rita at the casino. She was thrilled to hear from me and excitedly filled me in on all the comings and goings during my absence. Last night was the closing show for the Luis Prima and Keely Smith Revue, and tonight was the opening for The Penguins, The Coasters, and The Drifters. This weekend The Ike and Tina Turner Revue rocks the casino ballroom, and the following weekend James Brown and his Fabulous Flames. Her sister Lara, who managed the ballroom, was apparently enjoying being the queen in a bee hive of activity. The casino gaming venue upstairs continued to generate steady revenue and the traffic had increased along with the beginnings of a warm wonderful summer season.

I vaguely relayed my glacial progress thus far. She was painfully aware of the ups and downs, twist and turns an investigation may take. Rita knew what to say. She expressed confidence that somehow I would get to the bottom of the situation and bring it to a decisive conclusion. Rita and I had been around this carousel before. This was not her first rodeo. She wished me luck and told me not worry about things back on the island, as everything was running smoothly. "Like hot shit through a tin horn," she laughed. She told me she loved me, missed me, and was anxious for me to come home. She blew me a kiss through the phone, and we said our goodbyes. I sure miss that girl.

I showered, Burma shaved, splashed liberal amounts of some Old Spice I found in the cabinet, and a fairly limited wardrobe I found in the closet. With several impromptu swipes of the steam iron, I found myself decked-out in a pair of khakis with severely crisp creases, dark green woolen sweater with the rifle butt leather patches on the shoulders, a nice brown Eisenhower jacket and a pair of dark brown Buster Browns that were spit polished to a high gloss. I hoped that I wasn't too under dressed for the high-brow, haute' couture' crowd expected tonight. "Did you ever get the feeling that the whole world was a tuxedo, and you were a pair of brown shoes?" (George Gobel)

Main Street was still bustling with the stragglers of sun-burned sand bunnies and staggering hordes of 'Hodads and Grimmies' on their return migration to the last bus headed inland;' Highlanders.' I walked the short distance down the alley adjacent to the parking lot and entered the rear door of the *Bear*.

The kitchen staff was stoking-up the grill and the ovens in preparation for tonight's highly anticipated dinner shows. I went through the backstage area and into the main showroom. The lighting tech was high on a ladder adjusting the overhead lights to accommodate a fairly crowded stage. The audio guy was humping arm loads of cable and adjusting microphones in preparation of a lengthy sound check process.

Papa Nikos manned the reservation phone and the ticket booth until Nita returned. He seemed to be in good spirits and was confident that we would have a full-house tonight for both shows. However, I could sense his underlying apprehension regarding the on-going investigation.

Nita returned dressed to kill in a short, red lace dress that provided maximum exposure of her long gorgeous gams that seemed to extend to her neck. She wore bright red open toed pumps with matching red pedicure and manicure. Pouty red lips, real and spectacular girl parts. Her long wavy hair was ratted into immense proportions and her big brown eyes sparkled with excitement. Her 'hot damn' factor was way off the charts.

A dark haired waitress pixie arrived with her order pad at the ready and the finest un-tethered cleavage in town. They call her Paddles. I think they call her that because she likes it. There is another tanned, blonde surfer-girl waitress working tonight, with the most spectacular butt on the beach, and they call her Spanky. You can make your own inferences from that. Papa Nikos always provides dinner for his staff before show time. Cocktails were also available during the evening provided you didn't abuse the privilege. After my ravenous consumption of a melt-in-your- mouth fillet mignon, I retreated to the bar for a quick blast before the festivities began. Papa Nikos was already there pouring shots of ouzo for everyone to toast the 'promise of the evening'. "L'chaim!"

Seven P.M. was quickly approaching so I grabbed my Kiln light; a heavy black metal flash light that also serves as a short night stick to quickly subdue agitated inebriates, pulp flesh and pulverize bone. An unlikely scenario given the high-brow impeccably mannered crowd expected for tonight's shows.

The band's bus arrived and parked in the lot between the buildings next to the equipment truck and Vic Damone's white Lincoln town car arrived shortly there- after. Opening act comedian Shecky Greene stumbled in the rear door and headed straight for the bar, as was his usual modus operandi'.

I eventually meandered my way through the gathering crowd of musicians preparing for final lighting and sound checks, and proceeded through the show room and the entry vestibule. I opened the fire door onto the parking lot and scoped-out the first show crowd already cued-up all the way to the corner. Appeared to be a good crowd, well dressed, well mannered, and eagerly anticipating tonight's performance. It should be a fairly un-eventful evening. (I'll probably regret that I said that; jinxed it.)

Just prior to opening Papa Nikos gathered the bouncers, or doormen as he liked to call them, to deliver an inspiring pep talk, or instructional safety meeting as he liked to call them. It was a quick preview of what was expected for each show; how full the room would be, what type of clientele, special guests, late arrivals, etc. Tonight would be a top-drawer well -mannered crowd; big spenders, big tippers. There would be no rowdy oil field roustabouts or loud drunken cowboys with their ten gallon hats, ten gallon belt buckles, shit-kickin' boots and shiny spinning spurs. Add ten gallons of Lone Star beer to the rodeo, and you get to deal with a wild bunch of ignorant yahoos. (But I'm not bitter.)

I would work the front entry door and vestibule area this evening, taking tickets, checking I.D.'s and performing visual, and an occasional, un-obtrusive physical pat-down for those attempting to smuggle their own drugs, booze, or weapons. The process went smoothly and the room quickly filled to its posted 257 person capacity. The bouncers always kept a couple tables in reserve here and there for those late arriving inebriated idiots trying to impress their debu-tramp dates and willing to shell-out some long- green for their impromptu accommodations.

Shecky schlepped through his routine to spontaneous applause and uproarious laughter from an enthusiastic crowd thoroughly enjoying their evening of entertainment, dinner, and dancing. Following a brief intermission Vic Damone and the orchestra began their set to a warm and receptive audience and a crowded dance floor.

The first show concluded following several extended encores. Everyone in attendance had a wonderful time and tipped their waitresses generously. Once the hall was cleared, the bouncers made a quick sweep under the tables with their flash lights for jewelry, cash, controlled substances or any other contraband that may have been misplaced during the evening. The waitresses wiped and reset the tables and made a quick run with the carpet sweeper. When all was ready, Devin the floor manager made a tertiary perusal of the premises and then gave the O.K. to open the door and begin seating the crowd for the second show.

The second show drew a lot of industry people from Hollywood. Insiders and other top name entertainers that tend to frequent the trendy after-hours clubs, and the low-key dinner houses; high echelon high-brows that were too hip or too cool to hang out at the traditional Hollywood hot spots.

Halfway through Shecky's act a big black limo pulled to the curb out front. The large imposing driver got out and came around to open the rear passenger door. It was Johnny Stompanado, longtime boyfriend of movie star blond bombshell goddess Lana Turner, and personal body guard for L.A.'s infamous Jewish mob boss Mickey Cohen who emerged from the limo immaculately attired in a custom tailored seer sucker suit, beautiful cashmere overcoat, matching signature fedora, and severely shined Italian elevators. The self-acclaimed "*Haberdasher to the Hollywood Stars*," was accompanied by a gorgeous, bubbly, dark haired little cutesy-pie that looked like the real life version of Betty *Boop-Boop Be-Boop* cartoon pin-up girl. She seductively wore a short black lacey dress and an impressive full-length black ostrich feather cape.

Our paths had crossed on numerous occasions over the years, as we inevitably frequent the same night clubs, restaurants and after hours clubs along the Sunset Strip and Hollywood Boulevard, as well as the various sporting venues throughout L.A., like the Friday night fights at *the Olympic Auditorium*, the running of the ponies at *Hollywood Park* or *Santa Anita* and *the Hollywood All-stars* baseball games at *Gilmore Field*.

Mickey Cohen was a happy- go- lucky little mobster who thoroughly enjoyed his notoriety, his night life, and his beautiful exotic-dancer girlfriends. I have to reluctantly admit that I actually like the guy.

We have been known to throw back a few together in the wee hours of a long night. We respect each other's territory and don't interfere with one another's endeavors. Mickey even hired me a decade ago to shadow his partner-in-crime's girl-friend Virginia Hill, when Bugsy Segal was screwing-up big-time in Vegas while struggling to build *the Flamingo Hotel*. New York Jewish mob boss Myer Lansky had persuaded the other families in 'the Commission' to finance the construction utilizing borrowed Teamster pension funds. The original price tag for the project of one million dollars quickly ballooned in excess of six million, largely due to Bugsy's ineptness which caused construction delays, plan changes, material shortages or double-billing for such things as palm trees delivered through the front gate, then driven out the back gate only to be driven around to the front gate and delivered and billed a second time.

What concerned the five families the most however was Virginia Hill's control of the checkbook. Lansky and friends were not thrilled to discover that she was a signatory on the construction account. The project was out-of-control and there was no accountability for the cost over-runs or questionable expenditures. They wanted to know where the money went.

Lansky asked Mickey to go to Vegas and reign in the expenditures, get control of the cost over-runs, and expedite the completion of the project. Mickey then hired me to shadow Virginia's comings and goings, and with whom she was coming and going. Virginia loved the Hollywood night life, frequented the trendy hot spots, and hob-knobbed with the up-scale local wise-guys, film stars, producers and studio moguls. She had "A" list acquaintances and her dance card was always full.

I kept a close eye on her.........perhaps a bit too close. We bumped into each other on occasion, and it was an occasion each time. Virginia Hill was beautiful, smart, and seductive. She was alluring, aggressive, and manipulative. She had been around the block a few times, was attracted to the bad boys, and knew how the game was played. Over time we became trusted friends who shared many quiet moments together in our own intimate universe far, far away. I may have inadvertently tipped- her- off regarding the mob's apparent displeasure with Bugsy's performance thus far, and remind her of their usual 'modus operandi' regarding perceived misappropriation of company funds. That may explain why she skipped town just prior to Bugsy's assassination in her L.A. home.

A few years later Virginia was subpoenaed to testify at the 'Kefauver Traveling Circus and Trolling for Wise-Guys Expedition and self-aggrandizing photo-op commission'. She had the audience rolling in the isles with her compellingly irrelevant testimony and entertaining take-no-shit attitude. She was irritated, combative, sharp, witty, and yet divulged virtually nothing that wasn't already known about the mob. After that Virginia moved to Europe and married an Austrian Count or Swiss Duke or something.

"Dugan my friend, very nice to see you again," he said, as he came through the door and extended his hand. "Shalom Mickey," I responded with a smile. "It's always a pleasure Amigo. Nice threads Dude."

He slipped me a Franklin during his enthusiastic handshake and asked that I might procure a ringside table for himself and his lovely date Trixie, or Dixie, or Pixie, or whatever. Maybe it was Roxy. I assured Mr. Cohen that we would be honored to accommodate his wishes, and gave "Useless Guard Klopshinski" a quick flash across the room from my handy dandy kiln light.

"Good evening Mr. Cohen, nice to see you again Sir," the always polite 'diplomat beamed as he showed Mickey and his lovely companion to Papa Nikos' private table in the alcove just off stage right. Before returning to his station he stopped by where I gave him the Franklin to share with the crew. He gave me the sign of 'the sting' and smiled wide exposing his mouth-full of shiny braces.

I turned, just as two old friends stepped through the door. Officers Ron Mullins and Mike Mc Burney were old school chums of mine. They had joined the military together and served under Patton in North Africa. Since the end of the war they have been downtown 'beat cops' pounding the pavement to protect and serve the citizenry, and fight crime where ever they may find it.

"Aloha Amigos," I said, shaking their hands. "Aloha island boy. What are you doing back on the mainland, Brah?" they asked in unison. "Island-fever, it's like cabin fever," I responded.

Spanky arrived with two cups of Irish coffee, two fresh donuts, and tonight's modest contribution to the Police Officer's Retirement Fund. Mullins and Mc Burney were two fine cops who paid special attention to the real street crime and concentrated on keeping the tourists and locals safe and happy. They didn't much care about the gambling and upscale escort service activities as long as it was kept obscure, inconspicuous, and didn't cause any trouble. That tidy little contingency had gotten completely blown out of the water as of late.

I asked them about the girl in the dumpster, but they didn't have much to add beyond what I already knew, except to say that Chief Inspector Sven Golly was keeping a tight lid on the investigation. They confided in me that they suspected that Inspector Golly was probably afraid of Mona's little black book and client names contained within. There apparently wasn't enough evidence to support a search warrant at present, but they were confident that Golly was hot on the trail. He was chomping at the bit to get into Mona's place and find that book. They already warned Mona about the impending intrusion and advised her to find a secure location for her book of clients. The only thing Mullins and Mc Burney were able to add was that the girl in the dumpster, while associated with Mona' occasionally on an out call basis, she was fairly well known in the Hollywood and Sunset Strip circles.

They sucked the remaining drops of their coffee, wiped donut crumbs from their chin and prepared to resume their duties on the mean streets of Huntington Beach. They wished me luck and their parting piece of wisdom was to advise me that Chief Inspector Dickhead, as they fondly referred to him, was a total asshole most of the time, but became a real prick when confronted by a Private Dick schlepping around in an on-going investigation. "Mind your P's and Q's and stay the hell off Captain Dickhead's radar screen." With that parting piece of sage advice, Mullins and Mc Burney were off to fight crime and pursue criminals.

As I watched the two beat cops disappear around the corner, someone grabbed a hand-full of my behind from behind. I turned to find Nita Menage' and a beautiful young mulatto girl, both smiling in what I imagined to be eager anticipation. My pulse quickened and my mind raced from one implausible scenario to another. My grin grew noticeably wider and my trousers grew noticeably tighter. I was fantasizing that Nita had planned an enchanting evening worthy of her name. Perhaps I was being overly optimistic regarding this evening's imagined activities, as was the restless 'manaconda' stirring somewhere south of my moral equator.

Nita introduced her gorgeous ebony friend. Her name was Lola. She was a dancer. She was a dancer at the *Copa Cabana*. (Is anyone writing this stuff down? Some gay New York Jew boy should be in the recording studio as we speak.) Nita and Lola were good friends and Nita had entertained her friend with exaggerated tales of our legendary sexploits together. Once again my reputation exceeds me..........I mean precedes me.

As it turned out, Lola had a very rich friend who needed help. As my erogenous zone reluctantly began deflating, I listened patiently as she explained how a group of individuals were attempting to wrest control of her friend's enterprise by way of intimidation, implied threats, and perhaps even extortion or blackmail. Her friend was a novice with regard to such things, was not street smart, and sounded like a defenseless pussy; a wimp caught in the neon headlights of the mean streets. Her friend was in desperate need of someone experienced in such things and knows their way around the seedy underbelly and dark back alleys of stark reality. (Hey, wait a minute. I think I resemble that remark.)

I reluctantly agreed to meet Lola's friend, but with no commitments and merely to enlighten with personal experience, or perhaps to impart advice regarding street culture behavior. Lola and her friend would be waiting across Coast Highway next to the pier at *Maxwell's Restaurant*. Lola gave me a gentle kiss and held me close. She whispered thank you and then she was off down the sidewalk to the corner and across the highway to *Maxwell's*. I watched as she crossed the parking lot and entered the restaurant. "She's a sweet kid, Travis. Too sweet for you," Nita said with a sly smile. "But I know you'd get along great. You're both fuck- freaks; mattress- maniacs."

I asked Nita how well she knew Lola, did she know what she was doing, and could she be trusted. Nita assured me that she had known Lola a very long time and that they were roommates at one time. She said that Lola is a chorus line dancer on a nationwide circuit of mob affiliated clubs in cities including Dallas, New Orleans, Miami, New York, Chicago, Kansas City, Vegas and L.A. and international venues such as Havana and Toronto. "Lola is a sharp girl and knows her way around," Nita said. "I'd trust Lola with my life."

After 'touching-base' with Papa Nikos and the staff, I checked- out early and left them to an enthusiastic, well- mannered crowd.

I walked down the alley noting that there was no light and no music coming from upstairs in the lounge. I rounded the corner of the building and turned the key in the lock. Again, the place was uncharacteristically quiet and uncomfortably dark. I stayed close to the wall, keeping the floor squeaks to a minimum as I climbed the stairs. When I reached the foyer I began to hear the smoky sounds of Julie London softly playing on the phonograph. I quietly stepped into the moonlit lounge and found Mona on the plush couch resplendent in lavender negligee', stiff drink in one hand, cigarette in the other. She was sniffling and it was obvious that tears had been shed.

Since the plane crash that killed her husband, Mona had kept the place lively, fun and full of people as much as possible, in part to avoid experiencing melancholy nights such as this one; dark and lonely nights when sadness rushes over you like a relentless tsunami. All the 'what- ifs', and 'should-haves' flood your thoughts, overwhelm your emotions and cripple your soul. That loneliness that rips out your guts, leaves you hollow inside, and breaks a heart that can never be repaired. The desperation of a tragic loss, about which you can do nothing. I have a lot of empathy for Mona. Sadly, I know how she feels.

"Make yourself a drink Travis. How'd it go tonight? Sounded wonderful from here," she said slightly slurred. I poured myself a brandy and sat on the couch beside her. She was wiping mascara from her cheek and reapplying her lipstick. "It went pretty smooth,"

I replied. "It's a well-mannered crowd. Mickey Cohen was in for the second show. He says to tell you shalom baby." "Mickey Cohen, my tax evading, smartly coiffed little Boyle Heights Jew Boy turned Hollywood's 'A-list' mobster to the stars," she laughed. "I told him that you gotta' pay your taxes Sparky. It's like protection money or fire insurance; if you don't feed the bulldog, it will come back to bite you in the ass someday. How is that kosher little matzo ball? Haven't seen much of him since he got out of the joint." "He hasn't missed a step," I replied. "He's still a stylish, impeccably dressed little nebbish with a boob-boob d-boob trophy date draped over his arm."

I downed the last of my brandy and glanced at my watch. "Mona, I hate to leave you now but I have an appointment across the street." "Oh that reminds me," she said, as she got up from the couch and walked across the room to an armoire' in the corner. The silhouette projected through thin negligee as she passed in front of the big picture window was that of a taught, stunning twenty- year- old. I know girls half her age that would give their boyfriend's left nard to have a perky pair of protrusions like Mona's. She returned with what appeared to be a shiny, quilted hunting vest. "My friend Mary from *DuPont* dropped this off and asked me to give it to you for field testing. She says it's made from a new material she invented. She calls it *'Kevlar'*. She's especially proud of the fastening devices. They're designed to replace buckles, buttons, or zippers. She calls it *'Velcro'*." I removed my jacket and put the vest on over my sweater. It felt like a corrugated, cardboard egg carton, sown within a thick, laminated canvas outer and inner lining. The *'Velcro'* fasteners were different but seemed to do the job, though the sound that accompanied the un-fastening phase was similar to that of a long over- due' Brazilian wax job' in progress (what- ever that is?); sans the screaming in excruciating pain. It was a snug fit and my jacket went over it without too much restriction of movement.

While Mona fixed us another drink, I went to my room and on-loaded my standard issue P.I. pocket paraphernalia including blackjack, handcuffs, lock-picking tools, and of course my Popeil pocket pin light.

I removed my jacket and strapped on my shoulder holster and venerable .38 snubby. I probably wouldn't need any of these accoutrements, but I felt somewhat naked without them. They had become my suit of armor, or perhaps my security blanket. Funny, I didn't feel the need for any of those things while I was on the island being Casino Manager Extraordinaire'.

I rejoined Mona on the couch in the lounge. She had regained her composure and had Bobby Darin crooning on the phonograph about 'love beyond the sea.' I told Mona about the meeting tonight and the limited amount of information I had received from the lovely Lola. My intention was to listen thoughtfully, explain the realities of the streets and the criminals that inhabit them, offer advice, then refer him to Precious' nephew's *'Blackwater Security Agency,'* and then politely butt-out. "However, if I haven't returned by morning, then call out the cavalry."

Maxwell's Surf and Turf was an upscale joint with mahogany, walnut, and teak décor, and lots of brass and crystal appointments. It was elegantly furnished and subtly lit. I found Lola and her friend in the corner booth next to the large windows that overlooked the grand wide beach, the entire length of the pier, and the dark Pacific beyond.

Lola introduced her friend simply as Barry. We shook hands and I slid into the booth next to Lola across the table from Barry. The waiter arrived and I ordered another round of whatever they were having and a vodka martini for myself. Upon first impression, Barry appeared to be an uptight, buttoned down, pocket protected, low echelon corporate pencil pusher, who wore a conservative business suit, sensible shoes, and black horned-rimmed glasses. I guessed him to be around twenty five, clean cut, articulate, highly educated and the pride of his Ivy League Alma Mater. I imagine him prancing about with his junior varsity cheer leader sweater tied smartly around his neck while performing as water boy for the Lacrosse Squad, presiding as president of the chess club, or captain of the croquette team. Perhaps mommy and daddy raised young master Barry in the exclusive gated community just down the lane from the Cabot-Lodge and the Kennedy compounds or just across the cape from the Auchenclaus estate, where he watched Jacquelyn Bouvier ride her pony, Blackjack. Perhaps I judge too harshly. I may have issues with pampered, pansy-ass, arrogant little rich bastards………..but I'm not bitter. "Mr. Dugan, you come highly recommended by the people whom I have inquired regarding the situation in which my client currently finds himself. My client, nor myself have any knowledge of such dealings and we are in desperate need of help from someone experienced in such things and capable of bringing the situation to a satisfactory conclusion without involving the police or the media."

The waiter returned with our drinks then abruptly departed. "Who is your client and what is the current situation?" I asked straight away, while sampling my cool, clear elixir. Barry sipped from his brandy snifter and contemplated on how to begin his presentation.

"Mr. Dugan it is my understanding that you are a man who likes to get to the point, so I will cut to the chase, as it were. My client is a wealthy industrialist primarily invested in transportation systems. I will of course withhold my client's identity until such time as you have agreed to help us.

My client has been contacted several times as of late by a group of individuals using an array of acronyms and titles, who have indicated their desire to acquire controlling interest in my client's transportation empire. Even though, on each occasion they have been informed in no uncertain terms, that my client will not, under any circumstances, entertain their proposal, they have begun to threaten with subtle references of heavy handed hooliganism, such as labor disruptions, sabotage and blackmail."

"How do they contact your client?" I asked. "It's always by telephone using the guise of representing firms such as *Blue Haven Investments Inc.*, or *Occidental International Associates*, or *Peabody Property Investments*, and others. Of course we attempted to ascertain if these firms were legitimate. What we found was a labyrinth of front companies and bogus corporations. Furthermore, the paltry amount they are offering amounts to nothing more than extortion. This consortium of individuals has become progressively more threatening, and understandably my client has become progressively more dis-stressed about the situation. They told him specifically not to involve the police. I'm afraid my client finds himself in desperate need of assistance from someone experienced in such things." He paused and took a long pull from his snifter. He seemed fairly stressed himself.

"Okay Barry, let's see if I've got all the facts straight. The wealthy transportation industrialist that is your client is being threatened through phone contacts by unknown individuals wanting to purchase controlling interest in your clients business for what amounts to extortion. Thus far they have threatened labor disruptions, sabotage, and thinly veiled suggestions of bodily harm. Is that pretty much the gist of it?" I asked. "Yes Mr. Dugan, that is the situation in which we currently find ourselves and truthfully, we haven't got a clue as to what should be done or what precautions should be taken. That is precisely why my client requests that I seek your assistance. Apparently he is aware of a similar situation in your past that took place on Catalina Island that you brought to a successful conclusion. I believe that is where the recommendation for your services originated."

"Yes, unfortunately I do indeed have experience in similar situations and I believe your client has good reason to be concerned. These people are well versed in the art of extortion and they are not prone to compromise, nor will they fade away if ignored." I gave him a business card and wrote Precious Goodlay's number on the back. "I strongly urge you to call my business partner first thing tomorrow morning. Your client needs twenty-four hour personal protection as well as security for immediate family, business partners, or corporate CEO's. Our agency is capable of coordinating security staff as well as the logistics and personnel required to conduct an extortion investigation."

There was an audible sigh of relief from the young counselor. "Thank you Mr. Dugan, my client will be tremendously relieved to know that you are on the case." Lola smiled and gently patted the back of his hand.

I didn't need to pump him for further details regarding his client, contract arrangements, schedules or anything else; Precious would gracefully attend to those matters when and if Barry called. Barry reached across the table to shake my hand. He seemed relieved, the tension had subsided and he wore a smile for the first time since we met. Lola said that she would walk Barry to his car and then join me on the terrace for a night cap.

I stepped out to the terrace and lit a cigarette. I watched Barry and Lola walk through the gray mist to his car that was parked just beyond the dim glow of the parking lot's single light. Suddenly there was a terrified scream and the muffled sounds of an ensuing scuffle. I leaped from the terrace rail to a drain pipe and slid down the pipe to the parking lot. I hit the ground running. There were two hulking gunzels man- handling Barry into an idling sedan. Lola was furiously tearing at them and getting repeatedly elbowed or slapped away. I grabbed one of the immense meatballs by the back of his collar and smacked him behind the ear several times with my nasty little leather zap. He went down hard on the pavement with the back of his head. I reached in and dragged the second guy out of the car. I caught an elbow to the forehead in the process that slammed me back into the car parked next to us. I hit the ground hard flat on my back. The big ugly bastard pulled his piece and was prepared to blast me into the pavement. I grabbed the frame under the car and pulled myself under as he squeezed the trigger. The parking lot lit-up like daylight for a split second and the explosion that blew a huge chunk out of the asphalt next to my head echoed off of the store fronts down the beach and along Coast Highway. I pulled-out my snubby and shot him in the ankle. When he hit the ground I shot him in the head.

I could hear his compatriot, who had regained his senses, 'beat-feeting' a retreat across the parking lot back in the direction of Coast Highway. I dragged myself out from under the car and fired a quick shot at the fleeing miscreant. He returned fire from somewhere in the darkness and took-out the headlamp of the car next to which I crouched. I chased him across the highway, dodging traffic in both directions, and followed him through the vacant lot between *the Bear* and the truck repair on the corner. He ran down the dark alley behind the shops on Main Street. I ran into the alley and stopped in an alcove shadow of a brick building on the right. I couldn't see him and I didn't hear him. I have a bad feeling about this. I knew that I shouldn't go any further, but as always, I'm going anyway.

I took a quick peek around the corner. I would have to negotiate around half a dozen metal trash cans and about ten feet of open space to reach cover behind a large metal dumpster. I took a deep breath, pointed my .38 around the corner, fired two cover- shots, and ran for the safety of the metal dumpster. Suddenly I was blinded by a flash of light and what felt like a cannon ball hit me in the right shoulder. It spun me around and slammed my face into the brick wall. I hit the ground staring at the pavement where it meets the wall. I was numb, except for the deep, throbbing pain in my shoulder and down my right arm. It was like a firecracker exploding in your hand as a kid; that same, stunning pain that radiates all the way to the bone. "Freeze, Police!" I heard a shot, then a barrage of return fire. Then, deadly silence.

I tried to move; I couldn't. I lay there wandering if this is how it was going to end; face down in a filthy, urine-soaked, shit-hole of a back alley. Some I imagine would read the headline and say, how apropos. Maybe Precious was right. Maybe I didn't have what it takes anymore; seems like I've lost the edge. Seems like the thrill is gone...........at least from my current perspective.

I saw flashes of light streak across the white-washed bricks, and heard running feet. "Dugan, still with us buddy? Where are you hit?" It was Mullins. He rolled me over onto my back and shined his flashlight in my face. He put a finger into the entry hole in my jacket then felt the hole in my vest. With some difficulty he finally figured out *the Velcro* straps and ripped them open. He felt around on my chest for a corresponding bullet hole; there was none. There was no blood either. Apparently the new vest passed its initial field test with flying colors............thank God.

Within minutes the alley was lit-up like a carnival midway. Red and blue lights reflected off every window and danced across every wall, like it was the 4th of July. Sirens whaled in the distance and the place was crawling with cops, cop cars, ambulances and E.M.T.s. Eventually, the Coroner and the meat wagon arrived.

Mullins helped me to sit up against the wall as his boss arrived and began to bark-out terse orders to the cadre' of uniforms swarming about the area. "That's Inspector Golly," Mullins murmured. "He can be a real dickhead if he's in a foul mood..............and I have yet to experience anything otherwise."

Inspector Golly stomped over to where I slumped against the brick wall and shined a light rudely in my face. From what I could see beyond the glare of his flash light was what appeared to be the poster boy for 'Adolph's Aryan Super-race.' He was big and blonde and brutal looking with a severely angular crew- cut and piercing pale grey eyes. "Do you know this guy, Mullins?" he asked. "Yes sir, his name is Dugan, Travis Dugan. He's a P.I. out of Venice Beach." "Is he injured?" "He's been shot, but the bullet does not appear to have penetrated his vest." "Have the medical personnel give him the once-over, then you and Mc Burney load him into your squad car and get him over to my office. You bastards get your goddamn stories straight by the time you get there."

During the short ride to HBPD Mullins and Mc Burney cautioned me again with regard to keeping my cool during Mein Fuehrer Von Dickhead's not so friendly inquisition. He would be blunt, brutal, and abrasive. His arrogant, over-bearing, in-your-face rudeness is calculated to piss you off and provoke an unrestrained response. (Great, like I need to butt heads with some arrogant, smart ass butt-head cadet from the Third Reich.)

The impressive gold leaf lettering across the opaque glass door read; Chief Inspector Sven Golly. (No shit? Sven Golly?) Maybe that explains his over-all shitty attitude. Gee thanks mom and dad; like he didn't catch a load of crap from all the other toe-headed little Aryan punks in der grade school.

Sven Golly's office was impressively spacious, decorated with a humongous mahogany desk, and overstuffed brown leather banker's chairs. The walls were covered with gold and silver plaques, platinum framed awards, various citations for Meritorious Service, Valor, and a kaleidoscope of academic achievements and degrees from some of the finest schools in Europe, as well as prestigious American Universities.

Inspector Golly sat behind his desk fingering through an impressively bulging file folder. He motioned for me to sit down across the desk in a plush leather chair, while Mullins and Mc Burney stood at parade rest on either side of the office door.

Having mastered the art of reading files upside down, I could see that I was correct in assuming the file was chock-full of teletype background checks from the Department of Defense, the F.B.I., and LAPD. There should be some fairly compelling factoids within those multitudes of official papers. Sven should find them mildly entertaining.

The good inspector closed the file, folded his hands atop it, and gave me a rather puzzled look with those ghostly grey eyes. "Dugan, first of all let me commend you for your impressive war record, and salute your patriotic service to your country. Sixty-four B-17 and B-29 missions in the pacific campaign against the Japanese during World War II, then to return and fly A-26 night interdiction dive-bomb and strafing attacks above the 38th parallel in the Korean conflict. It takes guts to do that. You got balls Dugan I'll say that for you."

"However, the rest of this file seems pretty sketchy, man. There's a lot of discussion in various agency reports describing a loose cannon, unpredictable behavior, and un-orthodox legally questionable procedures. Phrases such as, 'short-tempered shoot from the hip cowboy,' or similar descriptions are peppered throughout those reports." "They're just jealous" I quipped.

He gazed at me quizzically for a moment then continued unabated. "You do however, eventually get the job done, but there inevitably seems to be substantial amounts of collateral damage and an unusually high spike in the casualty count arriving at the morgue. I briefly perused a rather descriptive memo in the file from a Constable LaFarge', Avalon Police Inspector, requesting a boat load of ice from the mainland, that he maintains was necessitated by the numerous corpses that you were stacking like cord wood, over-burdening the morgue and other available refrigerated space on the island. There were other terse comments from Constable LaFarge' regarding your smart-ass attitude and your unethical and no-doubt illegal methods of conducting an investigation, which after all, leads me to believe that Constable LaFarge' doesn't like you much."

I leaned forward and clasp my hands atop the desk. "You should have read a little further in that file," I replied. "LaFarge' eventually pissed me off, so I had to kill him. I beat him to death with an ancient Chinese statue of a golden dragon. I bashed his skull in until his brains looked like a mushy pile of bloody fish eggs."

Mullins and Mc Burney cringed in the doorway and rolled their eyes in consternation. Sven Golly was momentarily taken aback. He stared aghast, mouth agape, and the astonished look of disbelief etched across his ashen face. He looked at me like I'd just clubbed a baby seal.

There was a knock on the door. "Yes," Golly replied, without a change of expression or astonished stare in my direction. The department's ballistics tech entered carrying my super-bitchin' *Kevlar* vest and a large paper bag secured with bright yellow evidence tape. He placed the vest and the paper bag on the desk, and removed the tape. He reached in and pulled out a small clear plastic bag containing a slightly distorted, mushroom misshapen spent slug. "I dug this .22 caliber hollow point out of the vest."

He held it up to Inspector Golly. "Where ever you got this vest, I would contact them and order one for every cop in the department. This thing is a lifesaver." He then pulled the .22 automatic out of the bag. It had a half-assed, homemade silencer screwed on the end of it. "An assassin's weapon," the tech announced, placing it on the desk. "Good thing he used hollow points, a full metal jacket may have penetrated the vest."

Next out of the tech's bag was my venerable snubby and shoulder holster. "We performed ballistics tests on this weapon and the slugs match the two retrieved from the deceased male victim found in the restaurant parking lot. We ran tests on the deceased male's weapon and found that one round had been fired from the weapon, but we were unable to find the discharged slug, just a large divot in the parking lot asphalt."

Once the tech had departed, Inspector Golly sat down across from me with pencil and paper at the ready. "Okay Dugan, tell me what went down tonight." I explained that I was contacted by a girl named Lola at the *Golden Bear,* who asked me to talk to her friend named Barry. No last names for either. I met them later at *Maxwell's*, at which time Barry explained how his client was being pressured, backed by subtle, thinly veiled threats by unknown individuals to sell controlling interest in his transportation empire for an amount that can only be described as out-right extortion. Barry or his client have no experience with this type situation and requested some advice from someone who did. I offered insight as to methodology generally associated with such endeavors, and advice regarding available options to insure the safety of immediate family and associates. My suggestion was that they contact a competent personal security agency capable of defending persons and property against unwanted intrusions. Naturally, I suggested the services provided by my agency. Of course I strongly recommended that he contact the proper law enforcement authority and report the perceived threats. I continued my oration explaining that at the conclusion of the meeting Lola walked Barry back to his car in the parking lot. I stepped out onto the terrace and had a smoke while observing their progress to his car. I concluded my dissertation with a slightly embellished account of my heroic intervention in the parking lot and the ensuing gun battle into the alley behind *the Bear*, where the two alert police officers brought the very dangerous situation to an abrupt and satisfactory conclusion with no collateral damage to innocent bystanders or private property.

"Oh, nice touch there at the end, Dugan," Golly said, somewhat exasperated. "Should I pin a fuckin' metal on 'em now, or wait 'till the parade?" I glanced briefly at Mullins and Mc Burney dutifully guarding the door and got a wink and a quick smile from both.

Inspector Golly asked a few more questions regarding approximate time of occurrences, how long was the meeting at *Maxwell*'s etcetera. He asked where I was staying and contact phone numbers. He compared his notes with others within his file. He closed the file and folded his hands in front of him. He looked me in the eye and asked; "Why ARE you here? I know you're not here to hone you're back-door bouncer skills at *the Bear.*"

I simply explained about the late night distress call from Papa Nikos and how I had come to help calm his nerves and provide some sense of security for Papa, his daughter Caroline, and his employees at the *Bear.* I informed Inspector Golly that my agency had assigned a contingent of security personnel to the *Bear,* so if he notices a large cadre' of very large Samoans, that they will be us. "I made a promise to Papa Nikos that we would stay on the job until HBPD concludes their investigation and have apprehended the perpetrator or perpetrators and have them in custody."

"Boy, you've got all the right answers down pat, don't you Dugan? You've been around this carousel a few times before." He hastily gathered all the paraphernalia spread across the table, except for my personal belongings, and threw them back into the evidence bag. He shoved all my stuff across the table to me including the vest, my gun, all the cartridges, and my I.D.

"Let me give you a few facts, a word of warning, and some sage advice, Dugan. I know that you are cunning, ruthless, and potentially deadly. I am aware that you often utilize unorthodox, legally questionable and usually messy means to an end, which always result in unexpected consequences and disastrous collateral damage. Having said that, I am also aware that somehow you do eventually manage to get the job done to your grateful client's satisfaction......but, I remind you that you have been in town for two days and I already have two stiffs on ice in the morgue. So far you're batting a thousand on my shit list. My advice to you Dugan is, do not attempt to improve your average while you're in my ball park. Stick to your business and keep your nose out of mine. My word of warning is; if you don't heed my advice then I will pull your dance card, throw you in the slam, and prosecute the living shit out of you. Keep your nose clean or I will chew you up, shit you out, and ship your sorry ass back to where ever the hell you came from."

With those words of wisdom said, Inspector Golly gathered-up his evidence bag and prepared to depart. "Get this bastard out of here and take the Puerto Rican broad with you." He gave me one last hard stare from his ghostly eyes. "Nice talking to you Sven," I said with a smile. "Yeah, the pleasure was all yours asshole," was his reply before slamming the door behind him. I looked at Mullins and Mc Burney; "he seems kinda' angry." They just laughed and hurriedly helped gather my PI paraphernalia. "That was a tea party Dugan. Let's get outta here before he really does get mad and changes his mind."

Lola was waiting in the hallway. We gathered her up and headed for the squad car. They stopped in the parking lot *at Maxwell's* next to a bright red Chevy Cheetah; one of only a couple dozen prototypes built with a Ferrari inspired sleek, fiberglass body bolted onto a Corvette Stingray chassis. It was engineered with a 427 C.I., supercharged V-8 engine, four-speed manual transmission, tuned exhaust and racing suspension. The Cheetah was designed to compete against the best in world class European G.T. road courses.

I got down on all fours and ran my pin light up and down the frame of the red hot roadster along both sides paying particular attention to the starter and solenoid. Then I popped the hood and performed a thorough inspection of the engine compartment specifically the ignition and wiring. I wanted to make sure that the funny boys currently residing in the city morgue hadn't futzed with the car so that we'd blow ourselves up when the ignition key was turned.

We said goodnight and thanks to Mullins and Mc Burney and within moments Lola had the sleek red Cheetah screaming north on Coast Highway through the estuary at Tin Can Beach and into the quiet hamlet of Sunset Beach. She turned right onto Park Avenue, across the highway from *Woody's* neighborhood market and behind *the New England Live Lobster House*. She went about halfway down the narrow street on the short peninsula, across the channel from the bohemian isle *Huntington Harbor.*

We turned into the open door of a double car garage that had a quaint studio apartment above. We climbed the outside stairs to a neat, clean and comfortable size apartment with a small Kitchen and bath. The apartment had a nice view of the pacific across Coast highway and the main house in front had its own private dock and single mast sail boat.

Nita was right; Lola was a sexual maniac. She abused me in the most wonderful ways throughout the twilight hours until dawn. I didn't seem to mind... I didn't seem to mind numerous times.

Chapter Three

Day 3

In the morning we stopped for the early bird steak and eggs and bloody-Mary special at *Mother's Biker Bar and Grill*, before proceeding south, back down the highway to Mona's. Lola pulled the Bright red growling Cheetah to the curb in front of Mona's behind a shiny yellow '51 Ford Woody with three surf boards strapped to the top. It was the Yeager brothers, Denny, Benny, and Deacon; the 'Yeager-meisters.'

Benny, the youngest of the boys is a senior in high school and has already achieved world class status as a big wave surfing champion. Denny, the middle brother is the starting quarterback for the USC Trojans football team and Deacon, the oldest, lives the life of Riley. He lives the life we all wish we could. He's a yacht skipper for a select few super rich boat owners out of Marina Del Rey, Newport Harbor, and Dana Point. Deacon spends several glorious months every year cruising the rich and famous, the beautiful people, to Cabo, Mazatlan, Acapulco and of course the islands. "It's a tough gig but somebodies gotta' do it."

I fondly remember one glorious weekend that I crewed for Deacon and a boat load of gorgeous young Filipino nurses in Catalina. One of his clients is a doctor that owns about a dozen abortion clinics in Riverside and the Inland Empire. Each month one nurse from each clinic would earn the "Employee of the Month" award, and be rewarded with a weekend trip on the doctor's yacht to Catalina; glorious days of warm sun, scuba diving, water skiing, and nude sunbathing on the fantail.

Wild nights filled with dining, dancing, drinking and debauchery; everything I desire.

The Yeager brother's dad owned a thriving Cadillac and Oldsmobile dealership on Wilshire Boulevard in downtown L.A. and they lived on an oceanfront estate in Manhattan Beach. Life was very good for the Yeager-meisters.

Upon our arrival, it was apparent that the boys had ringed the doorbell incessantly looking for me and had awakened Mona in the process. She was leaning out of an upstairs window explaining my absence and where they could insert that bell-ringing finger. Handshakes and high fives all around, followed by introductions for Lola, Mona and the boys. They heard that I was in town and they were here to take me on a surfing safari. The Yeager boys were a wild bunch and their adventures were always exciting and unpredictable. I explained that I didn't have my board here and they said that was no problem because they were headed for Velzy's to the south and he would no-doubt have plenty of boards to choose from.

I went upstairs and found a well- worn pair of board shorts, my ever fashionable baggies and an old raggedy pair of Red Ball Jets. Mona threw me a towel on my way down the stairs and told me to watch out for sharks. (Funny girl)

I gave Lola a kiss goodbye and told her that I had an appointment tonight that may shed some light on Barry's situation. "We'll see if Barry calls Precious this morning or if he was scared-off last night." Either way, I told her that I would keep her in the loop and vice versa. I cautioned her to be aware of her surroundings and anyone that may be following her and don't get yourself into a situation that you can't get yourself out of. If she felt threatened in any way then call my office and arrange for immediate personal protection.

Just south of the Edison steam plant along the wide expanse of the Newport Strand near the jetty, we pulled into a large parking lot on the inland side of the highway in front of a boat storage lot. Under a big sign that read; 'Surfboards by Velzy', was a small Tahitian thatched hut. Dale Velzy , the legendary board maker and innovator of the' Velzy V-skeg', and the Malibu Express' surfboard design, emerged from the hut in his customary board shorts, flip-flops, and ever-present fine layer of Styrofoam dust. Velzy didn't look like your typical blonde beach bum, he looked more like a rough and tumble cowboy matinee movie idol. With his head-full of dark, windswept curls and his thick handle bar mustache, he looked like" Palladin" of TV's "*Have Gun Will Travel*" starring Richard Boone, only with big gnarly surf knots.

Dale greeted me with a wide smile and a big bear hug. We hadn't seen each other since I left Venice for the island. He made my first board when he first started in Manhattan Beach. That's where we first met the Yeager Boys and their dad. "Wait right here Dugan, I have a surprise for you." He ran back into the hut with the joy of a kid on Christmas morning. He reemerged with a bright yellow board, identical to the original he shaped for me so many years ago. It was an 8'2" with a full nose, thin rails and plenty of rocker. My little banana board had redwood and balsa stringers, a sparrow tail and of course the patented 'Velzy V-Skeg.' It was a lightning bolt that made instantaneous neck-snapping turns and shredded the face of the biggest, most ferocious big waves, as well as riding the nose through the intricate precision of awesome, smooth tubular perfection. (kawabunga dude)

We strapped the boards to the top, piled in the old woody and were headed south on Coast Highway. We barely got up to speed before the radio blast alternated between Wolf Man Jack on XERB, and the surf guitar twang of the Ventures. Soon after that, a giant yellow wheat-straw bomber circulated about the interior accompanied by a pungent aroma and engulfing purple haze. It wasn't long before my eyes glazed-over and the sides of my head folded over my ears. I was baked to a nice buzz.

We pulled to the curb in Laguna Beach where the town's unofficial greeter welcomed all who passed through town on Pacific Coast Highway. He was a scruffy old crusty with thick curly hair and a burly full beard. He wore a red and black checker-board lumber jack shirt, dungarees, and a pair of well-worn Buster Brown work boots. He was always happy to see everyone, but especially happy to see the Yeager-meisters and their bright yellow woody because they always brought a bag of fresh donuts and a big wheat-straw fatty.

The old guy reminded me of a kid named Dickey who lived in Seal Beach where I grew- up. Dickey was a few bricks shy of a load, but he was harmless, innocent and sweet.

Dickey was a happy-go-lucky kid who skipped around town with his five gallon paint bucket in which he carried his friend Mr. Crab and his trumpet. When he met you on the street, he would put your foreheads together and tap you repeatedly on the back of your head. "Hi! Hi! I'm Dickey. What's your name?" Once you had introduced yourself, Dickey would introduce you to his friend Mr. Crab (a lacquered exoskeleton discarded restaurant decoration) and play a tune on his trumpet. At the conclusion of his trumpet solo, the trumpet and Mr. Crab went back in the bucket and Dickey went skipping off to his next chance encounter.

The local surfers kept a watchful eye on Dickey to make sure he wasn't harassed or abused by the uninitiated tourists and inland Grimmies and Hodads. During one such encounter on the pier a group of inland barrio grease-balls were making fun of Dickey, tooting his horn and playing keep away with Mr. Crab. Dickey was becoming more and more desperate and when they tossed his trumpet off of the pier into the surf below, Dickey was panic stricken. A group of local surfers immediately converged on the scene and straightened out the situation which included tossing several In-landers off the pier to retrieve Dickey's horn; which they did. They were then escorted back to their low-rider 'Cholo-mobile' and directed to the quickest route out of town; which they took.

South of Laguna, PCH meandered through miles and miles of open grazing land along the bluffs that overlook the numerous intimate coves, pristine white beaches and beautiful blue Pacific. Eventually we turned off the highway toward the beach in the middle of a familiar nowhere. The bright yellow woody bounced along two ruts, masquerading as a road, and disappeared into an endless meadow of mustard weed, sunflowers and dandelions. The seldom traveled pair of ruts within the waving sea of bright yellow seemed to pass through some sort of space portal that time-warped us to a ramshackle dilapidated lean-to of a shack. On the porch, rocking in their chairs, sat two old dust bowl scrub farmers that looked like they just rolled out of Steinbeck's "Grapes of Wrath". They wore thread-barren overalls, well-worn, sweat-stained pork- pie hats, knee-high rubber boots and they were smoking wicker twigs in their corncob pipes.

There was a makeshift cloths-pole barricade stretched across the road, with a rope attached that went up through a rusty pulley hung from the porch roof, and then was tied to the porch rail next to the Clodhopper cousins, Gomer and Goober. One of the old toothless sodbusters extended another cloths pole that had a clothes pin attached to the end, into which we clipped a dollar bill. He pulled on the rope and raised the barricade to allow us passage.

We continued down the narrow path between the mustard weed, around a small hill that shielded Coast Highway and all things inland, and drove onto a pristine white beach that was Nirvana. One set after another of perfectly formed, glassy, pale blue tubular waves rolled in onto a smooth, desolate white beach. If it was good anywhere, it was always better at' Salt Creek.'

I waxed up my banana board and launched into the deep blue. It took the length of the paddle out to the breakers before the cartilage began to soften in my old decrepit surf knots on my knees and the top of my feet. The Yeager's and Velzy were already slicing through the smooth as glass translucent waves. The Santa Ana's were gently blowing off-shore which brought a warm breeze that blew the tops of the cresting waves into a sparkling mist. Wave after perfectly formed wave rolled in throughout the morning. They were overhead gentle rollers that held up for a long duration, then formed into transparent tubes and broke in smooth lines near the beach.

It took several swims to the beach to retrieve my board after some hairy wipeouts, before I got my sea legs under me and managed to catch a few impressive waves and demonstrated that I was actually pretty good at one time.

At the end of a long session, when everyone else was back on the beach, I paddled out to a big set that was rolling in. I waited for the biggest, most well- formed wave of the set, knee- paddled into perfect position and launched into a big overhead roller. I went left slicing across the steep face gaining velocity then, cut back hard right at the bottom. As the pale blue wave began to crest and the top began to wisp away, I cut back to the left just ahead of the advancing tubular waterfall. I was gonna' 'showboat' this last ride to show the boys on the beach who was still the alpha-dog in a pack of show-off hot dogs. As the big wave began to crest over my head, I crouched down and walked to the nose……in my case it may have been more of a shuffle. I was no 'Murph the Surf', but it would be the' play of the game' on the eleven o'clock news sports highlights, or so I imagined.

When I got within reach, I crouched down, stretched-out my left leg, and curled my toes over the nose. I held the rail with my right hand and stretched my left out ahead of me like a flying super hero. I held that pose as I streaked up the face of the tubular monster and went flying over-the-falls in a spectacular Evil Kneivel crashing wipeout.

The boys on the beach loved it. They alternated from spontaneous applause and boisterous cheers to hysterical, falling-down laughter. I mentioned that perhaps I should name that maneuver that I had just performed. Velzy laughed and informed me that a guy named Paul Strough, from the Gregg Knoll, Mickey Dora, and Hobie Alter Malibu crowd already claimed that move. "Maybe you could name that spastic shuffle to the nose after yourself," he joked. "No," Deacon interjected, "I think Soupy Sales already patented that 'Soupy Shuffle' you were doing." We all laughed. I should have known that I wasn't going to catch a break from this motley crew. (Hello? Call Tommy Lee, I have a name for his scruffy-ass garage band.)

From Salt Creek we went south through Dana Point to check out a couple of familiar surfing spots like 'Trestles' within Camp Pendleton, where the Marines simulate amphibious landings on the beach, and 'Doheny' where the steep rock bottom makes for towering shore break similar to the body slamming bone crushers found at the 'Wedge' in Newport Beach.

On the ride back, just past San Clemente, on the left side of the road and across a wide mustard weed meadow, I noticed a shiny-new black *Bell* helicopter sitting idle on the bluffs above the serene coves and wide blue Pacific. There was a group of about a half dozen short guys in dark suits and slicked-back hair milling about and pointing occasionally from one location to another across the wide field.

I asked Deacon to pull over and stop. I asked if there was a set of binoculars on board, and retrieved from under the front seat, I received a sand encrusted pair of opera glasses with several grimy French fries stuck to them. I blew-off the sand and the fries, adjusted the focus and could see what appeared to be a group of corporate 'yes men;' identical, mini-penis, Asian guys in cookie-cutter suits and screw-down hairdos, like some cats from Japan........ or spiders from Mars. (Ooooooh yeah! I need to cut down on the wheat straws before I morph into Ziggy Stardust.......who ever that is.)

"There's an opening in the fence over there," I said. Let's go down and take a closer look." We barely got started down the worn rut road within acres of mustard weed before the mini-men in black clambered aboard their shiny black chopper and the blades began to rotate. Within moments the helicopter lifted off, turned toward the ocean and flew away, disappearing into muted haze upon distant horizon.

We stopped in the spot from whence the helicopter departed. The boys walked to the edge of the bluff to check out the surf, I walked around staring at the ground. I picked–up a freshly discarded cigarette butt that had dark tobacco with a pungent aroma wrapped in a dark brown paper. Embossed on the dark brown paper was a golden dragon....................I stared at it for a few moments in disbelief. I couldn't fathom what I was seeing. A surge of blurred memories and confused emotions rushed over me, none of them good. I have a real bad feeling about this.

After dropping Velzy and my banana yellow rocket ship at his place, the Yeager-meisters deposited me back at Mona's. We bid each other adieu, adios and aloha before the bright yellow surf buggy made a tire screeching u turn in the middle of Main Street and a right at the corner headed north, destination Manhattan Beach, with *'La-Coo-Ca-Rocha'* blasting from the air horns as they disappeared into the setting sun.

I climbed the stairs and found Mona still on the couch in the lounge drinking martinis. She wore the same negligee' that she had worn last night, and the ashtrays looked like she'd chain smoked all night. I poured myself a martini and joined Mona on the couch. I apologized for not returning last night, but things had not gone as planned. She simply smiled, reached beside the couch and handed me a copy of this morning's newspaper. The headlines read; 'HB Police Gun-Down Two Robbery Suspects.' A single paragraph described how the assailants attempted to rob an unidentified Venice PI and his companion in *Maxwell's* parking lot next to the pier. One assailant was critically wounded in the parking lot and the second was killed after a brief foot pursuit and an exchange of gunfire. Didn't mention any names and noted that the investigation continues. "I'm so glad you're here Travis. I hate to think what would have happened to Lola if you weren't."

I informed Mona that Precious and I had a reservation at *the Hollywood Bunny Club* this evening to further the investigation of the murdered girl in the dumpster. Hef was to speak to the girl's ex-husband, Mort Stahl, and see what information he may have regarding motive or suspects.

"Oh, I almost forgot," she said. She went into another room and returned with my *'Harris and Frank'* custom tailored, fleecy white dinner jacket, and two pair of slacks. "That must be why Chang's cleaners, on the corner, rush-delivered these this afternoon." His only request," she continued with a smile," was that, for once, you return jacket without being spattered with blood. He suggests that you date nice docile and submissive women."

She laughed a hardy laugh, then sighed heavily, settled back into the plush couch, gazing melancholy and far away out the big window. "Boy it's been a long time since I've been to *the Bunny Club*. Not since the days when my husband and I ran around with Bobby Waterfield and his wife Jane Russell. We were a wild bunch back in those days. We made the rounds of all the trendy clubs with Norm van Brocklin, Tommy Fears, Crazy-legs Hirsch, Deacon Jones, Bogie and Betty the original 'rat packers', and occasionally Joey D. and dear Marilyn." Her voice trailed-off and her eyes filled with tears.

I held her close for a time, then gently picked her up and carried her into the bathroom. I slowly removed her negligee' and kissed her softly as it slid to the floor. We enjoyed each other's comforting embraces and the warmth of sudsy bubbles. When we finally emerged from the steamy shower, Mona wore a smile on her face and the checkerboard pattern of shower tiles imprinted across her butt. She didn't seem to mind. She didn't seem to mind several times. She spent so much time standing on one leg in the shower, with the other draped over my arm that I now fondly refer to her as 'my fabulous flamingo.' (And yes, she did live-up to her name. Great acoustics in the tile shower.)

Mona returned to her apartment and fell into a much-needed sound sleep. I flopped down on the couch in my place and drifted off wondering how Rita was, and how much I missed her. I tried to concentrate on the task ahead, but inevitably my thoughts always returned to Rita.

I was awakened by a phone call from my lovely Rita back on the island. She was cheerful and happy and said she missed me terribly. Things were going well, the casino was busy, the Commodore was excited about preparations for initial grading to begin in Hamilton Cove for the new Mediterranean inspired condo project, and Lara was about to debut a three-night engagement starring Rosemary Clooney and Les Brown and his band of Renown. The opening act is an old up-and-coming comic out of Vegas named Rodney Dangerfield. "From what I hear so far, nobody ever heard of him and he gets no respect," she laughed.

I gave Rita an abbreviated version of current events including subsequent introductions to HBPD's finest and the intrepid Inspector Golly. I relayed tonight's itinerary; an attempt to get a handle on the situation, though I have my doubts that we're going to gain any substantive information. I expressed my fear that we'll just muddy the water.

Rita cautioned me regarding my degree of patience in such situations. She knew that I was not much of a schmoozer. To me it seems a colossal waste of time to just sit around and shoot the shit. I usually don't have much shit to shoot, and I usually don't give a shit about the shit that's being shot. She also was aware that I have very little tolerance for annoying drunks. Drunks always seem compelled to tell you the same story over and over, each time a bit louder and more embellished. They always think what they have to say is so important and continually get closer and closer to tell their so important drunken drama. Drunks just love to hear themselves talk.

Rita has witnessed my impatience first hand on several occasions when some inebriate has encroached within my comfort zone at which time I simply knocked their ass out. It's my own personal way of telling the offenders that they have become annoying and to shut the hell up.

I assured Rita that I would be on my best behavior and that I was being accompanied by Precious Goodlay who was adept at the art of schmoozing while collecting information at the same time. Precious knew how to carry a conversation along without too much participation or input from me. She knew my strong suit was to be charming, amusing and unassuming; the strong, silent type.

There was a short silence and then Rita whispered how she missed me and was anxious for me to return home. She hadn't expressed it before because it hadn't been an issue for some time, but she was afraid for my safety and wished that I no longer took on dangerous cases. After all, it wasn't necessary. We had young bucks trained to do the leg work, and besides, I had a cushy job as casino manager on the island and a beautiful girl friend who loved me dearly. She was right and I agreed. I told her that I thought my enthusiasm for this line of work was waning, and in this profession that was a sure way to get myself killed. I assured her that this was a personal favor for an old friend and that when I got things under control then I would turn it over to our operatives. I missed her terribly and I was anxious to come home ASAP. We exchanged "I love you" and said our goodbyes.

I hung up the phone, then stood there staring at it. Still, I find myself reluctant to say the words, "I love you," or allow anyone to get close to my feelings. I tend to keep those feelings to myself. The few times that I have expressed such things to someone it always turned out bad; my feelings crushed, my heart broken, and my guts kicked in. You are left with a hollow feeling inside. You build an impenetrable barrier around your innermost feelings and allow no one to enter. Try as I may to deny it, I have indeed fallen in love with Rita Rigney.

It looked as though Mona's place was going to be dark another night or two, until the cooties, the crabs, and the heebie-jeebies had subsided. There will be some very lonely clients 'Jonesing' for some companionship and left to handle it themselves..........so to speak.

Precious and her robins-egg blue T-bird swept around the corner and whisked me from the curb precisely at the pre-arranged time. Precious was preconditioned to my lifelong proclivity to be fashionably late to most functions. That is why she tells me a time approximately twenty minutes earlier than the actual designated time, to ensure that I will be there when required. In school, I was the kid walking into class just as the tardy bell rang.

She stopped at the corner, leaned across and gave me a gentle kiss. "I'm glad you're not dead, asshole," she whispered close into my ear, and then she gave me a solid left hook to my tender right shoulder. She seemed quite satisfied at my obvious wincing pain.

On our way north up PCH, Precious gently reminded me, though it turned into more of a lecture, then progressively verged on an ass-chewing tirade sprinkled with liberal amounts of 'I told you so', that I was getting soft and my reflexes or instincts are not what they used to be. She finally began to lose steam somewhere between Santa Monica and Zuma Beach. I simply gazed upon her and smiled. She was a stunningly gorgeous blonde amazon; a statuesque bronze goddess shimmering in white satin and   glistening diamonds.

Her short satin skirt had risen to provocative heights upon her unbelievably gorgeous thighs. My smile grew wider as my trousers grew tighter. She glanced over and recognized the beginning of my subtle transformation to romantic, rakish charmer. That suave and debonair charisma draws you close and the dreamy bedroom eyes sweep you off your feet. She smiled, "what?" she asked playfully. I smiled softly and looked deep into her eyes. "Have I told you what a stunning, gorgeous beauty you are tonight, Precious?" Precious smiled; "bite me Travis." And so I did, softly on her inner thighs. Not hard enough to leave a mark, just hard enough to make her giggle.

She made the right at Sunset Blvd. and started up through the hills that would eventually take us past Cold Water and Laurel Canyon on our journey to the land of Oz; tinsel town. "Precocious got a call first thing this morning from your Mr. Kuda", she said while maneuvering the little T-bird along the winding up and down road. "Who's Mr. Kuda?" I asked. She looked at me like I'd just clubbed a baby seal. "Are you fuckin' kidding me? You attend an afterhours meeting with a guy, then pull his ass out of a wringer, almost get killed, and you didn't even get the guy's name? What are you a wet-behind-the-ears rookie? Kuda! God Dammit! Barry fuckin' Kuda! Hello! Does that ring a bell at all Travis?" "Geez, Precious, don't get your panties in a pucker," I provoked. "No problem dick-wad, I'm not wearing any," she snapped back. "Oh, Barry," I toyed. "Old Bar and I were on a first name basis. He was reluctant to disclose details, we spoke in generalities. That's why I advised him to call the office after I had listened to his sketchy story. He would have to divulge names, phone numbers, etcetera, if his client wanted protection and was prepared to sign contracts for such. I think the two gunzels in the parking lot probably sealed the deal. Barry Kuda sounds like an alias anyway. Otherwise, another gee thanks mom and dad."

"Barry Kuda is legit," she responded. "He is, in fact, the counselor for one Mr. Harry James Stanton, the railroad tycoon, who among other things, built and incorporated the city of Stanton, located just east, and adjacent to Huntington Beach. Stanton is a company town built to house the railroad employees and their families."

"Mr. Stanton owns the 'right of way' and the rail lines that run up and down the west coast and east to the oil fields of west Texas. He has established a virtual monopoly on all crude oil transportation along that route through Signal Hill in Long Beach, to the *'Flying A'* and *'Standard oil'* refineries in Carson and Wilmington, and north to the *'Richfield'* refinery near Hanford and *'Douglas'* in the bay area. A courier is to pick-up contracts for Mr. Stanton's signature this afternoon in order for us to initiate personal protection for individuals yet to be named. Manpower may be stretched pretty thin depending on how extensive Mr. Stanton's sphere of protection may be."

"Did Precocious receive any information as to a possible connection to the dead girl behind *the Bear*?" I asked. "No, and at this time we have no reason to suspect that there is a connection," she responded. "Mr. Stanton has requested a private meeting with you, and I presume that if there is a connection, then you will be made aware of it at that time. If that connection is made, then we will no doubt have a laundering of dirty linen assignment, as well as a personal security contract. However, I must remind you," she continued, "that you have advised them regarding the extortion attempts and I have a feeling that Mr. Stanton is going to want you to deal with that situation as well. I must caution you, as I have done on countless other occasions to no avail, that you could be getting in over your head."

We crested a small hill and emerged into the glorious brilliance of Hollywood and the Sunset Strip. The dazzling neon jungle was aglow and filled with excitement and anticipation. There is always a heightened energy within the glittering wonderland of restaurants, night clubs, ornate art deco movie theaters, and intimate playgrounds of the industry's moguls and stars. A fantasy play land where dreams are either fulfilled, destroyed, or both; where the eternal glow of the 'HOLLYWOODLAND' sign, high on the hill continues to attract the wide-eyed dreamers like gentle moths fluttering to a flame.

Precious pulled the robins-egg blue T-bird to the curb in front of *Ciro's*, one of Hollywood's most iconic upscale eateries; the place to mingle and be seen with the beautiful people, and one of the many trendy watering holes of the rich and famous.

We were promptly greeted by a proper maître d and shown to an open table on the patio near the bustling strip. Xavier Cougat's Latin rhythms wafted from within, and the open-space between the buildings across the street afforded a spectacular view down the hill overlooking West Hollywood, Pacific Palisades, and the last remnants of a glorious magenta sunset. The Wine Captain appeared and presented an extensive leather-bound wine list. I politely gave it a quick perusal then handed it back and ordered two vodka martinis, agitated not propelled.

A lovely young, dark haired girl with big blue eyes arrived at our table with likewise leather bound menus at the ready. She wore a provocative French maid inspired costume with great eye-popping panache'. (Kudos to the personnel manager.) I was already prepared to nominate this girl for 'Employee of the Month' and she hadn't said a word yet. When she spoke it was the soft voice of an angel. "Good evening," she whispered. "My name is Lolita, and it will be my pleasure to serve you." (Wow Lolita, how apropos.) (But again I digress............wait...........still digressing............)

I ordered two London Broil Flank Steaks, medium rare, smothered in sauteed' mushrooms; the house specialty, and baked potatoes with all the fixin's. Lovely Lolita departed with a wink and a smile. My lingering gaze of her lovely departure was not camouflaged by the arrival of the wine captain with our cocktails, nor did it go unnoticed by my alert, alluring, and now slightly annoyed, Norwegian goddess dinner date. "Really Travis, are you kidding me? She's young enough to be my daughter." I smiled wide and lifted my glass as if in a toast. "Even hotter, I like the way you think Babe. Are you suggesting what I'm thinking?" I asked with a widening grin. I tried to contain myself but it was futile, I couldn't do it. I began to laugh out loud anticipating her presumed reaction to my lecherously whimsical fantasies; didn't have to wait long.

"Oh! You sick perverted bastard. You immoral, carousing, horn-dog son-of-a-bitch." She could have gone on and on, but she couldn't hold back any longer either and broke out in uninhibited, boisterous laughter. "You know Travis, you're a womanizing horn-dog, you beautiful bastard, but you're a charming and funny womanizing horn-dog, and I love you, ya' big dick-head. It's always an adventure Travis I'll say that for you, it's always an adventure." We gently touched glasses and toasted a magnificent fading sunset. "Besides", she said, with confidence and a sly smile; "you couldn't even handle the stunning, robust piece of luscious arm-candy sitting across from you, much less the two of us together. Although I hate to admit, I like the way you think Macho Man. After all, we are in Holly-weird." (As I've said many times before, you gotta' love this girl.)

We enjoyed our meal under the canopy of twinkling stars and the glow of endless neon. Upon our departure I paid the tab and a generous contribution to lovey Lolita's modeling or film career, along with a business card from the '*Travis Dugan Talent Agency.*'

The T-bird made the glittering block-and-half journey to the *Bunny Club* and came to rest in valet parking. I slipped the swarthy attendant an Andrew Jackson and told him there would be another at the end of the evening if he parked the little blue bird close to the light where he could keep an eye on it. He assured me with a big smile that the beautiful automobile would be well taken care of. He handed me a numbered parking chit and then drove the car to a well-lit spot directly across from the entrance.

Precious wrapped her arm in mine and we strolled to the member's only private entrance. All eyes in the general admission line were on Precious and her every sensuous step, including the formidable Door Man, who couldn't take his eyes off my gorgeous trophy date and who couldn't get the door open fast enough. The smile on his face couldn't have been wider if it was painted on, and he barely gave my charter member platinum key with the embossed bunny head, a second glance.

We entered the world of the glamorous, the privileged pampered and chosen few. The elegant atmosphere was shiny and bubbly, sensuous and exciting; a subtly lit palace full of scantily-clad beautiful women bouncing about in various stages of giggly inebriation. There was lots of laughter, drinking and dancing. Headliners Steve Lawrence and Edie Gorme' were kibitzing back and forth on stage while smoothly segueing through their extensive list of chart topping hits.

A smart and snappy maître d welcomed us and invited us to enjoy a complimentary cocktail at the bar while our table was being prepared. After another round of martinis we were shown to an intimate table near the smooth-as-glass dance floor.

A sexy satin bunny arrived at our table complete with shiny satin bunny ears and a cute little cotton tail appropriately located on her shiny satin bottom. She took our drink orders and then disappeared within the swirl of the fashionable and wealthy upon the dance floor.

It wasn't long before Hef sauntered over in our vicinity dressed in his formal silk jammies, bright red satin bow tie and his finest red and black satin smoking jacket with silk lapels. He wore what appeared to be Patten leather Coco Chanel designer muck-lucks and of course, he was sucking on his signature smoking pipe. He did a Buster Keaton double take when he spotted Precious, ravishing in soft glow of candle light. His saunter quickly became more of a sprint as he hastened his approach. A wide smile formed his jubilant expression as he arrived to our table and gently kissed Precious on both cheeks, completely oblivious to my presence. He graciously welcomed Precious to the *Bunny Club* once again, and once again reminded her of the standing offer he made to her long ago. "You know Precious my offer still stands; a blank check centerfold pictorial anywhere in the world you wish."

"As always Hef, I'm extremely flattered by your very gracious offer, and I must admit that I have seriously considered it as of late, before I find myself in the land of hot flashes, cellulite, mood swings, or gravity submissive body parts. I have also discussed the idea with my niece Precocious, and she's all for it. In fact she expressed interest in participating as well," she teased with great relish.

Hef's expression grew far away and dreamy, as he sank back in his chair while fondly creating a mental picture of what that photo shoot might produce, besides the pup tent he was currently erecting in his jammies. Two statuesque and gorgeous blonde Scandinavian goddesses spread naked across the pages of his entertainment magazine for men, was obviously a titillating apparition for '*the robed one*'.

After a few reflective moments, Hef finally realized that I was there. "Oh hi Travis, good to see you again sorry I didn't notice you at first." "Perfectly understandable Amigo," I replied. "I wouldn't have noticed me either."

"We don't mean to piss on your parade tonight Hef," she began, getting to the point. "But, you do realize that we're here to talk about China Lei, and see if you might have any information that might help us find who is responsible for her murder."

"We assume that you've spoken to China's ex-husband, Mort Stahl, and most likely to the investigating police agency as well. Is that correct?" I asked. "Yes, an inspector Golly called to see if I knew Morty's present whereabouts. Of course I did, as he was fulfilling a weekend engagement at our Chicago Club. Morty called me immediately after having spoken to the inspector. You can imagine that he was extremely upset, totally distraught. I tried to comfort him as best I could, but he was totally un-consolable. I urged him to cancel his last show and fly back to L.A. immediately on the red-eye, which he did. My driver and I picked him up at LAX and brought him back to the mansion in the Holmby Hills. The police inspector arrived the next morning and asked Morty a litany of questions regarding China's background, current acquaintances, and possible enemies, grudges or motives."

"As Morty explained to the police, he and China had been amiably divorced for some time, but kept in touch when they both were in town. He was aware that she was loosely affiliated with a high end escort service in Hollywood, Brentwood and Beverly Hills catering to wealthy businessmen, movie people and sports stars. Other than that, he was not familiar with her current acquaintances, was not aware of any animosity from anyone, and certainly was not aware of a motive for murder. He's taking it pretty hard. Presently he's in seclusion at the mansion."

"I wasn't able to provide much in the way of useful information either, I'm afraid. Of course we still keep in touch. I see her in the club occasionally and at the mansion parties or special events. China was always one of our most popular models and spokespersons. Besides being exotically gorgeous, she was extremely intelligent; she could discuss any topic with knowledge and insight. China was sharp, always on top of her game, and she was ambitious. She navigated through the labyrinth of Hollywood decadence with poise and grace. The girls at the mansion and the entire organization are devastated by her passing and she will be terribly missed by all." He started to choke-up and had to graciously excuse himself.

Our satin bunny returned with our refreshments, and Hef soon followed. "Sorry folks," he said. "But you have no idea how this has affected me and everyone who knew China. I'm afraid I don't have any useful information. Believe me, I wish I did."

"I know this is not the best time to bring up another problem, but I have a friend who finds himself in a desperate situation with which you may be able to help. I told him that your agency was the best and that you would at least listen to his problem and offer some guidance. When I saw your name in the reservation book, I took the liberty of calling my friend, who is a wealthy land owner and cattle-baron in the southern California area, and informed him of your expected presence this evening. My friend is very anxious to meet you and has sent a representative to meet with you this evening to explain the current situation. If you are inclined to get involved, then the representative will arrange for a direct meeting with my friend. He asked that I not disclose his identity until you have decided if you wish to help." (I didn't have a good feeling about this.)

I leaned back in my chair and glanced over to Precious. She, being the consummate professional, stepped right up and confidently reassured Hef that we would, of course, listen to what his friend's representative had to say. Hef, visibly relieved sank back into his seat and a reassured look came over him. He thanked us and then excused himself to go and retrieve his friend's representative.

Precious and I looked knowingly at one another. "Seems like de je vu doesn't it Travis?" she asked, while gently coaxing the olive from her swizzle. I paused momentarily mesmerized by the dexterity of her talented tongue working in unison with her sumptuous lips in the process of coaxing the olive from her swizzle. (She could coax the olive from my swizzle anytime......... But, once again I digress.)

"Yeah, and I don't have a good feeling about it either," I responded. "It's like the convergence of conspiracies and conspirators we encountered on our last Avalon adventure. It's a reoccurring nightmare. My gut feeling is to get the hell out of here, but of course as always, I'm going to ignore my better judgment and instead stumble blindly into the quagmire of darkness and despair." (I hate when I do that.)

Upon the conclusion of that alcohol induced mini-rant, our saucy satin bunny returned with another round of 'martin eyes.' I was beginning to get a little fuzzy around the edges and in need of some fresh air and a change of scenery.

Hef approached with a small entourage in tow, one appearing to be the original rhinestone cowboy accompanied by two blonde bobble-head bimbos in their finest Dallas Cowboys cheerleader outfits. Precious glanced at me with a knowing grin. She knew that I generally regarded most cowboys as a bunch of ignorant, loud mouth drunken idiots. And they looked at me like I was a pansy-ass city slicker. Little do they know that I actually know one end of the horse from the other; I spent many summers at my cousin Sweet Loretta's ranch near the town of Norco in the unincorporated area of Riverside County. Her folks, my Uncle Stan and Aunt Bernice owned a horse boarding and training facility and managed the spring rodeo at the Grange in town. They boarded the Paint Ponies for *Monte Montana's Traveling Wild-West Show*, and trained cutting and roping quarter horses for the cattle industry in the area. Cutting horses can stop at the blink of an eye and turn on a dime. I learned to ride bare-back as a young buckaroo, and it requires skills to ride a cutting horse with only a handful of mane and a firm grip on the reigns.

"Travis, Precious, I'd like to introduce you to my friend's representative, Harden." The big cowboy with a wide grin removed his ten gallon hat and reached across the table to shake Precious' hand. "Harden Johnson Boehner at your service little lady," he said. "Well let's hope it doesn't come to that cowboy," she replied. "Spunky! I love a gal with spunk," he laughed. He then reached across and shook my hand. He attempted to fuse my knuckles, but I was prepared for the juvenile, alpha-dog exhibition and was having none of it. He smiled knowingly and reluctantly released his attempted death grip. He then introduced his bubbly cheerleaders as Bambi and Charlene. They came fully accessorized including white boots, hat, short little skirt, matching vest and enough cleavage to bury a Harden Johnson Boehner.

"What do your friends call you, Harden?" I asked, and was soon sorry that I had. The big cow- fart in the baby blue polyester Roy Rodgers outfit grew a big grin, pulled a big stogy out of his breast pocket, and broke into a *Second City* comedy routine in an accent that was somewhere between Fog Horn Leghorn and Al Jolson. "Well you can call me John, or you can call me Johnny. Or you can call me JJ or you can call me Junior. But ya' doesn't has to call me Mister Johnson." Harden Johnson Boehner broke out in boisterous laughter as did the bubbly bobble-head twins. Bambi reached into the cowboy's crotch and announced with a big smile, "I call him Big Johnson." Charlene reached in from the other side, "I call him Mister Boehner," she giggled.

"Why don't you girls go see if you can round up another round of drinks, while I discuss a little business with these nice folks," Mr. Boehner suggested to the bubble mint twins. Hef offered to escort the girls to the bar, and with one on each arm, a large grin across his face, they wondered away and disappeared into the crowd.

Big Johnson's demeanor abruptly changed once our host and the girls were out of ear-shot. His goofy smile and 'ah-shucks' persona morphed into a dead-serious, large and intimidating brute. He was a square jawed, steely eyed shit-kicker who was going to test my mantle by chest-bumping me around the corral a few times to see if he could scrape me off on a fence post or buck me off into the bleachers. Just as the feisty, mean little quarter horses discovered during the summers of my youth, I'm just as mean, you can't intimidate me, I'm scared of nothing, and if you piss me off I'd kill you or die trying......at least that was the persona that I was attempting to project. I chest-bumped my way onto his beach to do his bitches like a posturing Sea Lion Bull, and he was dually intimidated because he eventually backed-down from his contrived blow-hard bravado and moved on to the business at hand and the reason for this impromptu encounter.

Over a few more rounds, he explained that he was the ranch manager for a wealthy landowner, real estate mogul, and the largest cattle baron in the state, who was being pressured by way of thinly veiled threats and subtle intimidation to sell a large parcel of prime ocean front property in southern California. He went on to say that his employer had no current or future plans to sell said property. I asked if the property in question was part of a larger parcel that would require a survey, county permit application requesting a property split and separate deed documentation?" "No" he answered. "This particular property is already a separate parcel with corresponding deed."

Precious asked what type of pressure has his employer received, and by whom? 'Johnny,' as he informed us during our enchanting evening, was how he was normally addressed, began describing the same basic scenario that Barry Kuda had articulated last night at *Maxwell's*; an anonymous series of mysterious phone calls offering to purchase a controlling interest in an established rail line, or in this case, a parcel of prime ocean front property, for mere cents on the dollar of its actual worth. Commodities neither owner was inclined to sell at any price.

On a whim I asked if there was a rail line running near the property. He seemed puzzled, but informed us that several railway easements did indeed pass through the east side of the parcel, running north and south adjacent to Pacific Coast Highway.

An approving grin slowly formed across the cowboy's rugged face. "Well what do you know, you aren't as dumb as you look," he said. "You get a second chance at a first impression, Amigo." "That's why I get the big money and the beautiful women, Kemosabe," I responded with my own slightly veiled smirk.

He said that his employer was becoming increasingly concerned because the phone calls as of late have become more ominous, threatening contract interference, supplier backlogs, labor disruptions, livestock rustling, and insinuations of physical violence directed toward family, friends and key business associates.

It's the same shake-down that neighborhood thugs and organized crime have perpetrated upon the legitimate business owners and shop keepers since the days when 'Mustache Petes' extorted protection money from the push cart vendors on the cobblestone streets of Sicily.

The vivacious little cheerleaders with the crowd-pleasing pom-poms returned bearing another round of refreshments. I lit a cigarette and settled back in my chair. Star spangled Harden Johnson Boehner gathered his pom-poms and prepared to depart. "Travis, Precious, it was my sincere pleasure meeting you and I can assure you that I will recommend your firm to my employer. I have confidence in saying that I believe you to be the right man for the job, Travis." I handed him a business card and asked that his employer have his people call my people should he decide to contract our services. He glanced briefly at the card with a puzzled expression. *"Travis Dugan Talent Agency?"* he queried. "Oh shit, sorry, wrong card, man." I rectum-fied the situation and bid Harden 'Big Johnson' Boehner, and his traveling pep-rally and pom-pom revue, a hard-felt adieu'.

Precious turned to me with a wicked little smile and mischievous twinkle in her eye. She leaned close and whispered in my ear. "It's early, neither of us have been in Holly-weird for a while; how do you feel about painting the town red? Maybe you can expand the circulation and distribution of those talent agency recruitment cards you're carrying," she laughed.

We finished our refreshments, paid our tab, and left a generous gratuity for our vivacious and shiny satin bunny. Hef met us at the door and again reassured us that his friend was a high caliber straight shooter. We thank him for the reference and said good night. We met the valet who already had our keys in hand. I accompanied him over to the robin's egg blue T-bird sitting sprightly lit right where we left it. After a thorough inspection of the undercarriage and engine compartment, during which the young valet assured me that he had kept a keen eye on said T-bird and that no one had molested it, I laid another Jackson on him as promised.

Precious and I had the shiny bird cruising through the kaleidoscope of glittering neon that is the enchanted wonderland of Hollywood and the Sunset Strip. We danced our asses off to Hazel Scott's boogie-woogie piano at *'Mocambo's'*, enjoyed a refreshment and the smooth sounds of Nat King Cole at *the' Trocadero'*, and rubbed elbows over cocktails with Howard Hughes and Ava Gardner at the piano bar in *'Sheri's'*. We swept through *the Whiskey, Gazzarri's, and Pandora's*

Box in a blur of under-rehearsed grungy garage bands with names like '*Strangers with Candy*' and '*Flammable Jammies*.'

Precious and I enjoyed seeing old friends and acquaintances at many of our former after-hours stomping grounds like the '*Rainbow Room*', '*Chasen's*', the '*Cocoanut Grove*', and the '*Frolic Room*'. We dodged trollies on *the Red Car Line* and whizzed past *Angel's Flight*. We somehow wound-up at 8150 Sunset Boulevard, at the corner of Sunset and Crescent Heights; Mickey Cohen's '*Garden of Allah*.' How ironic, the '*Garden of Allah*', originally built by Allah Nazimova, silent screen star and nefarious hostess of infamously depraved Hollywood sex orgies, was once fertile ground for a young Boyle Heights street thug who was known to have relieved Betty Grable of her jewelry early in his stick-up career; Mickey now owned the joint and welcomed Betty and other Hollywood celebs as regulars and personal friends on a nightly basis. Mickey was a silent partner of course, unable to obtain a liquor license due to his felony tax evasion conviction and time served in the pen.

Mickey welcomed us at the door after I had made the same request of the parking valet that I had at the other venues; "keep the car close, in the light, and keep an eye on it." Mickey showed Precious and me to his private table within its own plush garden alcove. He was impeccably attired in a finely tailored double-breasted cashmere suit, immaculate silk shirt and tie, and severely shined Italian wingtips. He was gaga over my gorgeous blonde goddess of a date. He always is.

Mickey expressed genuine concern for Papa Nikos and his current situation and offered to help in any way he could. He said that he understood why Papa had shut down the wire service for the time being, but hoped that he could get it back up and running as soon as reasonably possible. Precious patted Mickey on the back of his hand and thanked him for his sincere concern, using the breathiest, sexiest whisper that I had ever heard come from her sumptuous lips. I know that I had a restless beast stirring under the table, and Mickey had a wide smile from ear to ear and a rosy blush on his cheeks. Precious snagged him, hook, line and sinker. Mickey would fulfill all of his Scandinavian Goddesses wishes; she need only ask.

I asked him off handedly if he knew any teamsters or railroad workers union representatives. He looked at me with a puzzled expression momentarily, then burst out laughing and gave me a playful slap on the cheek. "Dugan, you silly bastard, I know a lot of people. I'm sure one or two of them must be affiliated with a union of some sort." He gave me a momentary glint of a cold stare, then, just as quickly it softened into a warm friendly smile once again.

There was a noticeable hush in the room as blonde and busty B-movie bombshell Jayne Mansfield and her 'Mister Universe' muscle-bound husband Mickey Hargitay entered the establishment. Mickey Cohen hastily excused himself to welcome his newly arriving guests. "Try the knish before you go," he said, and then he was off to fulfill his role as benevolent host to the rich a famous.

It was long past the shank of the evening when Precious and I decided to turn this magical mystery tour around and head for the barn. Mickey walked with us outside. He handed me one of his *'Haberdasher to the Hollywood Stars'* business cards and two ringside tickets to the Friday night fights downtown at the venerable *Olympic Auditorium*, one of his favorite places to be seen. "I'd like to help any way I can, Dugan. Money, muscle, persuasion, whatever, just call me."

Suddenly there was a huge explosion and gigantic fire ball in the parking lot. The robin's egg blue convertible hardtop with portholes and the passenger seat were blown high into the sky and came to a flaming crash some twenty yards from the burning remains of the destroyed little T-bird. Luckily, the valet still had the driver's door open when he turned the ignition key, and the charge was placed on the passenger side of the transmission; meant to take out the passenger specifically. The valet was blown out of the car through the open door and out onto the parking lot. He suffered second degree burns on the right side of his body and his back, but the transmission took the brunt of the blast and he suffered no major, or life threatening injuries. In his zeal to look good for the boss, the zestful valet had run to retrieve our car before I had given him my parking chit or performed my inspection. His enthusiasm almost cost him his life.

Mickey Cohen went ballistic. He was having a conniption fit and spitting every kosher expletive in the book "Those ignorant Wops! Those no-class Neanderthal knuckle draggers!" he screamed. "They imported those Chicago bomb shmucks again to grenade my place of business this time. Those garlic suckin' sons-of-bitches blew off the front of my house the last time, ten years ago. They destroyed my entire wardrobe for Christ's sake. They're nothing but a bunch of crude, clumsy Diego idiots. I guarantee you Dugan, Jack Dragna and his band of grease-ball Guinea stumble bums are going to pay for this, and this time they're going to pay big."

Chapter Four

Day 4

The next morning arrived in bits and pieces of consciousness. I heard the crashing of surf onto a sandy shore, and the hiss as it retreated to the sea. I heard the shrill call of a seagull. The aroma was flowery, comforting and familiar. It wasn't until I finally opened my eyes to the brilliant pinks and greens that I realized that I was in my secretary Precious Goodlay's master suite.

Through the haze of a fairly impressive hangover I began to reassemble the events of the previous evening. I remember that Mickey Cohen provided a limo ride back to Balboa, after we spent considerable time with Inspector Ben Dover, LAPD Hollywood/Rampart division, unable to provide answers to questions that we were asking ourselves as well.

I became aware of a tantalizing aroma of freshly baked biscuits and piping hot coffee. I threw on a terry cloth robe that I found on the end of the bed and as I approached the kitchen I could hear the sweet melody of '*the Mango Tree.*'

"Good morning Travis," she said spritely; "how about a cup of coffee and a biscuit? I don't expect your stomach will be able to handle much more, do you?" "Yes, fine, what- ever, just do it quietly please," I begged as I sat at the breakfast counter and held my throbbing head gingerly in my hands. When I finally opened my eyes again, there was a tall cool condensing Bloody Mary complete with accessories; celery swizzle and bottle of tobacco. Precious was always able to drink me and anybody else under the table without suffering the traditional consequences the next morning. I envy her that, especially this particular morning. I look forward to the biscuits. They will help absorb the percolation process occurring in my fermentation chamber.

While I finished my breakfast, as it were, Precious went to shower and dress. She eventually emerged in white shorts and a white cotton top with horizontal stripes. Her long blonde hair was wrapped in a terry cloth towel. She smiled knowing how horizontal striped tops affected me and she was stunningly beautiful even without a bit of makeup.

The buzzer from the door man out front sounded. Precious pressed the intercom button. "Yes Barrington, good morning." "Good morning Miss Goodlay. Sorry to bother you this early in the morning, but I have a Mr. Stompanato here who has a delivery from a Mr. Cohen." "Thank you Barrington, I'll be right down," she replied.

I showered and shaved as quickly as I could while Precious brushed out her long golden locks. I believe I've mentioned before what effect watching a beautiful woman brushing her hair has on me. I found a complete wardrobe laid-out on the end of the bed. I dressed while she quickly applied eye liner and lip gloss, then we made our way down stairs.

There, sitting at the curb was a brand new robin's egg blue hardtop convertible with portholes, spinner hub caps, white side wall tires and continental kit; A little blue T-bird identical to the one that got terminated the night before.

Johnny Stompanato stood dutifully next to the car holding the keys. "Mr. Cohen feels terrible about the events of last evening and would like you to accept this small token of an apology, Miss Goodlay."

"Well that is extremely generous of Mr. Cohen," she replied while accepting the keys from Johnny. "Please express my sincere gratitude and my appreciation to Mr. Cohen for this very gracious gift. This is very kind, extremely thoughtful and tremendously appreciated."

It wasn't long before we had the little T-bird headed inland up Grand Avenue through the bean fields and the middle of scruffy downtown Santa Ana. I mentioned to Precious that I was concerned for her safety and that of Precocious' as well. I thought that we should close the office in Venice Beach and move operations to a new location.

She smiled and glanced over to me. "I'm way ahead of you Sherlock. I've already called Precocious at home, while you were still sleeping. Kato and Fia will escort Precocious to my place, and from there we're taking the last ferry across the channel to the island. I've also made arrangements with the Commodore and the Rigney girls for us to stay in the guest house, adjacent to the servant's quarters across the courtyard from the mansion. Precocious has spoken with her friend at the phone company and arranged to have all calls to the office re-routed to the guest house at the Rigney estate. We've beefed-up security at the estate with additional personnel and a K-9 operative as well; ETA at the seaplane tarmac in Avalon approximately noon today aboard your friend Kamikaze Steve's flying boat."

I smiled and settled a little more comfortably into my seat. This girl is good, she is really good. I'm glad that she's on my side, and I'm glad that we're partners because I would never be able to pay her what she's worth. Fortunately for us both, the celebrity personal and estate security business of her nephew's, called *'Blackwater Security Services'*, that Precious and I bought into some time ago, provides an abundant income, and funnels many lucrative clients toward our P.I. services as well.

We no longer accept cheating spouses, messy divorces, or missing-persons cases, with few exceptions. What *Travis Dugan Private Investigations* has become is' Hollywood's fixers.' We're the finders for the seekers, and the keepers of the well- kept. We recover lost, stolen or swindled treasures that traditional authorities are unable to retrieve, or treasures that cannot be reported to appropriate law enforcement because of the questionable ownership, heritage, or method in which the item was acquired. *Travis Dugan Private Investigations* smothers bad press, silences the rumor mongers and muckrakers, and eliminates extortionists, swindlers, and blackmailers who attempt to prey on high profile celebrities. We're lotus land's clearing house, where the pampered and rich inhabitants of the land of palm trees, launders their soiled and unsavory reputations, behavior and consequences of those behaviors.

We pulled into *Zody's* Department store parking lot across the street from *Aloha Family Motors* on the corner of 17th street and Grand Avenue. *Aloha Family Motors,* where you say aloha to your money, your dignity, and your wife, girlfriend or daughter if you don't keep a close watch on all the above.

We cruised through the parking lot behind the first line of parked cars just off the sidewalk. We were performing drive-by surveillance to recon the activities at the car lot and to see if anyone else was scoping-out the place. We drove across 17th street into the *Gemco* Department store lot, catty-corner from the subject location. We then crossed Grand Avenue into the *Montgomery Ward* lot and parked at the *Sambo's* Restaurant, directly across 17th street from *Aloha Family Motors.*

Precious and I sat in a booth at the front windows where we could enjoy a quick brunch and unobtrusively observe the comings and goings across the street at the used car lot. The 'previously- owned-automobiles' business was merely a' front' for the more lucrative drugs and hookers enterprise occurring out of their attorney's motor home parked in the back between the parts-car turd-boxes, the repos, trade-ins and returned loaners that were rolled on special 'oral agreements', rather than written contracts.

Charlie Straight and Joe Crooks, were the stereotypical plaid suit, white belt and tasseled loafers used car salesmen. They are the guys that give the car business a bad name. Charlie Straight and Joe Crooks put the sleaze in sleaze-ball. Soon as you walked onto the lot you could hear, coming somewhere from your subconscious, the '*bow chic-a-*

bow bow' soundtrack from a cheap porn film, and you feel slightly dirty, vulnerable and violated. Precious won't go near the place.

However, they had the right stuff for certain assignments that required something sleazy or scuzzy to be done. They also were always good for a loaner car, no questions ask. The only condition; "if you break it, you fix it. If you crash it, you own it."

It appeared to be a fairly slow, run-of-the-mill type day across the street at the converted gas station, turned used car lot. The porter was busy washing the front line treasures, and the greasy redneck mechanic was up to his elbows in the bowls of the latest shit-box acquisition from *the L.A. Auto Dealers Auction* in Rosemead. While the mechanic sweated in the shop with a car up on the rack, his nasty-ass red haired wife with her own magnificent rack, sat in their Caddy convertible, chain smoking Lucky Strikes, guzzling coke a cola, and sweating into her wife-beater, sleeveless men's undershirt; by days end, she could win any bar room' wet tee-shirt' contest in town. (Whatever those are?)

We finished our meal, paid the tab and walked to the car. I half joking ask Precious if she would like to accompany me across the street to *Aloha Family Motors* and say hi to the boys, knowing full well what her answer would be. "Oh hell no!" she exclaimed. " Those creepy bastards give me the willies. I'm not getting any closer than this. I already feel like I have to go home and scrub down with industrial strength Twenty Mule Team Borax and a course Brillo Pad. I'll call Mona's and leave a message when we've arrived on the island. In the mean-time, take care of yourself Travis. I love you, ya' big dick- head."

I ran across 17ᵗʰ street and onto *Aloha Motors* with the guitar twang of a cheese-ball skin flick playing in my head. The girls in the attorney's motor home greeted me from afar. "Hi Travis, did you come to party?" "Aloha girls, I'll have to stop by on the return trip. Looking good Ladies, love your work!"

Soon after the girls finished their union negotiated smoke break and went back inside the executive, luxury edition rolling whore house, a car load of drunken Jar heads from nearby El Toro Marine Air Base arrived, and did come to party; *'Bow chic-a-bow bow'*.

Joe Crooks met me as I cleared the front line; "Dugan, my friend, great to see you Amigo. Rumor has it that you've been living the life of Riley on some exotic tropical island. Judging by the few extra pounds and the deep, delicious Coppertone tan, I'd say the rumors were correct. What brings you back to our humble little piece of entrepreneurial heaven?" "I need a loaner for a couple of days, Kemosabe." "Did you want to go obtrusive and ostentatious, or un and non?" "I need to be Mr. Bland, Middle American Harvey Milquetoast in his incognito-mobile."

We walked around the back to where the 'crème puff' trade-ins are parked. "Previously owned and rarely driven by a little old lady from Pasadena. She only drove to her weekly Canasta party at the Vet's hall and Saturday night Roller Derby at the *Olympic Auditorium* with Dick Lane at T.V. Ringside; Whoa Nellie!"

It was a '53, Battleship Gray Hudson Hornet with gray mohair upholstery. It was a land yacht, a big gray tank. "She may look like a big pig, but she's got an in-line eight cylinder flat head that flies along the highway like you were riding a runaway locomotive," he began his instinctive sales pitch highlighting the feature benefits of a low mileage swat team crack house battering ram. (Whatever that is?)

I had the big gray Hornet rumbling down the road headed for Mona's. Joe Crooks was right, once you got this gigantic piece of machinery up to speed, it seemed to go faster and faster. It wasn't going to win any drag races, she was pretty slow off a dead start, but by the time you hit high gear she was flying. I took a superfluous route back to the beach, making sure I hadn't acquired a tail on my innocuous lumbering grey elephant already. I parked on Third Street at the alley that runs parallel to Coast Highway behind the Heavy Equipment Shop and *the Golden Bear*. It was still early in the afternoon, so the only stirring about *the Bear* were the bread and produce deliveries, the cleaning crew and the ticket office.

I turned the lock and climbed the stairs. Mona was supervising a small painting detail and had a carpet steamer at the ready. After the extermination of personal infestation and subsequent talent sabbatical, she decided rejuvenation was in order. I was still feeling pretty puny after last night's whirl-wind tour of our favorite Hollywood haunts and hot spots, so I retired to my apartment and crashed heavily onto the couch. I drifted away dreaming about Rita and the island paradise that I left behind. I sure miss that girl.

It was nearing sunset when I regained consciousness. I showered, shaved, dressed, and added my personal accoutrements before heading out the door. When I opened my apartment door onto the foyer, there was a note stuck to the door from Mona. She said that Precious had called and that everyone had arrived at the mansion and they were getting settled in. She would call you again tomorrow. Mona added a P.S., F.Y.I. She would be across the street at *Maxwell's*. Stop by for dinner if you get a chance.

I skipped down the stairs and feeling surprising good. I planned to stop by *the Bear*, then across the street to rendezvous with Mona. Once on the side walk, I locked the door, went around the corner and down the alley toward *the Bear*. The diminishing glow of sunset made its final plunge into the depths of the pacific far in the distance as I reached the junction where the alley behind *the Bear* meets the alley that runs behind Mona's and the shops along Main Street. Suddenly from the shadows a hulking monster jammed a bag over my head then grabbed me off the ground from behind in a rib-crushing bear hug, pinning my arms to my sides. I tried to head-butt him, only to thump the back of my head against his chest. I tried to kick him in the knee caps, only to get squeezed tighter. I got sucker-punched in the gut that knocked all the wind and fight out of me, then took a whack from a blackjack behind my left ear. It didn't knock me out, but I was unable to make any of my faculties respond or function properly. Several of my neurological circuits seem to have been disrupted. My receptors disconnected.

I got stripped of my 'snubby' and carried limply like a dime store marionette to a waiting sedan. The Ogre released his bear hug and put his gigantic hand on top of my head. "Watch your head," he growled, as he rammed the side of my head into the top of the car while stuffing me into the back seat. At least I will have matching cranial lumps behind each ear. Two meatballs mashed in on either side of me and a third got in at shotgun. The driver went to the end of the block and turned left onto Walnut Avenue. I was having a hard time trying to regain my breath, I heaved heavily within the confines of my black bag. I felt like I was about to hurl my cookies.

I tried not to lose consciousness, or my lunch, and still pay attention to where we were going. I kept thinking what an idiot I was; I keep telling everyone to be aware of their surroundings and don't allow them-selves to get into an un-safe, or compromising situation from which there is no escape; and yet here I was, snatched off the street like a naïve school girl by a grimy creep in a windowless panel truck.

We bounced over every cross street from Main all the way to Golden West, where we made a left and then a quick right onto PCH. I finally began to regain my breath as we descended the mesa cliffs and across Tin Can Beach. At the end of Tin Can Beach we turned right and proceeded up Warner Avenue with the estuary wet lands on the right. I couldn't believe it when we pulled to a stop and the Gunzel riding shot gun got out and opened a familiar chain link gate. Once we passed and he closed the gate behind us and remounted, we then proceeded down the drive and came to a stop under what I believe to be an open carport between a small cabin and a one car garage. I was rudely yanked from the car and assumed my position as a bear-hugged marionette. I was carried through the doorway and another knuckle-dragger pulled the bag off of my head. I looked around while my feet dangled a foot off the floor. I had to smile; it was the familiar cabin where Raven and I shared, what was probably the most glorious summer of my life, between the wars.

"Welcome Mr. Dugan, I'm so glad you accepted my invitation," said the hulking gravel voiced no-neck with the pushed-over nose, packed into severely stressed pinstripe suit, sitting behind a desk with a friendly smile on his broad, square-jawed mug. "Well, how could

I not, with such a gracious and refined concierge' to retrieve me," I responded while still hanging helplessly from the vice like grasp of 'The Incredible Hulk.' "And soon as this big sum-bitch puts me down I'm going to kick his ass." The pinstripe suit behind the desk paused momentarily, then looked at the other two guys in the room, then broke out laughing, and the others boisterously followed suit. I eventually, reluctantly joined-in.

"I like this guy," laughed burly pinstripes. "Please, Mr. Dugan, have a seat my friend. Relax, have a drink while we talk. I mean you no harm. I simply want to ask for your assistance with a project in which I am currently involved." 'The Incredible Hulk' placed me in a chair across the desk from pinstripes and then released his death grip

Pinstripes poured two shots, courtesy of my buddy *Johnny Walker*, and passed one across the desk to me. "Mr. Dugan, my name is Salvatore' Manila and I represent the International Brotherhood of Railroad Workers and Engineers." I reached across the desk and swapped shot glasses, then leaned back and took a strong pull. "No shit, Sal Manila? I find that gut-wrenching." He smiled, glanced at the other guys, then responded; "yeah, you mean like the big 'Doogie' I took this morning?" We all laughed. "Touche', Mr. Manila, touche'," I toasted and downed the last of my *Johnny Walker Re*d.

Pinstripes enjoyed our humorous repartee' momentarily and then abruptly got down to business. "Mr. Dugan you may or may not be aware that we are currently in negotiations with Mr. Stanton and his representatives regarding future unionization of his *Western Pacific Railroad* line." He paused, poured both of us another shot, offered me a cigar which I declined, and then snipped and lit one for himself before continuing.

"*The Western Pacific Railroad* is one of the few rail lines in the entire nation that is without union representation for the protection and the benefit of its workers and their families." (So far sounds a lot like bureaucratic politico speak.) "We are aware of your recent contact with a representative of Mr. Stanton and we simply wish that you campaign in our behalf when you have made personal contact; put in a good word so to speak."

"Well, you seem to know a lot of stuff," I responded. "Unfortunately, I'm afraid you've placed more importance on my influence with Mr. Stanton than actually exists. I haven't even met the man. I merely met some pencil-pushing sissy, whom I advised to hire the services of a reputable personal security firm." Sal Manila looked at his two knuckle dragging minions and smiled. "I like this guy. He's a funny guy. You're right Dugan I do know a lot of stuff. For instance I know that you got involved in an unfortunate altercation in *Maxwell's* parking lot and wound-up blasting the shit out of a guy. Don't get me wrong, I think you handled the situation as you should. In fact, I was so impressed with your instinctive reactions, your talent, and your coolness under fire that I want you on our side, and I'm willing to make it well worth your while."

"I appreciate your confidence in me Sal, believe me I do. However, I'm only here to hold a few hands and sooth a few nerves until the cops catch the person or persons responsible for the dead girl in the dumpster. I didn't want to get involved in the first place, I don't want to be here now and I want to get the hell out of here ASAP. I have no problem supporting your cause, but again I doubt that my two cents are going to amount to a pile of shit to a man like Mr. Stanton. He's going to be a tough nut to crack and even with my limited knowledge of his reputation, it's my understanding that his railroad workers are treated pretty well. Hell, he built an entire town for his workers and they seem to be happy and fairly content. I gotta' tell ya Sal, I don't envy you in this endeavor and the pitfalls that lie ahead. I'm glad to help in any way I can Sal, but again I don't think I'm going to make a world of difference, and besides how would you know?"

"Doesn't make any difference Dugan, if Stanton signs a union contract, you get paid. I'm very generous to my friends who do favors for me. I would like to make this transition as painless as possible for all concerned and I think you can assist in that capacity, much like the babysitting duties you are already performing; hold a few hands, sooth a few nerves, and gently promote the benefits and advantages of unionization when the opportunity presents itself. Subtlety, Mr. Dugan, I prefer the art of subliminal suggestion, though I'm not opposed to negotiation with an iron fist cloaked in a velvet glove."

"Were the two gorillas in *Maxwell's* parking lot your idea of subtle," I asked with a little attitude. "Or the attempt on my life at *the Garden of Allah* in Hollywood? Was that to be interpreted as subliminal suggestion? I have a hard time representing someone that I have to keep looking over my shoulder to insure that I don't get throttled from behind."

"Dugan I can assure you that I had nothing to do with that, despite the crude and clumsy behavior my two unsophisticated and socially inept associates have thus far demonstrated. I do not condone, nor do I employ the methodology of common thugs and degenerates. I find that procedural formula to be counter-productive, and I strongly suggest you look elsewhere to vent your only slightly veiled pent-up vengeance." (Wow, pretty articulate for a guy who looks like he's taken too many blows to the head to even put a coherent sentence together without a liberal amount of de's, doe's and youse guys sprinkled throughout the gravel-voiced delivery.)

"My legal counsel and I are currently in negotiations with Mr. Stanton and his attorneys. We of course are promoting the benefits of unionization with regard to his overall operation, as well as the health and pension benefits available to his workers once they have voted to accept union representation. We will handle the details and legalities involved. All I'm asking is that you ease any anxieties or calm any misgivings, should you have the opportunity." He rose to his feet and extended his hand; a really big and meaty one that had done its share of hard work, but not lately. "So if we have an understanding Mr. Dugan, I will bid you so long till we meet again, and have my associates drop you where-ever you request."

I stood and firmly grasp his hand. "We have an understanding, provided that you can assure me that no physical harm will come to

Mr. Stanton, his family, or his business associates, ...and that your two representatives present will keep the bag in which I arrived, to themselves. I know exactly where I am, so you're not fooling anybody."

"I represent thousands of Railroad workers across the country, and I personally guaranty the integrity of our intentions and the sincerity of our commitment with regard to the welfare of our union brothers and their families. I apologize for my associate's prior behavior, but they were concerned, based on your reputation and previous demonstration, that you would be reluctant to accept my invitation. They were attempting to insure your safety as well as their own."

He motioned to one of his minions and my .38 and the cartridges they had removed, were placed on the desk. Sal Manila looked at my venerable antiquity of personal protection, with trepidation. He handed them to me and told his two knuckle draggers to take me back to where they found me.

We pulled to the curb on Third Street at the end of the alley that runs behind the equipment shop and *the Bear*. The big side of beef that snagged and bagged me earlier opened the door on my right and got out. I slid out, leaned back into the car and thanked the other two Neanderthals for the ride, then closed the door. I turned and brought my fist from the door handle, with all I could muster, to a solid uppercut that landed squarely on the big palooka's chin. It didn't even snap his head back, but after a moment, he collapsed flat on his back like a fallen red wood; who would have guessed that the big bastard had a glass jaw? "Yeah baby! A cold-cock one-punch knock-out," I yelled. "I told you I was gonna' kick your ass, ya' big ugly fuck!" Just then he began to get up and the other two shmucks began scrambling from the car. "Uh Oh" I said aloud, then turned and ran like a scared rabbit down the alley into the darkness. I rounded the corner of the repair shop and ran into the open lot between the buildings. I plowed into a couple of teenage hub cap thieves attempting to steal the vanity plate off the back *of BB King's* white Caddy convertible. "Run you dumb little shits. There's a guy chasing me with a gun, and we've got to out- run him," I yelled while trying to scramble to my feet. "We don't have to out-run him, asshole," they responded as they streaked by. "We just have to out-run you;" and they did, with relative ease.........punks.

I stopped at the corner of *the Bear* before I got to the bright lights out front on the sidewalk, and looked back. I didn't see any pursuers, and I didn't see their car come around the corner onto PCH in front of *the Bear* either. I took a moment to catch my breath, regain my composure, and dust-off my duds.

The second show was already well underway and the house was sold-out, so the ticket booth was closed and Nita had probably gone home. I walked through the parking lot to the alley and knocked on the rear door. Tommy Manson let me in after a sketchy synopsis of the evening highlights and current status, including the resumption of the wire service in the attic as well as the private gambling venue in the basement.

I found Papa behind his desk sipping ouzo and counting cash. He looked quite content. He smiled wide when I entered and poured a drink for me. "Dugan my friend, I'm so happy to see you. I hadn't heard from you and I was beginning to worry. Are you well, son? Is everything ok?"

I sat and sipped and propped my feet on the desk. The first shot gave me a visible shiver that inspired a chuckle from Papa. It was good to see him laugh again. Caroline entered with her bag of cash from the dinner and bar register. She smiled, threw her arms around my neck and smothered me with kisses, then smothered me with her lovely Greek puppies. "Oh Travis, you big jerk, we were all worried about you. Are you alright?"

"Everything is wonderful when you're near, my enchanting Greek goddess," I replied with the most sincere smile, of which I had practiced my entire life. "All I need is a warm caress and a comforting embrace." She smiled, sat on my lap and put her arm around my neck. "Boy, you had me going there for a moment Casanova," she laughed. "I imagine you've practiced that routine since you were capable of sporting a stiffy. But you know what, works for me. Let me close-up the club, grab my toothbrush, then I'll come and press your buzzer." She kissed me on the cheek then skipped off to her closing routine.

Papa held up his glass as if in a toast, he had a warm contented smile on his face and the familiar twinkle in his eye had returned. "Dugan my son, I have been thinking for a long time that you might someday realize what a beautiful and warm hearted woman my Caroline has become. She is not the young child that you remember. I would be thrilled to turn the *Golden Bear* over to you and Caroline; then I could retire a happy man and spend my days with the beautiful grandchildren that you and Caroline will produce." He laughed, leaned back in his chair and downed the last of his ouzo.

I ran into Mullins and MC Burney as I was heading for my digs at Mona's. They had no inside information to divulge other than the identities of the two Goombahs that ate the big weenie in the parking lot and the alley the other night. They were two low-level knee-crushers out of Chicago, loosely affiliated with the Luciano crime family. No one knows how they got here or why. That was unsettling information and threw another wrench into the works. I don't have a good feeling about it. I don't need this shit.

I turned the lock and climbed the stairs to the foyer. Music and laughter emanated from the lounge and Mona emerged with a cigarette in one hand, a stiff drink in the other, and a warm smile, slightly transparent evening gown, and a twinkle in her eye. Alana and Swallow came prancing out in their baby- doll chiffon nighties and gave me exuberant bubbly hugs and kisses, then danced back into the lounge to rejoin their corporate love interests for the evening. It was apparent that Mona was back in business. She told me that Precious had called and asked that I return her call ASAP. I thanked Mona, then retired to my corner apartment and dialed the number to the guest quarters at the Rigney estate. After the customary series of buzzes and clicks, Mabel the island phone operator, managed to insert the correct cable into the corresponding hole in her switchboard and the phone began to ring in the courtyard guest house. Precious answered on the third ring.

"Good evening Precious, how is life in paradise?" "Good evening? What fuckin' time zone are you in dick head? It's three in the morning you dumb shit. I've been trying to get ahold of you all day. Is everything ok? Have you had any trouble?"

"Well, I miss you too, and everything is peachy. Thank you for asking, and to answer your final question; nothing I couldn't handle..... even with my diminished reflexes, questionable intelligence, and fading physical capabilities." "I'm sorry Travis. I didn't mean to bite your head off. It's just that nobody had heard from you and nobody knew where you were. You scared the hell out of me."

I waited till she could catch her breath and settle herself before I continued. I told her about my impromptu adventure into the realm of well- connected union bosses and organizers. I wasn't sure that I bought the notion promoted by Sal Manila that the union push was on the up and up, and that they had nothing to do with the altercation that resulted in two fatalities. The Chicago connection was right up their alley, and they demonstrated a well-known modus operandi.

I related how I played along in order to avoid a good thumping and played the role of the blissfully ignorant, brilliantly challenged, pedestrian, run-of-the-mill, pin-head PI who couldn't find his own ass with both hands in broad daylight with a map, who knows nothing and is no threat to them. "I performed the role brilliantly, I might add." "Wasn't much of a stretch," she replied. (I make a good straight man who can set'em-up, lob a soft ball, and then walk right into to the punch line.) It made her feel better to give me a good-humored zinger. What can I say? She's a giver.

Precious asked if I still had the ringside tickets to the Friday night fights that I received from Mickey Cohen several nights prior. When I answered in the affirmative, she informed me that Precocious had appeared in a television and radio commercial for *Gillette* razors and foamy shaving crème. *Gillette*, being the corporate sponsor for the televised fights from *the Olympic Auditorium*, wants her to make a personal appearance during pre-fight celebrity introductions to coincide with the launch of the commercial nationwide. "It's running locally on all the channels, started yesterday after midnight. Kato's sister Fia, is scheduled to accompany her, but I knew you would want to meet them at the sea plane tarmac in San Pedro. They will be arriving on the last flight from the island on your friend Steve's plane."

"The other reason that I've been trying to reach you," she continued," is because Mr. Harden Johnson Boehner called this morning and requests a meeting between you and Mr. James Ervine tomorrow around noon at his home on the ranch. I also wanted to let you know that we ran checks on Boehner as well as Mr. Kuda. Barry Kuda is a bona fide ivy league educated preppie from a well-connected, wealthy old-money family on the Cape of Cod."

"Boehner, however, is a real handful. He seems to have gone to considerable effort in an attempt to conceal his true identity or his actual past. It has taken some digging, in some unusual places, to try and zero in on this guy. I'm not convinced the information we're uncovering is authentic. It's too neat, seems manufactured. I'm working on it."

I assured her that I would call after the meeting with Mr. Ervine. We said I love you, goodbye then, hung up the phone. I went over and switched on the ten inch black and white *Dumont*. It began its warm-up process with the appearance of a small, bright dot in the middle of the screen which slowly grew to a fuzzy horizontal line that gradually stretched across the middle of the screen. Eventually the entire screen was a black a white electric blizzard accompanied by an audible static buzz. Horizontal bands began to roll up and down the screen. Finally the screen cleared to a static shot of an American Indian Chief in full head dress against a backdrop of radiant broadcast signals along with a consistent, annoying signal tone.

A few clicks of the dial and I came upon Jack Par attempting to stutter his way through and interview with pianist Oscar Levant' on the *Tonight Show*. A couple more clicks of the dial and local LA political muckraker, and resident conspiracy theorist Joe Pine sitting in single spot, in what was otherwise a completely dark studio, chain smoking and ranting about the governments 'Big Brother' conspiracy to fluoridate our drinking water. According to him it was an impending disaster and only the beginning of a massive government takeover of every aspect of our lives. He predicted that the next thing will be that your sons will be required to register for the draft and induction into the military complex, and eventually shipped off to some god forsaken jungle to be impaled upon a pungy stick or come home addicted to heroin and other opiates. *Be the first one on your block, to have your son sent home in a box;* All over a paranoid, trumped-up communist containment policy based on the Pentagon's *Domino Theory*.

A few more clicks on the old *Dumont* dial and I found it. There she was as gorgeous as I had ever seen her, with her long blonde hair, deep delicious tan, and radiant blue eyes. Precocious watched seductively as the *Gillette* Manly Man removes the foamy shaving crème from his rugged jaw with the new *Gillette* razor and double edge blade to the tune '*The Stripper.*' And Precocious' close-up tag line, in her seductive Scandinavian accent; "*Take it off. Take it all off.*"

There was a soft knock on the apartment door and Mona entered carrying the '*Kevlar*' vest that I had personally field tested the other night. The opening stanza to the theme of the late night reruns of '*Tales of the Highway Patrol*, starring Broderick Crawford' began to buzz through the *Dumont*; (You pencil-neck geek.)

"My friend at *DuPont* asks that you field test the vest awhile longer. She is concerned that a full metal jacket bullet would have penetrated completely through the vest. That's why she's made a few improvements including this thick aluminum-mesh inside liner. It is designed as a last line of defense in stopping a projectile from penetrating completely, and works similar to medieval chain-male. She asks that this time, for comparative analysis of course, that you try and get shot by a high-powered rifle like a *Manlicher* 6.5 millimeter firing *Carcano* case-hardened copper rounds. (Yeah, I'll get right on that)

Just then, the rousing opening bars of '*The Stripper'* again began blasting from our ten inch black and white. We both turned and gazed at the stunning apparition that magically appeared within the sound and picture box. "Is that Precocious?"

"Sure is," I replied while staring mesmerized at the T.V. "She scored a national T.V. and radio commercial. I'm escorting her to her first personal appearance since the spots began running, to the Friday Night Fights at *the Olympic*." "Good for her, and aren't you the lucky boy," she said with a smile. After Precocious delivered the tag line, Mona turned to me with a wicked little smile and a mischievous twinkle in her eye. "I don't know about you Travis, but I'm getting wet, and growing a clit woody." "Me too," was my only response while still staring at the screen. "Damn Travis, she's so gorgeous, **I'd** do her." "Me too," I replied.

"Well, I must get back to my guests," she said, turning to go. "Oh, I almost forgot. I told my friend about your mishap at *the Garden of Allah* the other night, so she sent along something that she has been working on. She said you'll find it in the breast pouch of the vest, designed for a badge… if you had one. She said you'd figure it out. The only clue and I quote; like Mona's girls, functionality can be found at either end." Mona kissed me on the cheek, put her cigarette butt out in her now empty shot glass, and danced her way back to her guests in the lounge.

I found Professor Peabody's newest invention protruding from the breast pouch as instructed. It looked like the hard rubber hand grip off of a motorcycle handle bar. It was solid like a fist pack, with a fist-guard at both ends. Upon closer inspection, I noticed a small button inset within the inside of the fist- guard. With a push of the button and a subtle flick of the wrist, a small solid black night- stick telescoped from the handle and locked into place, like a stiletto or a light saber. (Whatever that is?) I smacked it against the palm of my hand a couple of times. It was about the size of a souvenir replica they give away on 'bat night' at *Gilmore Stadium* when *the Hollywood All Stars* are in town. It will make a nice knee-crusher or bone-cracker.

I remember the clue regarding the versatility of Alana and Swallow. I turned the fist- guard on the butt-end of the handle and pulled. An array of small, highly polished aluminum mirrors deployed like an umbrella, and a pin-light illuminated the reflected image. Wow, what a freaking genius. Why didn't I think of this? It's a fist-pack that transforms into a formidable, bone crushing Billy-club. *But wait, that's not all; not only does it slice and dice, but it makes Julian potatoes. And that's just the beginning; when the party's over, you simply twist the handle and the tiny aluminum umbrella deploys for ease of use when inspecting the undercarriage of your automobile for those pesky and annoying explosive devices. No more clumsy compact mirrors and separate flash light. Say goodbye to that humiliating, back-breaking exercise of crawling around on all fours scuffing your shoes and soiling that hard-pressed crease in your trousers. But wait, that's not all; call right now and we'll double your order. That's right, we'll double your order, and not only that, we'll pay for your express shipping and handling charges.*

A pebble bounced softly off one of the windows that faced Main Street. I opened the window and looked down to the sidewalk at the door of the stairwell entry. It was Caroline. She smiled, waived a bottle of wine, two wine glasses, and from my vantage point, an abundance of robust cleavage as well. I dropped the door key down to Caroline, spun the smoky sounds of Pattie Page on the phonograph, dimmed the lights, and anticipated an enchanting evening with a sensual Greek goddess. (Yea !)

Chapter Five

Day 5

("I Wanna' Be a Cowboy Baby!")

Late in the morning, under a beautiful clear blue sky, and after a quick breakfast with Caroline and the girls at *the Sugar Shack*, I had the battleship gray Hornet steaming south along Coast Highway in high gear. After an enchanting evening with the abundance of sensually soft, warm and spongy Caroline, I was in an unusually good mood. I whistled a tune that I couldn't seem to get shed of, that I heard along the way on L.A. AM radio; *"Stanley, Stanley, Stanley Chevrolet, two blocks off the Santa Ana Freeway, 1 1 9 8 0 East Firestone, Stanley Chevrolet."* (it's funny how stuff like that will probably stay with me forever; useless trivial crap. Like Sheriff John's Lunch Brigade; *"Put another candle on my birthday cake, a wish I'll make on my birthday cake. Put another candle on my birthday cake, I'm another year old today. Happy birthday to me, I'm another year old today."* Don't get me started, because I still remember the second verse as well.)

I turned east on Ortega Highway, just shy of Laguna Beach and was fixin' to mosey out yonder. It was pert-near high noon by the time I turned onto Ervine Ranch Road. As near as I can rectum, I rode along a not-so-dusty-trail for pert-near a mile until I came upon two immense steel gates with a well-staffed guard shack in the middle.

I pulled to a stop at the gates and was promptly greeted by Preston Foster of the Yukon Mounted Police, complete with knee-high riding boots, traditional riding breeches, and Smoky the Bear Hat. "Yes, how may I help you sir?" "Howdy Amigo, my name is Dugan, Travis Dugan and I have an appointment with Mr. Ervine today at noon." He consulted his official clip-board then nodded in the affirmative. "Yes Mr. Dugan, if you'll proceed through the gates and up the drive, bear to the left and follow the corral fencing, you'll see the main house at the top of the hill." He gave me a proper gate guard salute, pushed a button somewhere within his command post, and the enormous gates slowly swung open. "Much obliged Muchacho. Adios and hi-ho Silver!" I saluted. "And away!" I could see him in my rearview mirror shaking his head in serious un-approving constipation as I drove away.

I drove along a wide, well-maintained gravel road lined with tall pine trees and sparkling white corral fencing, all the while whistling *'Happy Trails to you.'* The endless expanse of blue grass pastures were dotted with impressive Kentucky influenced spired horse stables and hay barns topped with copper steeples and weather vanes. Bearing left along the road I could see the sprawling log cabin mansion long before I arrived to the top of the hill. It reminded me of *the Ponderosa* on Sunday night T.V.'s *Bonanza*, in living color......on *NBC*.....bing, bing, bong. Cue the peacock.

I parked the Hornet in front of the huge double door entry. I noticed one of our smartly dressed operatives dutifully standing his post. "I assume, by your menacing presence, that Mr. Ervine has officially contracted for our services?" I asked after climbing the wide steps up to the entry doors. "Yes sir, I arrived at zero six-hundred this morning and two other associates are due, along with a K-9 unit, e.t.a. fourteen hundred hours." "Very well, carry on, as you were," I responded smartly.

A proper old-world butler named Gregory answered the door and escorted me into an enormous parlor or foyer that afforded a magnificent view of the huge and impressively designed living area, as well as the acres of citrus groves visible through mammoth sheets of floor to ceiling plate glass windows and doors. The room was decorated, naturally, in authentic western motif of oversize raw hide furniture, cow hide throw rugs, and Texas Longhorn steer horns mounted over an immense, indigenous slate fireplace. There were intricately crafted show and parade saddles, bull whips, spurs, rifles, gun-racks, and mounted trophies on the walls of every horned and antlered mammal on the North American continent. There was even a stuffed Grizzly Bear standing menacingly in the corner, poised to attack. The area was festooned in wood carvings and statuary of horses, eagles, bears, and coyotes. The chandeliers, sconces and table lamps were fashioned from wagon wheels, rattle snakes, and cowboy boots. There were faded silver-plated lithographs and photographs of old buckaroos in battered dusty chaps, hats and boots posing proudly with their prized horse, dog and side arm. Portraits and autographed pictures of famous western movie stars like 'the Duke' John Wayne, Gene Autry 'the singing cowboy, Roy Rodgers, Clayton Moore the Lone Ranger and his loyal Indian side-kick Tonto, played by Jay Silverheels. Wow! Kemosabe, I'm impressed. Ya'll come back now ya' hear?

Gregory returned and escorted me along an interior courtyard festooned in bright blooming flowers of every size, shape and color. There were small waterfalls and other water features within a meandering stream that ran through several ponds stocked with large, exotic and colorful Koi fish. He knocked on an intricately carved solid oak door depicting a vigorous cattle drive or perhaps an ensuing stampede. He opened the door and stepped in. "Mr. Dugan to see you sir," he announced.

Mr. James Ervine was about six feet tall. He was thick across the chest, broad across the shoulders and sported an impressive set of guns. He had a tanned shiny dome with silver grey around the sides and a big bushy mustache of the same hue. He was around sixty, tanned, burly and robust. He had a firm grip, and his hands were no strangers to a hard day's work. He had a broad, friendly smile and sparkling, happy blue eyes. Mr. Ervine was attired as you would imagine a land-baron gentleman rancher to be. He wore a Roy Rodgers shirt with pearl snap buttons and an Indian design turquoise slip-tie. Of course he wore crisp, fresh blue jeans with a big shiny belt buckle, and an impressive pair of Gila monster, rattle snake, or ostrich skin, pointy-toed, stirrup-heeled cowboy boots. There was a big white broad-brimmed cowboy hat and a pair of shiny silver spurs hanging from the wood- carved Cigar Store Indian in the other corner opposite the big scary Grizzly Bear.

He invited me to sit across from him at the large impressive desk and poured both of us a small snifter of brandy. After a small sip he leaned back in his high backed brown leather banker's chair, and propped his boots up on the desk. "Mr. Dugan I know you're a busy man of few words," he began straight away. "That suits me fine Dugan, I'm not big on cocktail party banter or useless ass-kissing bullshit. That's why my good friend Commodore Rigney recommended your services. He expressed his extreme satisfaction with the manner in which you dispatched his seemingly impossible situation. So let me explain our current situation and perhaps you can figure how, and where we go from here."

"Boehner has previously explained that we have received phone calls from some outfit that nobody ever heard of and can't be identified by the Stock Exchange, the Securities Commission, the Better Business Bureau, or any other god damn agency or acronym you can imagine. Their initial contacts seemed legitimate enough until they made an unsolicited offer on a pristine, unbelievably beautiful parcel of land located on a fairly secluded stretch of southern Orange County coastline."

"They were informed early on that we were not interested in selling that parcel of land at any price, however they persisted and refused to take' no thank you' for an answer. It was at this point in the conversations that their ridiculous offers of land purchase began to be accompanied by veiled threats of unspecified business disruptions and livestock disappearances. We've already experienced cattle rustling occurring in the outlying perimeters of the grazing pastures located close to roads, ruts or firebreaks that would allow access and egress to a big-rig livestock transporter. It happens in the pre-dawn hours and they're in and out quickly. We haven't found any evidence that they haul in cowboys or their horses to round-up the cattle, so our only conclusion is that they must use a helicopter. They simply back the transporter into a hole they cut in the fence and use the chopper to drive the cattle straight into the trailer. They're in and out before dawn and long gone by the time we discover the breach in the perimeter fencing and loss of livestock."

I asked if he had contacted any official authority or police agencies regarding the threats or the cattle rustling. He informed me that the local police were not equipped to investigate the alleged property extortion unless an actual crime was committed. The Sherriff's Department was investigating the rustling and property damage of course, but he wasn't particularly optimistic that it would amount to more than a pile of pasture pastry. "The rustlers could drive that load of cattle across the border into Mexico within hours and that would be the last anyone would ever see of those cattle. We contacted the FBI, but they were only interested if the thieves were driving stolen cars across the border, for god sake."

"What would you like me to do, Mr. Ervine, other than provide personal security for you and your immediate family and select business associates?" "I was hoping that I could persuade you to take this case and find out who was originating these threats, and eliminate that threat by whatever means, before they actually harm one of my family members. Mr. Dugan, I'm a widower who has raised three great kids by myself on this ranch. My older son works for the corporation and has a wife and twin baby girls. I have a son attending Cal Poly Pomona and my daughter is a freshman at San Diego State. I would do, or pay anything to insure their safety. I would not hesitate to kill anyone that would bring harm to my family over a parcel of land or a bunch Black Angus Cattle. I would be much obliged to you Mr. Dugan if you could put an end to this; and I don't care how or what you have to do to accomplish that."

There was a soft knock on the door and a tall, beautiful dark-haired girl stepped in. "Oh I'm sorry Mr. Ervine I didn't realize you had a guest. You asked me to check-in with you once I had delivered the chuck wagon to the west corral. Would you like me to prepare lunch for two?" she asked. "Miss Randi Andretti, I'd like you to meet Mr. Travis Dugan. Perhaps you could persuade him to stay."

We had barbequed beef ribs, chili beans, and corn on the cob, on the patio that was adjacent to James Ervine's office through sliding glass doors. The patio floor was fashioned from huge slabs of the same dark grey slate utilized to create the immense fireplace in the living area. Overhead was wooden lattice covered in grape vines, similar to the vine covered riding trails found at William Hearst's mountain top castle overlooking the wide Pacific and the central coast shoreline to the north near San Simeon. Randi provided an ice bucket plumb-full of chilled bottles of Lone Star Beer.

Over and extended lunch and a bucket full of beer, Mr. Ervine confided that he was extremely worried about the situation. He has a large extended family who are scattered from Orange County to west Texas and he can't possibly effectively protect them all. Beyond that, there are key business associates, property and infrastructure as well as livestock and equipment; they're all vulnerable to determined individuals intent on doing harm.

I sensed his desperation. In a way he reminded me of Mr. Rigney; the Commodore. Like the Commodore, Mr. Ervine was accustomed to being totally in charge of whatever enterprise in which he was currently involved. He knows every aspect of the operation and rarely takes no for answer. He's not afraid to get down in the trenches and put in as hard a day's work as the next man. He is the boss, and he is used to being in control. His general reaction to a foreseen threat would be bold, brash, confrontational and combative. This is different. This is not an obvious threat that can be confronted by conventional means. This is not a face to face, man to man street fight that can be decided at the end of a fist in a knock-down drag-out bare-knuckled street brawl. This is a situation in which he is not familiar. He doesn't have a handle on this and he is not in control. He's lost. His decisions are reactionary rather than proactive. Like Mr. Rigney, I have empathy for the guy. I feel compelled to help. (I hate when that happens.) Again, like all the other times that I had a bad feeling about something and my gut tells me to pass, vamoose, don't go under any circumstances; I'm probably going, and I'll be lucky if I live to regret it.

With that said, and conspicuously right on cue, enter the bombastic Harden Johnson Boehner. He wore a toned-down work-a-day version of the rhinestone cowboy costume, only suitable for Hollywood, worn the night we met he and his bubble-boobed cheerleading strumpets Bambi and Charlene.

"Ah Johnny, glad you could make it. You remember Mr. Dugan." Boehner walked over with a big smile and a big handshake; "Howdy Dugan, good to see you again partner. Where is that pretty palomino filly you were with the other night?" "Rode hard and put away wet," I replied. "Bambi and Charlene seemed to be having a good time. I assume the rest of the evening grew even more festive?" "You know what they say partner? What happens in Holly-weird, stays in Holly-weird," he responded with a smile.

"Johnny, I'd like you to haul Dugan out to the west corral to meet Bucky Strayhorn. Dugan, Bucky is the trail boss on the ranch and he's in charge of the ranch hands and the livestock. He can give you a more detailed, first hand explanation of what has occurred and his take on the whole deal. Don't let his ornery disposition throw you, he knows his way around a cattle ranch and you may find his knowledge useful."

I found myself reluctantly bouncing with Boehner along a cattle trail that went through some of the most breathtaking landscapes and afforded unbelievable views of the wide Pacific Ocean, in a Willy's Jeep painted to look like a zebra. According to Boehner, the ranch bought out the entire motor pool inventory, including pick-up trucks, jeeps, and livestock transporters from an ambitious but defunct attempt to bring a real life African safari experience to Southern California. The concept behind 'Lion Country Safari' was for the entire family to drive, in their own car, through a sanctuary well-stocked with free roaming African wildlife such as lions, leopards, elephants, giraffes, wildebeest and gazelle. After a mass wild animal escape, a tourist lion mauling or two, and skyrocketing Insurance liability payments, not to mention an onslaught of regulatory agencies and numerous law suits, '*Lion Country Safari*' found itself unsustainable and wound-up selling off all of its assets and taking down its creditors in bankruptcy court.

We pulled to a stop at a dusty corral, where a bunch of dusty cowpokes in dusty chaps, boots and hats were leaning or sitting on the corral fence. In the middle of the corral a rowdy little chestnut quarter horse was resisting ferociously the attempt by a half dozen cowboys just to put a saddle on his back. One cowboy on a horse had the chestnut pony lassoed by both hind quarters and another had a rope around his neck. They had him hobbled and hog tied, but he was still putting up a spirited fight.

After a lot of whooping and hollering, cussing, bucking and biting, and furious swirls of rising dust clouds, the saddle eventually got cinched down tight onto the back of the rebellious little spit- fire. The first bronco buster approached the little horse with his spurs a-jingling. Just the sound of those spurs set the horse into a raging frenzy. His ears laid back and his eyes bugged out. He was having none of this. He was dead set against any attempt to tame his wild spirit and was prepared to dole-out some punishment to any of these redneck dust-bowlers who had enough balls to try.

Finally, after a lot of thrashing about, the cowboy was astride his mighty steed; a mighty 'pissed-off' steed. He gathered a handful of reigns in one hand and a white-knuckle death grip on the saddle horn with the other. He gathered his cojones,' took a deep breath, and with obvious trepidation he nodded his head that he was ready. With a flick of the wrist, the cowboys slacked their ropes, and the little horse exploded out of his restraints with a vengeance. He took off at full speed across the corral, head down and bucking for all he was worth. He twisted and turned and made several attempts to scrape the monkey off his back along the corral fence posts. The other cowboys hooped and hollered and laughed with delight until the little horse made a tight circle then, leaped off the ground with all fours and body- slammed the hapless cowboy into a fence post knocking him unconscious. The cowboy hit the ground like a sack of potatoes and the little horse circled back around to stomp the shit out of him. The other wranglers rushed in and dragged the unconscious cowboy out of the corral. After several minutes and a pail of cold water poured over him, he slowly regained his marbles and found himself sitting in a puddle of fresh mud.

Randi Andretti appeared riding over the hill, bareback on a big black and white Paint horse. The beautiful apparition reminded me of the enchanting summer I spent with Raven, and her Paint horse Dakota, in the wetlands estuary within palm covered paradise, adjacent to 'Tin Can Beach,' that now seems so long ago. She dismounted and tied her horse to the back of the chuck wagon she had delivered earlier. Randi was a gorgeous, statuesque brunette who looked more Navajo than Italian. She wore a wide brimmed hat that was tied around her neck and hung on her back. She had on a plaid, long sleeve western style shirt that her impressive puppies danced the dance of youth proudly beneath, and a pair of jeans that fit her stunning, pouty butt like she was poured into them. Her knee-high leather moccasins tied tight below the knee with a fringed leather strap. Her skin was smooth as silk and glowed with a golden brown hue. When she arrived, all the cowpokes turned their attention to the statuesque beauty.

She walked over to where Boehner, Strayhorn, and I leaned on the corral fence. "I see Rocket Dog is still batting a thousand, ay Bucky?" she asked with a wide smile. "Still piling-up the casualties and notching the fence posts? You have to admire his spirit and his spunk. If you ever figure out how to get that little horse to cooperate he's gonna' make a hell of a cattle pony and cuttin' horse."

Bucky Strayhorn leaned on the fence and stared at the little horse across the corral, who taunted him with snorts of bravado and by pawing the ground like a bull preparing to charge a Matador. "If that little horse doesn't get an attitude change real quick, I'm figurin' he'll be gettin' a one way ride on the tallow truck straight to the glue factory," he responded, with a big spit of chew as an exclamation point.

I had to smile, the feisty little horse posturing 'bravado' across the corral, reminded me of a 'macho' little chestnut pony, coincidently named Rocky, that took great pride in bucking me to the ground for the first time in my illustrious equestrian debut. He also tried to stomp me into the dirt before chasing me up a fence post. This initiation into the equine world took place when I was five or six years old at my cousin Loretta's ranch in the Corona/Norco area of the Riverside County Inland Empire, where I spent much of my summers as a youth. As I recall, being the hard-headed tenacious little bastard that I was, the next time that little horse came running by my fence post perch trying to bite me, I jumped on his back, grabbed him by an ear, and yanked the living shit out of that horse's ear until he pooped himself out spinning in circles and eventually became reluctantly obsequious. (obsequious? Must'ah gots me a college edumacation somewheres.)

"Have you tried riding him without the saddle?" I asked out loud, and was immediately sorry that I had. I should have known to edit the thoughts that scroll across my scanners before making such audible. I constantly counsel my young PI recruits that you will learn a lot more if you keep your mouth shut and just listen.

Bucky Strayhorn slowly turned to me with a look of consternation etched into his weathered expression. "Why the hell would I want to do that? ya fuckin' greenhorn. The whole point of this exercise is to turn this god damn little pony into a saddle horse. Real genuine, bona fide cowboys ride on saddles; they are an essential working piece of equipment. But having said that, by all means Buckaroo, I'll bet you fifty bucks that you can't stay on that horse more than eight seconds saddle or not." Again, he punctuates his sour expression with a big jaw of chew spit into the dust.

I smiled, with a little bravado of my own, reached in my pocket, counted out fifty bucks and handed the cash to Randi. "I believe I'll take that bet Bucky. But ya' gotta' spot me one fall, after all, I am just a fuckin' greenhorn." Bucky smiled wide, dug around in his jeans and came up with a wad of severely crumpled bills that he gave to Randi. She followed me over to the chuck wagon and asked, quietly concerned, while I retrieved a bright shiny apple and quartered it, if I really knew what I was doing? I put the quartered apple in my pocket and said to Randi, as we walked back to the corral where the other cowboys were having trouble finding anyone to cover their bets against me, that I hoped it was like riding a bike;" once you know how, you never forget." She didn't seem all together confident with my response and her expression indicated that she questioned my sanity. "Don't worry baby, I've got this," I said with confidence. Take all their bets; I'll cover any losses."

I climbed the corral fence to the top rail, where I sat and began to remove my Buster Browns. The assembled wranglers began laughing loudly and there was an immediate up-tick in the action against me. The cowboys on horseback managed, with some difficulty, to once again rope the little chestnut horse and had him restrained in the middle of the corral.

I walked over to where the hog-tied pony snorted and pawed the ground, to the "watch-out for pasture pastry" and "don't step in the meadow muffins," cat calls from the gathering peanut gallery. I unbuckled the saddle, removed it and the blanket from the lathered –up little horse, and set it atop the corral fence.

When I gently offered an apple wedge, it took the little horse a considerable length of time to settle-down and allow me to approach cautiously. He was not a happy pony. His ears were pulled back and his eyes bulged; he was stressed, but he did eventually lean down and sniff the offering. He finally acquiesced, and lipped-up the apple wedge with enthusiasm. While he munched on the juicy morsel I firmly held his bridle and gently stroked his neck. He eagerly accepted another crunchy treat and while he indulged, I slowly eased onto his back and gathered the reigns.

He didn't like it a lot. He glared at me with Bette Davis eyes, as if to say;" buckle your seat-belt it's going to be a very bumpy ride." I grabbed a handful of Rocket Dog's mane, slid up to his shoulders, and tucked my legs and feet tight around his girth. I gathered my cojones, took a deep breath, and nodded my head; it was go-time.

The fired-up little horse burst out of his constraints at full-steam across the corral just as he had done before. Suddenly he stopped and dropped, catapulting me over his head. I flew through the air, landed on my left shoulder, did a tuck and roll somersault back to my feet and leapt back astride the stunned little horse, and still had the reigns in hand. He seemed impressed. He seemed impressed only momentito', then he seemed pissed. "That's your one gimme' greenhorn," yelled Strayhorn. "You got eight seconds starting now asshole!" Randi clanged a round on the chuck wagon chow bell, and we were off in a cloud of dust and a hardy; "High-ho Silver, away!"

Rocket Dog streaked across the corral and attempted to pull that same stunt again. This time I was ready for him however; when he finally took his abrupt duck-dive into the terra firma, I wound-up on his neck, staring over his head from between his ears. The mean little shit twisted his head around and tried to bite my foot, for which he caught a right-cross up-side his head. Now he was really pissed. He reared-up on his hind legs, furiously thrashing the air with his front hooves, and screaming like a raging banshee. With me stuck to his neck like a vampire Chimpanzee, he went over backward and hit the ground hard flat on his back at the clang of the chow-bell. I pushed-off just before he hit the ground, and leapt back on to his neck as he struggled off of the ground to his feet. The cowboys lining the corral were howling with laughter and falling all over themselves. The money they lost in their wagers with Randi was worth the price of admission. The mad little horse took off across the coral once again only this time he tried to scrape me off on the fence posts. I performed a movie stuntman, hang from the side of the horse trick, then grabbed the runaway maniac by the right ear and yanked as hard as I could. I had his head yanked around so that he was looking from where he had come, but he was still running straight against the fence posts. I was up on the little bastard's neck, had him in a headlock, and was twisting the hell out of his ear and he still ran amuck. He was a stubborn little horse I'll say that for him.

He eventually began to tire and after a few more rebellious pirouettes he finally settled down, snorting and frothing at the mouth, and covered in lather. I released my grip on his ear and settled back behind his shoulders. I gave him a soft kick and he began to trot across the corral and responded smartly to subtle movements of the reigns. Before long he was doing figure eights in the middle of the arena and sharp, clean lateral movements right and left. He wasn't real skilled in reverse, but with a little time and effort Rocket Dog will make a spunky and quick cattle horse.

I dismounted and led him to the watering trough for a quick drink, then gave him another apple wedge from my pocket. He started nosing my pocket once he figured where they came from. He was my best friend all of a sudden. I gave him the last piece of apple, stroked his neck, spoke a few soft words and remounted.

With a swift kick to the ribs and a genuine "he-yah!" Rocket Dog streaked across the arena at full speed straight toward Bucky Strayhorn sitting on the fence. As we thundered toward him the other cowpokes began to scatter. At the last second I pulled back on the reigns bringing the charging little pony to an abrupt dust-swirling stop knocking Bucky backwards off the top rail. He did a back summersault and landed on his back pockets to a chorus of howling laughter from the other wranglers.

I slung the reigns over the top rail and walked over to where Randi waited, as the other cowboys helped Bucky to his feet. "Are you sure you want to antagonize Bucky Strayhorn?" she asked. "He's kind of a psycho with a short fuse." I smiled, "second chance at a first impression."

Bucky came flying over the corral fence like a Tasmanian devil; He was a raging bull, charging forward head down, wild round-house rights and lefts coming somewhere from right and left field. He was a barroom brawler. He had no skills. He was a clubber. I backed up, ducking his crude swings from the bleachers. I decided to give him a lesson in pugilism. I stepped inside and gave him two quick left jabs to his nose, followed by a straight right to the chin that straightened him up in time to catch another one two left and right that set him on his pants. He got up and came running, attempting a tackle or wrestling take down. I grabbed his shirt collar and used his momentum to roll back and kick him in the gut as he flew over me and landed flat on his back. I quickly jumped to my feet and waited for him to get off the ground. "Eat this jujitsu boy!" he yelled as he came off the ground and threw a handful of dirt in my face, then landed a couple of those roundhouse clubs that he throws, on my shoulders and the top of my head. I backed-up and took momentary refuse behind my best impersonation of a Kenny Norton 'peek-a-boo' defense. He continued to rain blows, clubbing my arms and shoulders, as I peered between my forearms held out horizontally, waiting for my eyes to clear. It was sort of a horizontal 'rope-a-dope.' (Whatever that is?)

He began to tire, his wild clubbers came less frequent, his legs got rubbery, and he was huffing and puffing; he was ready. I waited for his next feeble barrage of looping bombs, then began a counter-punch carpet-bombing barrage of my own. Two left hooks that got him looking the other way, then a series of uppercuts that stood him up and started him rolling backward on his spurs.

I stepped in close when he was back on his heels back- stroking his arms wildly, and delivered the 'golden boy' straight right that KO'd the ugly knuckle-dragger last night, with the same pre-ordained outcome. He hit the ground hard, flat on his back in a big cloud of dust. There was total silence from the assembled peanut gallery. I walked over to where Randi sat mouth agape and asked for two cold Lone Stars. I carried the fresh and frosty brews over to where Bucky sat bewildered in the middle of the arena. He smiled wide when I handed him the cold one. He tipped it high and downed half the bottle in one gulp. I fished around in my pocket and came up with a now severely crumpled pack of Lucky Strikes. I gave him one and lit both with the familiar 'chink' of my trusty service lighter with the Air Force wings emblazoned upon it. Bucky grabbed my wrist and stared at the shiny metal lighter. "You were with the 539th bomber group," he asked, suddenly enthusiastic. "Affirmative, *'the Cross-town Boys'*, B-17's and then 29's out of Tinian in the Marianas." "So you were there when *the Enola Gay* was on the island?" "Yep, sure was. She was down on a very secure end of the island surrounded by concertina wire and its own security detail. We knew something was afoot because she was stripped of her gun mounts and turrets." "My brother was assigned to that bomber squadron," he said. "He's some kind of atomic brainiac. I don't know what he does exactly, but he still works for some secret government outfit in Washington D.C."

I motioned for Randi that I was buying one for the house. A round of whoops and hollers signified that I had suddenly become everyone's best friend. They all grabbed a beer and joined Bucky and me in the middle of the dusty arena. Randi brought us a 'freshy' and sat beside me.

Bucky took another big pull from his amber elixir, then looked at me and smiled. "You know Dugan I didn't like you much when you first showed-up." There was a long poignant pause. Laughter began to ripple across the gathered masses. I finally had to laugh. I looked over at Bucky and he had a big grin on his face as well. "I figured you for just another Hollywood pansy, a lot a show and no go. I thought you'd be another *playhouse 90* tough guy, a lot of talk, but can't walk the walk. But I've got to admit partner, you talk a lot a shit, but you can back it up. Anybody that can kick my ass in a one on one fight has earned my respect." I looked at him and smiled. "That wasn't a fight. You assaulted my fist repeatedly with your face and then fell on the ground." Uproarious laughter broke out among the assembled wranglers. I had them rolling in the dust, although the open bar may have had some influence on their receptiveness to my high-brow humor. "Well, I can't rightly argue with that observation," he said with a smile. "And it ain't worth another ass-whoopin' to try." More laughter from the peanut gallery ensued.

"Why the hell ARE you here anyway? You're sure not here to be a bronco buster, and I don't figure you for a boxing coach, so what's your story Dugan?" "Mr. Ervine has requested that you haul Dugan out to the parcel on the coast that we spoke of previously," chimed Johnson Boehner, perched atop the corral fence with a big smile and a cool beer. Bucky slowly turned and gave Boehner a look of contempt. "You think I want to spend the rest the day driving this limp-dick yahoo out past Timbuk-Three?"

"I can give him the lay of the land," Randi volunteered with a smile. "I know the territory, he can get a feel of the place....I mean a feel FOR the place," she laughed, as did the dusty misfits rolling in the dirt. "Is that what ya'll call one of them-there Freudian slips?" asked Boehner falling off the fence with laughter, and perhaps one beer too many.

***

The big Paint horse moved swiftly with a smooth stride that covered a lot of territory in a short time. I rode behind her with a firm but gentle grip around her trim smooth waist and her robust, strong thigh. At the crest of a tall grass covered hill we paused to reflect on the unbelievable beauty that lay before us. Rolling green hills dotted with oak trees and running creeks in the valley floors that stretched before us to the shores of the endless deep blue Pacific, and of course, beckoning from muted horizon, my island paradise, Catalina.

We took our time descending the lush green hills along a narrow cattle trail shaded occasionally by massive oak trees and dappled sunlight. Her long dark hair had the fragrance of wild lavender and reminded me of the many moonlit rides along the beach that Raven and I enjoyed together that enchanting summer so long ago.

Once we reached the bottom of the hill we followed a wide sandy creek bed that meandered along the low-lying grassy bluffs and gently rolling dunes. As we approached the concrete tunnel under Coast Highway, that allowed the creek to flow to the sea, the horse spooked a little and we immediately could hear and see why. About twenty feet ahead was a monster size rattle snake agitating the biggest set of rattles I'd ever seen. Randi reached under the fringed cuff of her moccasin and from a neatly concealed pouch she brought forth a 9mm Berretta semi- automatic. She aimed and squeezed-off one round. The giant diamond shaped head of the fearsome snake-zilla instantly vanished and the remainder of the fat four foot snake fell limp to the sand.

"Damn, Annie Oakley, if you can do that backward over your shoulder with a mirror, you could be a star in Buffalo Bill's Traveling Wild West Show," I exclaimed. "Oh hell that's nothing. I can shoot the nuts off a gnat's ass at twenty yards from a galloping horse," she responded with a smile. (Good to know) "Remind me to fetch that up on our way back," she said as we rode by. "What the hell for?" I asked. "That big fatty will cook-up nice," she replied. "Tastes like chicken."

We rode through the tunnel under PCH and the train trestle and emerged onto a huge, flat parcel of land overlooking a rugged coastline with rocky outcroppings that shield many secluded coves and pristine white sand beaches. "This is the parcel of land in question," she began. "Its three-thousand acres that stretch three miles up and down the picturesque shore line and extends inland as far as that first set of coastal foothills where the highway and the rail line run."

We dismounted and walked the horse along a narrow path that led down the bluff face and onto a pristine white beach. She let the horse go to wonder among the wild flowers and sparse clumps of long grass that grew near the bluff face. It was low tide, which allowed us to walk in shallow water around a craggy outcropping and onto a secluded white beach within a small intimate cove.

"This is my favorite cove," she said in almost a whisper. "There's a serene, deep grotto out there by the big rock that shields the grotto and the cove from the incoming waves, and some amazing tide pools on either side."

"Come on Monkey Man," she said, let's go for a swim." She removed her moccasins, peeled-off her jeans, and removed her blouse with a sly smile, proudly exposing one of the most beautiful female bodies I had ever seen. Randi had good reason to be proud; all her girl parts were real and they were spectacular.

As she waded into the shallow water, with the sun glistening upon the gentle waves, I frantically ripped off my cloths and followed her lovely round derriere' into the pale blue Pacific. She watched, with the same sly smile as I casually strolled into the water. "Oh my goodness, I see you're no stranger to goin' commando, hey Monkey Man? Nice tan. Love the meticulous manscaping too. Self- performed, or do you have that professionally done?" "I have a girl that comes on a regular basis," I responded with my own sly smile. "I'll bet she does," she said with a slight blush. "And goodness has nothing to do with it my dear," I added. "Is she under contract?" "No, it's more of an oral agreement."

We casually swam about in the calm grotto and strolled among the many tide pools. Randi knew a lot about the flora and fauna found within the craggy rocks and shallow pools that were replenished with each gentle incoming wave. There were urchins, snails, small crabs, octopus, abalone and bright orange and purple starfish. Farther out in the surf there were happy sea otters floating on their backs and cracking abalone shells on rocks they balanced on their chests.

I gazed in awe as she strolled from the water a short distance up the beach, turned and leaned against a large smooth rock absorbing the warmth of the fading afternoon sun. "Oh my god," I whispered to myself. There could not be a more sensually arousing vision than the one I was currently etching into my memory receptors.

Her head was tilted up toward the warm sun, and her long dark hair blew gently in the afternoon breeze. Her radiant smooth skin was a deep golden brown and her beautiful taught breasts reached gently toward the pale blue sky, as did her playfully erect chocolate kiss nipples. Her softly rounded hips, butt and thighs as well as her lovely, pouty mound of sweetness, were that of an innocent young Indian girl. I couldn't help thinking that Hef would cream his jeans for a photographic reproduction of the visual to which I'm obviously enjoying despite cold ocean water and scourge of the inevitable 'shrinkage factor.'

I strolled to the alluring vision before me, put my arm around her waist, gently pulled her close and kissed her softly on her neck. "Oh my goodness Monkey Man, though I'm sure goodness has nothing to do with it, but I can see you have no pockets, so I assume your assault with that friendly weapon is just because you're happy to see me. Maybe you should come up and see me sometime big boy!"

Chapter Six

Day 6

(In world news today; Russia has announced the successful launch of Sputnik 1, the world's first earth orbiting satellite. It will be visible to the naked eye on any clear night sky throughout the northern hemisphere. Russia also announced the successful test firing of its latest ICBM long range nuclear missile, capable of striking virtually all of Europe, most of Canada and vast portions of the United States. The Eisenhower administration seemed surprised by the announcement and Vice President Richard Nixon suggested that it merely was the Kremlin's knee-jerk counter reaction to the recent speech by the President proclaiming the implementation of the 'Eisenhower Doctrine' whereby the U.S. government will provide military and economic aid to any and all countries struggling against the insidious scourge of communism.

In entertainment news; Leonard Bernstein's 'West Side Story' opens on Broadway this week, bringing teenage gang violence to the Great White Way.

'Bridge on the River Kwai' and 'Twelve Angry Men' topped the box office receipts this weekend, followed by 'Sayonara,' 'Peyton Place' and 'Witness for the Prosecution.'

CBS is proud to announce the series premier of its newest family comedy 'Leave it to Beaver' staring Hugh Beaumont as Ward Cleaver, Barbara Billingsley as June, Tony Dow as Wally, and Jerry Mathers as the young Beaver Cleaver.

From the mountains to the desert, from the desert to the sea, and to all of southern California, this is Jerry Dunphy wishing you a good day and returning you to Dick Haynes at the Reigns, on KNX news, talk and sports radio.)

I grumbled, and fumbled around with my hand on the night stand until I discovered the clock radio alarm, of which I wasn't aware that I owned. With eyes still closed, I turned nobs and pushed buttons to no avail. Sweeping it off the nightstand onto the floor had no effect either. I finally came upon the cord, followed it to the wall socket and yanked it out of the wall; silence.

Didn't last long, the phone began to ring incessantly, no matter how I tried to ignore it. Whoever it was on the other end of the line seemed awfully persistent. Must be Precious. It comes to mind that I should suggest to Mona that her friend at *DuPont* should invent some kind of telephone answering device. After a specified number of rings, leave a message or just hang-up.

"Good morning Precious," I cheerfully greeted. "Good morning my ass, you horny bastard, do you realize that you haven't spent one night in that apartment since you arrived?" I was correct in my assumption as to the origin of the call. "I beg your pardon? My dear, you do realize that I am a professional investigator currently conducting an active murder case, which, of course, at times requires late night or after hours covert surveillance, utilizing undercover investigative techniques, or un-orthodox methods of research." "Yeah, unorthodox undercover techniques?" she responded. "Save it for the young, dumb and impressionable sand-nymph sun-bunnies. Get over yourself asshole."

"Not only that," I continued unabated, " I single handedly tamed a raging, wild bucking stallion that stood ten hands high if he was a foot. And you had the audacity to accuse me of losing my touch, my lightning fast reflexes, my keen instincts, and my deadly abilities. Well I'm here to tell you baby, I'm a bad ass, and I'm pretty; I'm pretty bad ass!"

"Oh piss-off Cassias, stop flappin' your yap. It's not kosher to toot your own kazoo," she scolded. "Tell me Buckaroo Palooka, did you actually gain any useful information during your brunch with Mr. Ervine yesterday, or were you just inflating your ego and increasing your hat size, or more likely, you were showboating for the sole purpose of getting laid? Bull's eye, hey Casanova? You're such a disingenuous, narcissistic, sanctimonious, self-indulgent son-of-a-bitch. I'm surprised Rita puts up with your bullshit." "She's a pretty liberal girl," I responded. She generally lets me do who I want.....I mean **what** I want."

I explained that Mr. Ervine wasn't forthcoming with any information of which we weren't already aware. It was another hand-holding-session. However I spent considerable time with a girl named Randi Andretti who seems to know a lot about the situation around the ranch. She confirmed that Mr. Ervine and China Lei had a familiar, long term relationship that had grown very close over the years. China often accompanied Mr. Ervine to social functions like philanthropic charity balls, museum openings, art exhibits, theatrical productions, movie premiers, cocktail parties and so forth. They went on several vacations together; Hawaii, the Bahamas, and Acapulco. China was educated, sophisticated, and knowledgeable on any number of subjects, well versed regarding current events and was capable of conversing on many levels and in several languages. According to Randi, Mr. Ervine became quite despondent over China's death and feels personally responsible for her murder; if she were not associated with him, then she would not have become a target in the on-going extortion campaign.

I further explained that I had gotten a firsthand look at the parcel of land at the center of this situation. It is unquestionably a pristine stretch of unbelievably beautiful shore line, but so are many others along the southern California coast. There has got to be something special about this property, and there has to be a common denominator between this property, Mr. Stanton's railroad line that runs through it, and the on-going extortion campaigns being played out against both. What could it be that makes this risky and complicated endeavor so lucrative as to create these convergence of conspiracies? Oil, gold, buried treasure, some type of smuggling operation? That's the sixty-four thousand dollar question isn't it? I'm afraid that we won't know the answer however until we successfully fit all the pieces of the puzzle into their proper places before we realize the entire picture. Unfortunately, that may be too late.

"The other reason I called Travis," she said, abruptly changing the subject, "is because tonight is Precocious' scheduled personal appearance at the *Olympic Auditorium*, remember? Kato will escort her to the seaplane tarmac for Kamikaze Steve's last flight off the island of the day, ETA Wilmington at dusk. She's your baby from there."

I waited at the end of pier B as the little red *Grumman* came in low and flew down the length of the channel with a brilliant golden sunset in the distance. Kamikaze set her down with a smooth hiss as she skimmed across the water and eventually came to a slow taxi to the pier. He opened the exit door and tied-off the nose while I snugged her up aft. We greeted each other with a big handshake and a familiar smile, as we pushed the gang-way to the opening in the fuselage. Kamikaze went aft, opened the cargo hold and began off-loading passenger luggage onto the pier, while I helped those disembarking across the gang-way and thanked them for flying *Avalon Air Express*.

Precocious was the last to emerge onto the gang-way and looked dick-stiffening devastating in a stunning, sparkling silver sequin dress, that was both low cut and revealing, and likewise short and revealing; revealing the most beautiful Norwegian, Barbie Doll girl parts you can imagine… (Go ahead, I'll wait.) Her long blond hair cascaded over her golden brown shoulders and down her smooth back, and her big baby blue eyes shined with enthusiasm and twinkled with innocent delight. She came rushing to me with a big hug and kiss, and a big beautiful smile. "Oh Travis, I'm happy to see you. Thank you for being my date for tonight. I love you so much Travis. I'm so excited in anticipation of tonight." I opened the door to the Hornet and helped her in. "You look fabulous baby. You'll knock 'em dead tonight. I'm looking forward to tonight too."

While we loaded Precocious' luggage into cavernous space of the Hornet's trunk, I asked Kamikaze if he'd seen a shiny black *Bell* helicopter flying over the channel between the mainland and the island. He looked at me with a puzzled grin. "Funny you should ask that, Bombardier. It just so happens that I have seen that particular aircraft on several occasions over the last few months. When I first spotted it, I immediately thought of you for some reason. At the time I thought it curious that you would come to mind. I must be psychic." "You didn't happen to be curious enough to get the registration numbers did you?" I asked. *"Any one for tennis,"* he responded, with a strange grin, obviously extremely proud of himself. "What the hell are you talking about?" I asked slightly dumbfounded.

"Nebraska- Echo- 1 4 1 0- Sierra. NE 1-4-10-S," he repeated. "Oh for Christ's sake man, it's really scary how your mind works. You're not psychic, more like psychedelic bordering on psychotic. Did you see where it went or where it landed?" "The last time I saw it was on the other side of the island heading out toward the shipping lanes. There was an impressively humongous black Magnum Raptor Mega Yacht anchored out there, but I didn't fly close enough to get names or numbers. I actually had a fleeting thought that you would want that info, but on second thought it seemed silly. Damn you Bombardier, you've made me suspicious of everything now, ya' overly suspicious, paranoid sum-bitch."

During the ride up the coast and across the *Santa Monica Mountains*, Precocious and I got caught up on old news. She told me that Rita missed me terribly and was weary of running the Casino alone without me. I explained that I only returned to the mainland originally as a favor to an old friend. It was only to be a temporary hand-holding nerve-calming session. Since my arrival however it has morphed into a convergence of intertwined conspiracies, reminiscent of *the Big Casino* and *Golden Dragon* adventures. I wasn't thrilled about it either. I missed lovely Rita and I missed our life together in paradise. I really miss that girl.

We arrived at *Schwab's Deli* on *Sunset* just after dark and parked the Hudson at the curb between the deli and Mickey Cohen's bookmaking front down the street; '*Michael's Haberdasher to the Hollywood Stars.*' *Schwab's* was the un-official introduction to the Hollywood scene. It was the place to be seen if you were famous and the place to be discovered if you weren't. *Schwab's Delicatessen* became the 'touch stone' for every starry-eyed innocent who arrived in 'tinsel town' after it became known that 'Sweater Girl' Lana Turner was discovered sitting at the counter *at Schwab's* wearing a revealing fuzzy angora. Perhaps that's why pubescent predator Groucho Marks held impromptu auditions there on a daily basis even though he had an office across the street. Plus he liked the corned beef on rye.

I knew Precocious had never been here and that she would thoroughly enjoy the experience. She already looked like a movie star and she would definitely create a buzz upon her entrance. The entire place fell momentarily silent as we entered and all eyes followed Precocious and her unobtrusive, apparently invisible escort to a booth in the back. Groucho's infamous eyebrows arched high and his ever-present stogy fell from his gaping yap into his gaping lap as she passed.

Precocious was all smiles and goose bumps. She could barely contain her exuberance and it was obvious that she was having a great time thus far. I ordered two hot pastramis on rye, mustard, pickles and one with onions and sauerkraut, from a cute little Jewish girl behind the counter.

Upon my return to Precocious' side, she quietly squealed with delight and grabbed my thigh, and-then-some, with both hands, under the table. I was flattered, youthfully robust and aroused. Then I realized that she was goo-goo over the new arrivals; Television producer and comedic star Ernie Kovacks and his wife, stage and screen singing star Edie Adams who popped in for a 'to go' order. They waived to Groucho on their way out and Ernie pointed at Groucho and shouted in a heavy

Yiddish accent; "no soup for you!" and then did a double take when he noticed Precocious. Being the showman he is, he waved goodbye to the adoring crowd, making special effort to blow a kiss and wink to my gorgeous blonde companion, and exited to spontaneous laughter and applause. (Buzz-off hambone, I thought to myself. I knew that I would spend the entire night running interference and hammering would-be interlopers with cross-body blocks, forearm chucking, and an intimidating shitty attitude.)

After a thorough inspection utilizing my 'Professor Peabody' combo night-stick and illuminated undercarriage reflector- wand, we had the gray Hornet buzzing along under the glow of the 'HOLLYWOODLAND' sign high on the hill, the clear night's twinkling canopy of stars, tall Hollywood palms, and the dazzling neon flash and glitter of *the Sunset Strip*. Fast talking, street-hawking, side-show-Johnnies loudly touted the attributes and talents to be found within the darkened caverns beyond the neon glare of the various strip joints and exotic dance venues dotted here and there along the glittering boulevard. It was reminiscent of the strip clubs such as boob-job pioneer *Carol Dota's, The Condor Club, and the Bunny room*, along *Broadway,* near *China Town* in San Francisco. I am aware of these things due to weekend passes from the confines of boot camp on *Governor's Island* in Oakland Bay at the inauguration of my military service.

We cruised past the *Rainbow Room*, next door to *the Whiskey, Gazzarri's and the Palladium*. I turned on San Vicente Avenue then turned again on Hollywood Boulevard and went past *the El Capitan'* and *Gramann's Chinese Theatre* where the hand and foot prints of film, T.V., and recording stars are virtually imbedded in concrete for eternity, along with the polished granite slabs of the *'Hollywood Walk of Fame.'*

We went back to Sunset, past the *Gower Street Studios* to Alameda. At the corner the traffic signal clanged, the stop sign arm rose into position and the light turned red. *A Red Car Line* trolley whizzed by with sparks flying from the overhead electric connectors as it clanged its way into downtown. The bell sounded, the stop sign retracted, to be replaced by the go sign, and the light turned green. The Hornet swept down the dark street with *the Southern Pacific* rail yards on the left and past *Union Station* to Olympic Boulevard. We drove past the auditorium, around the block several times, down a few alleys, and confident that we hadn't acquired a tail, I pulled into the V.I.P parking lot.

Inside it was packed and abuzz with pugilistic anticipation. *The Olympic Auditorium* was an immense   concrete arena for modern day gladiators. There were ringside, V.I.P., and general admission seats on the main floor surrounding the boxing ring in the middle, and lounge seating in the balcony. There were vendors hawking peanuts, popcorn and cracker jacks. Others peddled hot dogs, beer, or Bonbons.

A heavy- set floor manager type babe in charge of VIP accommodations and appropriately equipped with impressive earphone headset, walky-talky, and multi-paged clipboard, escorted Precocious and myself to our seats in the middle of the second row behind the ringside seats. With all the spraying of blood, sweat and snot, the ringside seats at a professional fight are like the front row concert seats at the stand-up comic Gallagher's watermelon smashing, and sledge hammering of assorted fruit extravaganza, requiring foul-weather gear and drop-cloths. (Whoever that is?)

I casually gazed around the immediate area looking for anyone suspicious, sketchy, or threatening. I didn't have to look far; the whole place is full of sketchy looking sleaze-balls. As ring announcer Jimmy Lennon began to gather the invited guests within the boxing ring for the beginning of the televised main event, a somehow familiar face arrived at the end of our row, smiled as if he knew us and began to make his way toward us. He was clean cut, well dressed, and extended his hand as he approached.

"Hi, sorry to interrupt your evening Mr. Dugan, but a Miss Precious Goodlay, from your agency, informed me that you may be in attendance this evening and that I might find you here. Please allow me to introduce myself. My name is Dwayne Hickman and you may recognize me from my CBS television show; *The Life and Loves of Dobie Gilles.*" Precocious leaned forward and asked if that was the show with the beatnik character named Maynard G. Krebbs? "Oh yes, everybody remembers Maynard," he said, mocking sarcastic. "Maynard was played brilliantly by my good friend Bob Denver and I'm flattered that you're familiar with the show."

"Tonight however," he continued, " I represent the advertising firm of '*Feindham, Bindem and Boikom*'; formerly' *Dewey, Cheatham and Howe*', the agency that represents *the Rigney Confection Corporation* with regard to all T.V., radio, or print media promotional advertisements. It has come to our attention that Precocious has an equally- photogenic twin sister named Precarious."

"We are starting a *'double your pleasure, double your fun'* campaign for the *Double Mint Gum* franchise, and we are using identical twins as spokes persons. It will run nationwide on T.V., radio as well as print, including bus stops and billboards. Your faces will be seen in more places than *the Burma shave* signs. The entire campaign utilizes very high production values and will be filmed in a variety of tropical locations. It's a tremendous opportunity, not only do you get to experience some of the most exotic locales in the world and pampered like a princes, but you will be paid at the top of the standard pay scale. Believe me Miss Goodlay, this is a sweet deal. I don't wish to take any more of your time this evening and you of course will have to discuss it with your sister. I will leave you my card and I look forward to your call once you have had time to think it over. It's been a pleasure to meet you Miss Goodlay and you as well Mr. Dugan. Please enjoy the rest of your evening." He shook our hands and then retreated to the isle and disappeared into the swirl of smoky darkness.

The ring bell sounded, the overhead lights flickered, Dick 'Whoa Nellie' Lane, took his seat at T.V. ringside, and ring announcer Jimmy Lennon grabbed the microphone suspended from the rafters. The live broadcast of the '*Gillette Friday Night Fights from the Olympic Auditorium*' was about to begin.

The heavy-set floor manager babe with the headphones and the clipboard appeared at the end of our row of seats, pointed at her wrist watch, and motioned for Precocious to follow her to the bright lights and the big city within the boxing ring. I gave her a big hug and kiss, wished her good luck, and assured her that she would knock'em dead.

I watched as she followed the floor manager to the ring steps and managed to navigate her way up the steps, climb between the ropes and into the ring in her minimalist skirt and spiked heels. There was a stampede by the honored assemblage to spread the ropes and assist Precocious into the ring. Whatever Jimmy Lennon was saying over the P.A system was ignored by all male members of the crowd and half the females, while they watched, mesmerized by Precocious' enchanting journey through the enthusiastic crowd and ascent into the ring.

The glaring television lights snapped on, the ring bell rang frantically, and Jimmy Lennon stepped to the mike. "Good evening sports fans, ladies and gentleman, and welcome to *Gillette's Cavalcade of Sports*, tonight brought to you live from the *Olympic Auditorium* in downtown Los' Angeles', California." He points to the time keeper and the bell rings several more times. He shuffles the handful of 3x5 cards he carries and brings the mike to his mouth to continue.

"Ladies and Gentlemen it is our pleasure at this time to introduce our special guests of this evening;" more pointing and bell ringing. "Boxing fans around the world please help me welcome Middle-weight Champion of the World and local hometown hero, Emile Griffith." Emile, looking a little older and a little more grey, circled the ring waiving, smiling and acknowledging the applause of the fans. After a nod, a point and several more rings of the bell, he announced former heavy- weight champ Floyd Patterson to more applause, and after another round of nods and clangs, the same procedure for the guy who took the championship belt from Patterson in a packed house *at Yankee Stadium*; 'The Swede,' Ingemar Johansson, followed by applause and a smattering of boos.

"And finally sports fans, we saved the best for last. Please welcome *Miss Foamy Gillette* who has something to say to all you men out there." He handed the mike to Precocious and the soundtrack for '*The Stripper* 'began to play over the sound system and the crowd went wild. She raised the microphone to her lips and the place fell silent in anticipation. She smiled, tilted her head, flashed those beautiful baby blues, and whispered; "*Take it off, take it all off.*" The auditorium erupted in wild applause and whoops and hollers. They loved her. A star is born.

While I watched Precocious gracefully exit the ring and down the steps, I noticed nebbish Barry Kuda a few rows down scanning the crowd and looking completely out of place and obviously uncomfortable. He eventually zeroed in on me and made his way to our row of seats and then shuffled his way across to the empty seats next to me and sat down. "Mr. Dugan I apologize for the interruption, but your secretary informed me that you may be in attendance here tonight. I would normally not be found in such surroundings, but Mr. Stanton, who is presently attending a charity function at *the Pantages Theater*, asked me to invite you to a late dinner with him at *the Players Club*, after the pugilistic exhibition of course. Are you familiar with the establishment or shall I provide directions?"

I kept a close eye on Precocious as she acknowledged the accolades of her many adoring fans and new best friends along the way back to where I waited. I assured Barry that I was familiar with former film director Preston Sturgis' eatery and that Precocious and I would humbly accept Mr. Stanton's gracious invitation. "Shall we say ten-ish." "Marvelous!"

Barry Kuda retraced his steps back along the row of seats to the isle just as Mickey Cohen arrived on scene dressed to the nines and accompanied by his two familiar stripper girlfriends Liz Renee' his main squeeze, and Candy Barr just in town on the mob circuit from Jack Ruby's *Carousel Club* in Dallas. Cohen and his stunning entourage' waited for Barry to clear the isle then shuffled single file down the row of seats toward me with big bright smiles, big bouncy boobs, and lots of sparkling bangles and baubles. Once the girls got settled, Mickey made his way down the row and leaned in close. "Dugan glad to see you my friend, but I was hoping that you were going to be accompanied by your gorgeous Scandinavian companion in the baby blue T-bird. What happened man? Did she blow you off after you blew- up her T-bird?" he giggled. "Have you become too dangerous to date?" I simply smiled and pointed to the stunning apparition waiting to rejoin me at the end of the row. Mickey turned and was momentarily mesmerized. "Oh my God!" he muttered. "I mean holy shit! or shalom. Are you fucking kidding me; twins? Who's the lucky boy? You dog! Man, some guys have all the luck. You have got to be hung like a porn star man. Enjoy your evening you lucky bastard." He backed away and allowed Precocious to squeeze past and rejoin me with a big hug and kiss. I smiled at Mickey who was simply shaking his head, humbled and bewildered; perhaps envious and obviously in awe.

We enjoyed several bouts between up-and-coming fighters including Patterson New Jersey's Ruben Hurricane Carter and former Golden Gloves Champ Joey Barnum, now professional middle-weight contender by night and Orange County bail bondsman by day, then between bouts we graciously excused ourselves and went to our dinner engagement and rendezvous with our host, railroad tycoon James Stanton.

The Players Club was an upscale eatery catering to the 'A' list Hollywood crowd. Preston Sturgis, a movie director with several hits under his belt, didn't like the food *at Chasen's, Ciro's, or Frank's Grill*; the local watering holes for the likes of Billy Wilder, Spencer Tracey, Garbo, Gable, Harlow and Hughes, so he built *The Players Club*. It was built on three levels; the lower level was a car-hop drive-in and drive-thru, the second level was casual dining, and the third was the high-brow, suit and tie, candle light and violin serenade haute couture' dining.

A prim and proper maître'd rushed to greet us upon our entrance and efficiently led us to Mr. Stanton's private dining area near the fireplace in the back of the room. Stanton was accompanied by the nebbish

Kuda, and two of our operatives sat nearby. They rose to their feet when we approached and old man Stanton seemed particularly pleased to meet Precocious. We completed cordial introductions, I assisted my trophy date with her chair and we all made ourselves comfortable.

A lovely, well versed young waitress promptly arrived and took our drink orders; whiskey and Rye for the old rail jockey, a Rob Roy for the spectacled one, Mai Tai for the exotic Norwegian beauty in sequins, and Vodka Martini agitated not propelled, for yours truly of course.

We exchanged pleasantries and talked boxing until the waitress arrived with our drink orders on a tray. Mr. Stanton recommended the Filet Mignon' and it was unanimous all around. He waited for the waitress to retreat and for everyone to enjoy the initial test-run of their respective thirst quenching refreshments, before starting right in. Stanton had similar build and features as did Mr. Ervine.

"Dugan, I apologize for hijacking you and your stunning companion's evening, I owe you big time, but I felt it important that I talk to you as soon as possible. You see, the previously veiled threats over the phone have now escalated to a deliberate act of sabotage resulting in a serious, multiple car derailment in west Texas. The route will be off-line for several days while we initiate repairs to the rails and ties, and upright the damaged cars." "Have you received any communication since the derailment?" I asked, to which I received a negative response.

"Mr. Stanton, allow me to speak freely and bluntly. With all due respect, I've been pussy-footin' around here for almost a week and don't feel as though I've gotten the entire story. I don't believe that you've been completely honest or candid with me. I originally came to hold hands, sooth frayed nerves, and offer some insight and advice. That advice has led to a huge commitment by my agency on your behalf to provide personal security for a large number of individuals scattered in several distant locations, which has stretched our staff to the limits, including hiring Pinkerton's to secure the Rigney estate, so as to allow us to place personnel where more urgently needed. All of which is fine, that's what we're here for. However, the situation has escalated to a more dangerous level. There have been attempts on my life, as well as the people associated with me. I have become the target. It makes me wonder how and why these people think that I'm involved other than providing personal security through my agency. Therefore, having said that, and again with the upmost respect Mr. Stanton, I have several blunt, but poignant questions to put forth, and unless I get some straight-forward answers, then I'm afraid we will be forced to terminate our relationship."

Old man Stanton gestured for the waitress to bring another round, then settled back in his chair with a wide grin. "Dugan, I was wondering if we were ever going to get to this phase of our relationship. If you'll recall, at your initial meeting with Kuda, I got the distinct impression that you definitely didn't want to get involved and that you were merely here, as you stated, to hold hands, sooth nerves and offer advice. I need someone with big enough cajones' to take charge of this situation and bring it to a swift and decisive conclusion; and I don't particularly care how that is accomplished. The word around town is that you are the man for the job. Your recommendation comes with accolades by all. I can't tell you how disappointed I was at the conclusion of the initial meeting. I was afraid for the safety of my family and associates at that time. I'm even more so now."

"Very well Mr. Stanton, tell me about the relationship between you and China Lei." Our lovely waitress arrived with the second round, and he waited until she departed before responding. He took a long pull on his Whiskey and Rye then settled into his chair. He held his drink with both hands and gazed into it. He got a melancholy look on his face and stared off into space.

"China was an exceptionally beautiful person, both inside and out. She was intelligent, articulate, and had a wonderfully whimsical sense of humor; she was a joy to be around. I know it sounds like the ramblings of a foolish old man, but it was true; she really made me feel twenty years younger. She was vibrant, enthusiastic and had an effervescent outlook on life that was wonderfully contagious. She of course was also exotically sensual, sexy and gorgeous. She knew how to make a man feel like a man; a very lucky man. We were great friends and I thoroughly enjoyed her company. We went to many charitable functions, plays, operas, and several vacations; the Bahamas, Bora Bora, and Tahiti."

"I am not naïve' Mr. Dugan, nor am I delusional. I am well aware that China has other 'friends', if you will, who take her to charity balls, theatre performances, and exotic vacations as well. I learned long ago to accept the circumstances, and she made no attempt conceal anything from me." "Are you aware that she had a similar relationship with a Mr. James Ervine of Orange County?" I asked. He paused momentarily with a slightly puzzled look. "Yes, I was aware of their relationship, I had seen them together at several functions over the years." "Do you know Mr. Ervine personally?" I asked. "We have been introduced at several functions, and he ships his cattle to the auction stock yards in Texas aboard my rail line, but that's about the extent of our relationship. If you don't mind my asking Dugan; what does James Ervine have to do with this? I'm sure there are other rich business men who have had similar relationships with China?"

"I'm quite sure there were similar relationships, however I know of only one other who is experiencing the same type of extortion threats to which you are currently enjoying. The odds of it being a coincidence are slim to none, and there are several common denominators; China Lei, and a prime section of Mr. Ervine's ranch, along a pristine stretch of shoreline, that not so coincidently, your rail line runs through."

"What could be so damned important about that parcel of land with your rail road running through it, as to be worth extortion and murder? China's murder was a wake-up call for you and Ervine. You both had a long standing relationship with her and you both had sincere affection for her. China meant a lot to you both, and her death hurt you both deeply. It got your immediate attention, and made any further threats that much more ominous. It's only going to get worse if we don't figure out what the connection is, and who's behind it."

"Dugan I implore you to take this case and bring it to a swift conclusion. You are the only person experienced in these types of situations and from everything I've heard from whom I consider to be very reliable sources; you are the only individual with enough hutzpah to confront these individuals and dispatch them post haste. Dugan I'm begging you to take control of this situation. Without you to run roughshod over this operation I wouldn't know what to do or where to turn. The authorities are getting nowhere and they're telling us nothing. I gave them the benefit of the doubt in the beginning, hoping that they were being prudent by keeping the investigation close to the vest. Now, however I'm beginning to think that they are just inept or that Inspector Golly is being compromised in some manner."

Precocious and I exited the *Players Club* at the conclusion of a scrumptious dinner and walked across the parking lot to the Hornet. I had her stand back several yards before we got there, so that I could perform a preliminary check for unwanted pyrotechnics with my Professor Peabody combo nightstick and illuminated reflector wand. Satisfied that all was well, I motioned for her to approach, unlocked her passenger side door and helped her in. I went around the front of the car to the driver's side as she slid over and leaned across to pull-up the door lock. Suddenly there was a huge explosion and a blinding flash of light under the car parked next to ours. The explosion blew the roof and the doors off the car, which slammed me into the side of the Hornet, sandwiching me between the two vehicles, but in the same instant shielding me from the ensuing fireball.

It took me a few seconds to gather my marbles, reconnect my neurological receptors, and realize what had just happened. I was glad that I had on my *Kevlar* vest because it kept my innards intact when I made sudden contact with the Hornet's door. The Hornet's door was now seriously concave and all the paint was singed off that side of the car. I opened the door and found Precocious on the floor, covering her ears and screaming like a banshee. Suddenly, from between the parked cars across the way, several gunmen advanced and began peppering the Hornet with gunfire. I turned the key and stomped the starter-peddle. The Hornet roared to life, I yanked her into gear and mashed the go peddle to the floorboard. We raced across the parking lot with a barrage of bullets impacting the screaming gray battle wagon. One of our attackers stepped out from the line of parked cars and before he could fire his weapon the angry Hornet swept him up and spit him out. We caught a second lingering too long in the open and he slipped trying to escape; he thumped along under the Hornet as we rolled over him. I glanced off the side of another car mashing a third garbanzo in between.

Round after round smacked into the fleeing Hornet as we screamed out of the parking lot in clouds of burning blue rubber and out onto Sunset heading toward Santa Monica over the mountain to the coast. Several cars began to pursue and suddenly I remembered the ambush on a lonely mountain road I drove headlong into during *the Golden Dragon* adventure; I yanked the wheel to the left and made a sweeping U-turn in the middle of Sunset Boulevard scattering traffic in all directions. The roaring gray Hornet side-swiped a car parked at the curb then removed the right front fender from a small sports car sending it into a spinning pirouette in the middle of the street.

We had the Hornet careening down Sunset in high gear, dodging traffic and blowing through stop lights like a chrome ball in a pinball machine. There were parts and pieces falling off, or dragging behind the Hornet that became high velocity shrapnel when they eventually dislodged and flew off.

There were still several cars in pursuit no matter how I tried I couldn't shake them. We flew over the *Rampart Street Bridge* and slammed the pavement hard upon landing; Precocious continued to scream, from the fetal position, on the passenger side floorboard. They continued to gain on us and began to ricochet' rounds off of our fleeing tank. I reached under the seat and grabbed Moms O'Malley's .45 and began returning fire out my window. I emptied the clip then threw the weapon into the back seat.

We roared down the back alleys of South Central, scattering trash cans, blowing through dark neighborhoods, and leaving chaos and destruction in our wake. Sirens and flashing lights were everywhere screaming through the downtown streets attempting to catch-up to the ensuing rampage.

I swept the Hornet around the darkened corner of a building at high speed, and then stomped on the brakes. The first car in pursuit flew around the corner and slammed into the rear of the Hudson, smashing the front of their car back to the windshield, and launching the occupants through the windshield and onto the trunk lid of the Hornet. I mashed the go pedal and we screamed away in a cloud of smoke, scattering twisted and battered bodies from the trunk lid across the road. The remaining pursuers went in all directions attempting to avoid the carnage but still managed to rumble over their mangled comrades. Suddenly, an early morning milk man in bright white uniform carrying his metal basket of milk bottles, cottage cheese and butter, darted out from the side walk directly in our path. He looked like a deer caught in the headlights. I yanked the wheel to the right and pancaked the side of the Hornet off of *a Good Humor* ice cream truck parked at the curb. We careened back across the street, hit the curb and went airborne. The sign on the side of the panel truck we were hurtling toward read; *Helms Bakery, Boyle Heights*. We T-boned the panel truck and came to a grinding stop, like a screeching train wreck in scattered heaps of smoldering metal, bread, donuts, and steaming radiator water.

This is not the Jewish enclave of Boyle Heights in which Mickey Cohen grew up; we were attracting enough colored folks to make a Tarzan movie. The door opened and I fell out onto the pavement; fade to black.

Chapter Seven

Day 7

The consistent clip-clop, clip-clop of railcar over rail ties, the pungent aroma of a robust stock yard, and the flashing strobe of a rising sun through the bulkhead slats of a slow moving cattle car. I lay on my stomach, feet tied at the ankles and hands tied at the wrist behind my back. I performed an internal inventory audit to determine what condition my condition was in. (I flashed on Kenny Rodgers and the First Edition). I had a constant ringing in my ears, an impressive egg forming between eyes where I impacted the handcrafted, simulated Tortoise shell steering wheel of my, now newly purchased and severely depreciated, battleship gray Hudson Hornet. I also became aware that I was lying in a congealing pool of my own blood. Nothing seemed broken and I felt no pain.

I began to think about Precocious and became extremely anxious, guilt ridden, and really fuckin' scared that I'd failed to protect her and now I've lost her. I had to get the hell out of here and find her, before it was too late; if it wasn't already too late. I can't imagine what I would tell Precious if anything ever happened to Precocious; or how I would ever live with myself, the guilt would be overwhelming.

Suddenly the door at the end of the cattle car slid open and two sketchy-looking weirdoes entered as the train continued to clip-clop along the scenic shoreline of the deep blue Pacific. The tall one, wearing a conservative business suit, black turban, dark beard and intensely stern expression, looked like a Middle Eastern extremist that was nuttier than a Holiday fruit cake. The second guy looked like he thought he was Tashiro Mafuni; only he looked more like Poncho Villa. He had a scraggly Fu Man Chu mustache, a funny top knot pony tail, black gee made of stiff sail cloth, and a big-ass samurai sword. Together, they looked like traveling side-show freaks or a macabre' circus act. Maybe Fu Man Chu swallows that sword; I'd like to make him sit on it.

Samurai Poncho dragged a cane-back café chair from the corner and set it in the middle of the floor. He then produced magically from somewhere up his sleeve, a big impressive handle that after a series of elaborate arm waves and twists of the wrist brought forth a big impressive butterfly knife blade; Shazam! He then took the knife and cut the bottom out of the chair. (Oh please, really? You shmucks can't be more original than that? We're on a moving train for god sakes!) He dragged me off the floor by my wrists, inflicting as much pain to my arms and shoulders as he could in the process, and slammed me down hard in the chair. For his next trick, from somewhere up his sleeve, he produced a set of Chinese nunchucks; two small night sticks about a foot long connected at one end of each by a six-inch strand of rope, that can be utilized as a defensive weapon by spinning it like a baton, or an offensive one by lashing out with it similar to a bull whip. Used properly it will snap bones and pulverize flesh. Samurai Poncho whipped it around his neck and waist, over his shoulder and under his arm, switched hands back and forth and snapped it to within a whisper of my face, just to assure me that he was proficient at his craft.

"Who are you fuckin' idiots and what the hell do you want?" I asked. "Why am I tied to a chair and where's the blonde girl?" Poncho Samurai stepped forward and delivered an open-backhand to my left cheek bone splitting the flesh, and to be followed soon after by a big purple welt. The open-backhand, which is closed into a fist just before impact, is designed to rip flesh and create lots of blood. It's a cheap shot from a chicken- shit that had himself all pumped-up like a show-boating- peacock.

"Mr. Dugan, you are in no position to ask questions," piped-up Turban boy. He had a calm, self- assured demeanor, yet his eyes were intense and stern. It wouldn't take much to turn him vicious and cruel. "My advice to you Mr. Dugan is that you cooperate, answer my questions forthright and with little hesitation. If you choose to resist, then your experience, as well as your beautiful companion's experience, will be very difficult and very painful. Mr. Dugan you have two options; you can do this the easy way, or you can do this the way my friend would prefer. Please excuse my manners, Mr. Dugan I have not introduced myself or my associate. I am Mohammar Kadjetski, and my associate is Toby Juan Cannole'." (Oh bullshit; too many Ian Fleming novels, I suspect.)

"It is very simple Mr. Dugan you need only tell me why you're here and why it is that you seem to be in the middle of several confrontations that result in a number of fatalities. You are making my clients very nervous with your unwanted interference. You don't seem to play well with others do you?"

"And who are your clients Mohamed? And why do they give a rat's ass what I do?" Apparently I don't follow directions well either. Fortunately, we had Samurai Poncho there to set me straight. He set me straight-up with some kind of strange front chicken kick that caught me under the chin and snapped my head back, then followed with a spinning back kick that hit me upside my head and sent me, and the chair I rode in on, tumbling to the floor. He finished with several elaborated katas and a number of quick whacks with his nunchucks to my shoulder and thigh. He then set me and the chair back into position in the middle of the cattle car as we continued to roll along, clip-clop-clip-clop. He then punched me in the face drawing a trickle of blood from my nose and upper lip. "You are to answer questions not ask them!" he yelled in my face. He seemed perturbed. I was a little perturbed myself.

"You know, tough guy," I began, smiling at Poncho, "for an asshole who thinks he's such a hard-ass, you really are just a pansy-ass sissy. It takes a real pussy to beat-up somebody tied to a chair, you fuckin' queer." That's all it took; Samurai Poncho flew into psychotic rage, kicking and screaming, punching my chest and head. Somewhere along in his elaborate spaz attack Poncho produced that ridiculously complicated butterfly knife and began whipping it around like a thigh-heavy cheer leader twirling her baton at Pasadena's Rose parade. He kicked me in the chest toppling me over onto my back, in the next instant he cut the rope around my ankles, brought the chair upright and cut the restraints at my wrist. I bounced out of my chair and faced the little creep with the funny knife. He smiled, spun the knife a few more times, and threw it past my head to stick into the bulkhead slats. He then removed his big-ass Samurai sword from its sheath, twirled it around with much pomp and ceremony, raised it over his head and stuck into the floor. Banzai!

He attacked, punching and kicking in an attempt to steam roller over me. I stood my ground and blocked most of his incoming offensive barrage. I caught a couple of solid roundhouse kicks to the chest but my *Kevlar* vest absorbed most of the punishment that Samurai Poncho could dish out. He pushed me to the bulkhead with his continuous onslaught where I' rope-a-doped' him along the wall until I backed into the corner, then braced my foot against the wall and sprang out swinging. I drove my knee into his chest and followed with a flurry of blinding rights and lefts. I stayed close, moved forward and kept laying into him with powerful combinations including more ripping elbows and pulverizing knees. He stepped back and delivered a powerful side kick that knocked me, with surprising force, into the bulkhead. Once again I pushed-off with a straight right and left, only to be pummeled back to the wall under his relentless onslaught. This time however, I backed into the handle of his butterfly knife stuck in the wall. I spun around grabbing the knife from the wall and continued around slashing him across the throat with a backhand swing. He retreated holding his neck as blood began to seep from between his fingers. He backed into the sword still stuck in the floor. He yanked the sword from the floor and began to advance whirling the sword in flashing circles as he came.

Suddenly a rapid barrage of gunfire erupted from the Pullman car attached behind the cattle car. I threw the knife and it was promptly batted away by the whirling propeller blade of Poncho's sword. The rear door of the cattle car flew open with a crash, and Turban Boy fired two rounds from my snubby through the open door. Two rapid return rounds were fired from somewhere near the floor outside the door that hit Turban Boy in the chest hurling him against the bulkhead then falling flat on his face to the floor. Poncho made one last desperate overhand swing with his sword attempting to take my head off. I ducked at the last second and he buried the sword in the bulkhead. The next two shots took him out, sprawling him across the deck.

She stepped through the door, cleared the room, then ejected the spent clip from her Berretta, replaced it with a fresh one, and snapped back the slide, loading a live round into the chamber. It was Randi Andretti, and I was real happy to see her. "Are you OK?" she asked, while checking the pulse, or lack there-of, on Turban Boy. I answered in the affirmative and reiterated how glad I was to see her.

"I presume this antiquated blunder-bust belongs to you?" she asked, removing my venerable snubby from Turban Boy's death grip. She also recovered my magic nightstick, penlight, lock-picking kit, and my I.D. "The blonde girl is tied-up in the Pullman car behind us. I want you to get her off the train and back to the safety of her island sanctuary. The train will slow at the trestles before crossing into the Marine training base at Camp Pendleton. You can bail before the train crosses the trestle. You're on your own from there."

"I would have preferred to interrogate these two shmucks, but that's obviously not going to happen, so I'll take theirs pictures, collect finger print samples, and go through their pockets to see who they are, with whom they associate, and try and figure what they're up to. I'll take care of this mess and ride the train to the end of the line and see who or what is waiting."

"Who are you?" I asked. "And how did you know where we were?"

She looked at me, debating whether to confide in me or not while she rifled through Samurai Poncho's ninja suit. "I'm with the F.B.I.

temporarily assigned to Federal Customs, investigating a white slavery ring operating along the west coast and the border between Texas and Mexico. It began as a white slave trade investigation, but there seems to be other players from different backgrounds, and their own motivations, converging on the scene. An association of conspirators working together, each for their own piece of a pie; a pie that is yet to be discovered, and is the key to this investigation. I'm still trying to connect the dots."

"As to how I knew where you were; we've been keeping close tabs on you, though you tried your damnedest to shake all our tails. A mutual friend of ours asked me to keep an eye on you. He said you tend to create a lot of chaos, cadavers, and collateral damage. You cause a lot of destruction, and generally need to be rescued from your own calamity. He did emphasize however, that you always quickly get to the core of the situation and deal with it decisively; it's not always legal, it's never pretty, but always pretty conclusive." She never divulged who our mutual friend is, but she didn't have to; I assume it was my old buddy Inspector Lugar, formerly of L.A.P.D, and currently Chief Constable of Avalon's Police Department.

I found Precocious lying on a leather couch in the Pullman car, bound hand and foot. She was shaking with fright and had been crying hysterically. There was the familiar coppery smell of blood and the stale odor of death. I stepped over two bloody stiffs and untied her. I held her close, comforting and calming and assuring her that she would be back on the island safe and sound before the day was out. Her quivering calmed and she seemed relieved. It had been a tough night for Precocious; from the exhilaration of her celebrity debut at *the Olympic*, to the chaos of a terrifying high-speed car chase through the streets of L.A., and the depths of despair aboard a south bound Pullman.

Chapter Eight

Day 8

In the morning I borrowed Mona's big white Chrysler Imperial, and after breakfast at the *Sugar Shack*, and a heartfelt warm adieu' on the seaplane dock, I put a much calmer and happier Precocious on Kamikaze Steve's morning flight back to Avalon; I know I promised her that I would have her back before yesterday was over, but she was not prepared to fly, and I didn't want Precious to see her in that condition.

We spent the night in my apartment at Mona's after we had by-chance been picked-up at the trestles that afternoon by the Yeager-meister's woody mobile on their way back from Grandview's 'old man break' in Escondido. During the ride they offhandedly informed me that they had seen that black chopper again on that same piece of ground as before, only this time they had a pair of powerful binoculars with them to spot migrating whales along the way. They wrote down the number on the aircraft; *NE 1410S*. The disheartening disclosure however, was that all the occupants aboard the shiny black helicopter were well-dressed, distinguished looking Chinese executive types. (I have a bad feeling about this.)

Precocious and I enjoyed a quiet, intimate dinner in Papa's private alcove *at The Golden Bear*, after she had lingered in a warm, soothing bubble bath, and emerged looking content, shiny and new. We laughed along with the opening act comedian Jackie Vernon, who was a big overweight dufus with a big uncontrollable shock of curly hair. He stood in front of a slide projector screen and held a clicker in his hand; there was no projector or slides, he just described each imagined slide with a dead-pan delivery of a befuddled, mid-level, middle class, disheveled bar-fly schlemiel. He could walk into his favorite bar and the entire bar would shout, Jack! "Three things I always told my buddies at the local bar that you would never catch me owning, because only old men owned them were; a trailer in a retirement mobile home park, a golf cart, or a pontoon boat," he began. Click-click; "Here I am cruising in my golf cart past the bow of my pontoon boat in the marina, on my way to pot-luck dinner and bingo night *at Del Web's Leisure World* community in Sun City."

We danced the night away to the cool, smooth velvet tones of tonight's headliner Johnny Mathis, and *chances are I wore a silly grin.* We held each other close on the dance floor and all the trials and tribulations of the previous events seemed to fade into the night, and Precocious eventually relaxed and enjoyed the evening. An evening of dining, dancing and a few cocktails, and Precocious was satisfied, exhausted and slept through the night like a baby.

When I got back to Mona's I called *Bailey Brothers Towing and Auto Salvage,* and now stood on the sidewalk waiting. Jerald, Jerome, and Jermaine Bailey were big, bad-assed brothers from Pomona who ran a towing and repo business on the mean streets of Compton, South Central and East L.A. They are intimidating and scary and they command a healthy amount of respect where ever they venture. I'm glad they're my friends and they're on my side.

I arrived at *Aloha Motors* riding shotgun on a tow truck, unceremoniously dragging what was left of the old gray Hornet, with assorted accessories daggling from various locations, a pocket full of cash and a big pink box full of assorted donuts, because everyone knows; the way to a car salesman's heart is through his donut hole.

We pulled around the back and parked the crumpled heap next to the other turd box trade-ins. Jerome lowered the singed hulk to the pavement, removed the hooks and leaned on his rig barely able to keep his giggles under control. He couldn't wait to see the reaction when Joe Crooks and Charlie Straight get a gander of their 'cream-puff' loaner car.

I placed the big pink box on a relatively flat and undamaged portion of the hood, opened the top and waited for the enticing aroma of fresh, warm donuts to waft across the lot and infiltrate the sales office. Didn't have to wait long; Charlie Straight was the first to wonder around the corner of the building. He did a double take when he first glimpsed the pitiful Hornet carcass lying helpless and mortally wounded in a growing pool of its own fluids. He paused, looking exasperated and perplexed, in a pose reminiscent of Jack Benny searching for answers from the wings, then made a bee-line for the big pink box poised majestically atop the venerable Hornet's bonnet. Jerome Bailey could not contain himself any longer and burst out laughing. "This is better than an episode of *Amos and Andy*," he laughed. "And you are The King Fish, you crazy sum-bitch. Like you always tell me man; it's not just a job, it's an adventure."

Charlie slowly strolled around the remains of a once fine automobile surveying the assortment of damage and dangling accessories. The left front fender was severely crumpled and the headlamp dangled from its socket. The driver's door was now concave and had a permanent impression of my torso embossed within, and the entire side of the car was scorched and crinkled. The left rear fender was hanging by the gas tank filler tube and the trunk lid was mangled and tied down to what was left of the rear bumper. The right side of the car was the T.V. side, except for the numerous bullet holes that riddled the entire side of the car from what resembles a bumper to what appears to have been a bumper in the days of her 'showroom ready' debut.

Joe Crooks was next on scene with coffee mug at the ready, followed by the grubby redneck mechanic in greasy overalls. They each found their respective donut of choice within pink box and then began the same morbid procession that Charlie Straight had solemnly performed. The mechanic lightly tapped the large mouse erupting from the sidewall of the left rear tire with his foot, and the tire immediately began to make a continuous, pitiful 'poo-poo cushion' fart, and that side of the car slowly sank to the pavement. Jerome Bailey rolled around on the ground, abandoning his effort to subdue his uproarious laughter.

The mechanic's sexy wife with enormous sweaty breasts that stuck to her thin wife beater undershirt like it was wet toilet paper, and her short shorts, made the obligatory stroll to the pink box, *all good things come in a warm pink box*, then she began to bend over and inspect the undercarriage, under the hood and under her tee-shirt for wayward donut crumbs, all to the extreme delight of a beaming Jerome Bailey who simply shook his head in disbelief and wore a smile that spread from ear to ear.

When all had second donut in hand, I opened the door, turned the key and punched the starter peddle. The venerable Hornet roared to life and purred like a kitten save for the continuous rap of the fan blade rhythmically striking the radiator and cowling. "How much for trade-in value", I boldly asked. Joe Crooks blew his mouthful of coffee all over himself, Charlie Straight began to choke on his glazed twist, and Jerome Bailey rolled on the pavement in convulsive laughter.

The two lovely lot lizards emerged from the attorney's motorhome attired in Daisy Duke-shorts and crop-top wife-beaters. I raised the pink box over my head and made the girls jump for it; 'bouncing for donuts.' The girls jumped up and down with anticipation of the sweet treat delights within pink box, and to the sweet delight of my man Jerome whose eyes grew as big as his smile. It brought back fond memories of the Korean laundry girls we taught to play volley ball during the war. They also wore short toreador' single button tops that rose to exciting heights when they jumped in the air to block a shot at the net or spike the ball to the opponent's side. We gathered quite a crowd, could have charged admission.

We eventually negotiated a cash price for my newly purchased Hudson Hornet, and I was ready to roll in another 'loaner.' It was a high-mile, two-tone Desoto Adventurer with white side wall tires, enough vista-vision front and rear windshield glass to simulate a rolling fish bowl, and the gigantic angled rear ailerons of a super-sonic sabre jet with the tri-tower tail lights.

Before I departed *Aloha Motors* I phoned Precious to make sure Precocious had arrived safely back on the island. She assured me that Precocious had returned safe and sound, and after she had settled in they would schedule a debriefing session. Precious also informed me that she had received a pre-dawn phone call from the County Sheriff's department regarding the fire-bombing of our Venice Beach Office. The fire department kept the inferno from spreading to the *Dome Theater* next door or the other adjacent businesses, but *'Travis Dugan Private Investigations'* is a total loss.

The Sheriff is sending an investigator regarding our recent or current clientele that may harbor a grudge or have other motive for the bombing, even though she explained that we have no current clientele and that all our operatives were currently assigned to estate and personal security details, and I was here only to hold hands and sooth nerves. The fire department arson investigator also requests an interview once his on-scene investigation concludes. Preliminary investigation indicates multiple I.I.D.s; Improvised Incendiary Devices; 'Molotov cocktails'.

Precious also informed me that she had run a background check on Randi Andretti through all her normal channels and came up with nothing, nada, het, zero, the big goose egg. I told her about my recent conversation with the alleged Randi Andretti and her current federal affiliation and on-going investigation. "That is why you came up with nothing."

I pulled the two-tone green Adventurer to a stop at the big impressive wrought iron gates and the guard shack in front. A crisp and clean red-coated Mounty greeted me and asked how he may assist me. I asked that I might have an audience with Mr. Ervine, it was of extreme importance. Sargent Preston of the Yukon Mounted Police asked for my I.D. which I produced, then excused himself and disappeared within guard shack chalet. Moments later he re-emerged with official clip-board in hand, walked to the rear of the Desoto and jotted down the license number. He politely returned my I.D. and gave me explicit directions to proceed up the drive and bare left to the Ponderosa Palace in the sky.

I passed two of our operatives patrolling the grounds in one of the ranches Zebra striped jeeps and several more as I approached the top of the hill. There were numerous cars parked around the drive in front of the Ponderosa. It looked like a social function of some sort; champagne brunch, cocktail party, or a gathering of mourners.

Gregory met me at the door and invited me to follow him out to the terrace. The mansion was teaming with humanity of all shapes and sizes; from golden oldies to teens and toddlers. I asked Gregory if I had interrupted a family function and was informed that I should discuss that with Mr. Ervine who was anxious to talk to me.

I arrived on the terrace just as Mr. Ervine was concluding a phone conversation. "Dugan, please have a seat. I have just received a series of disturbing telephone calls," he began with obvious concern in his tone. I took a seat across from Mr. Ervine and Gregory poured me a mint julep. "I realize its early sir, but you'll thank me later," he said before his departure.

"Dugan that was Captain Crawford: UCSD Campus police on the phone. It appears that my daughter, Jamie and one of your female operatives have been abducted from the parking lot adjacent to her dorm room. They found the car with the trunk open and their suitcases inside. Her keys were in the ignition, her purse, wallet and I.D. on the seat. No one saw or heard anything. They have called San Diego P.D. and investigators from the County Sheriff's Department are in route."

"I had insisted that she return to the ranch immediately when I talked to her day before yesterday, but she had one more final exam and had to reschedule her summer school classes to the fall semester. She was to complete her exam and reschedule her classes yesterday, and be on the road home this morning.

Dugan no piece of property, regardless of its pristine beauty or financial value is worth the life of my daughter or your operative, the other lives now in danger, or the lives already lost. I've decided to agree to their terms and relinquish the property. The situation is spinning out of control and I must put a stop to it before anyone else is placed in harm's way. Upon their next communication I'm going to acquiesce and cooperate fully. I see no other viable option."

Mr. Ervine fought back the tears and struggled to control his emotions. It was apparent that he was experiencing fear, anger and the embarrassment of appearing vulnerable and impotent in the face of eminent danger. This was not business, it was personal, and generated emotions of which Mr. Ervine was not accustom. He was having a hard time dealing with the rush of alien thoughts and feelings.

I sipped my mint julep while Mr. Ervine regained his composure. I needed to garner as much information as I could before I called Precious back on the island. I wasn't looking forward to that conversation; the likely operative assigned to protect Jamie Ervine would be Kato's little sister Fia. I love that girl and have known her all her life. I would never forgive myself if anything happened to her.

"I need to call my office, Mr. Ervine may I use the phone in your study?" "Of course Dugan, but there's more that you should know before you make that call. Bucky Strayhorn's brother, who works for the *Atomic Energy Commission* or *Nuclear Regulatory Commission* or some such government program, was found floating in the Potomac yesterday. Bucky took the 'red eye' to D.C. last night."

"Where's Boehner?" I asked. Ervine looked at me slightly puzzled. "He's in Austin riding herd on the head of cattle we shipped by rail to the stockyards, then to the auction house. Once the sale is over, he flies to Chicago to sell cattle futures at the Commodities Market for next season's calving."

I went to the study and dialed the number to our temporary digs in the guest quarters on the Rigney estate. After the obligatory series of buzzes, clicks and static fuzz, Mabel the island operator, managed to stick the correct cable into the corresponding slot in her switchboard and the phone in the office began to ring.

Precious answered on the third ring. *"Good morning Travis Dugan Private Investigations"* sang sweetly over the phone. After brief greetings and affectionate gestures of missing one another, she gave me a quick synopsis of current events on the island, which thankfully were calm, under control and running smoothly thanks to my managerial expertise and procedural protocol that I initiated for just such circumstances when I was going to be unavailable for short periods of time.

She told me that Precocious and Rita were enjoying a much-needed day-off at Little Harbor. They packed a lunch including plenty of refreshments and plan on spending the day on the beach enjoying the surf and warm sunshine, with Kato along as driver and beef-cake personal security.

Precious then informed me that she had received an early morning phone call from a very uneasy railroad tycoon. Apparently a rail inspection and repair crew found four bodies strewn along the tracks between Solana Beach and La Jolla yesterday. It didn't appear as though they were struck by a train, but rather thrown from it, and they all appeared to have multiple gunshot wounds. The authorities were summoned and are on scene, including the NTSB.

She finally asked about the situation here on the mainland. I paused, took a deep breath and then told her about the early morning abduction of Mr. Ervine's daughter Jamie at UCSD. "Oh no Travis!" she gasped. "Fia was assigned that detail."

"You know Kato is going to freak out when he hears about it. He's going to drop everything and go-off half-cocked. I doubt if anyone here is capable of talking him out of it or stopping him." "That's OK Precious, let him do what he thinks is necessary. He's going to do what he wants anyway, and it may be for the best. Kato prefers to work alone, so let him do what he can. I may need him."

Before we concluded our conversation I asked Precious to run a background check on Mohammar Kadjetski, Toby Juan Cannole', and Bucky Strayhorn's brother Billy, who worked for the *AEC* or the *NRC*. She told me to be careful, keep in touch, and that she loved me very much.

***

So here I am, under the cover of bright darkness and a blue moon, standing high in the trestle over the creek between the Ervine property and Camp Pendleton where Precocious and I had recently detrained. I stood high up on a cross member hugging a support beam waiting for the southbound train. I called Mr. Stanton from Ervine's study earlier and received a tentative schedule for both the northbound and southbound trains running on parallel tracks and on the same rail bed.

According to Stanton a train leaves each morning from opposite ends of the line. The southbound train from the bay area stops at the refineries along the route in Nipomo, Wilmington, Carson and Torrance, and retrieves the empty tank cars that were delivered the night before by the northbound train coming from the oil fields in west Texas and along the Pacific coast. In the Hayward/Hollister area, and the Ervine ranch to the south, the train picks up cattle cars loaded with livestock waiting at side spurs for transportation to the stockyards in Texas. Occasionally the train picks up flat cars loaded with oil rigging, pipe, tubing and generators, as well as private and corporate Pullman cars.

At the end of the line the empty tank cars are dropped on side spurs at the various oil storage facilities to be refilled and ready for the northbound return train the next morning. The cattle cars are dropped at the stockyards to be evacuated, mucked out, and ready for the return trip north. The Pullman cars are dropped at a pre-determined side spur nearest their ultimate destination.

Likewise, the northbound train picks up empty cattle cars and full oil tankers for the trip north where the whole process starts all over again. There are two trains running day and night schedules in each direction. It's a very efficient system.

The *Union Pacific Railroad* transports heavy freight, truck trailers and international shipping containers on tracks that run mostly northern and southern routes through the central valley, and east through the Cojone Pass. The *Southern Pacific* runs its popular *'Coastal Flyer'* passenger route including *'sky view'* formal dining cars and private berthing super liners, on tracks leased from Mr. Stanton's *Western Pacific* line and scheduled between his commercial runs.

I sat on a trestle cross-member, lit a cigarette and gazed out over the Pacific and the twinkling lights of Avalon in the distance. I was alone, melancholy and homesick.......again.

The moon illuminated the soft white waves as they gently rushed up the sandy shore and the hiss of their inevitable retreat to the sparkling dark sea. The view from the trestle down the creek bed, across the smooth white beach to the sparkling waves, the wide dark ocean, and the twinkling lights of Avalon was breathtaking, extraordinarily beautiful and romantic, yet at the same time, lonely with stark shadows and bright contrast of alien moonscape. I felt like a *stranger in a strange land*.

The sound of a pair of outboard motors approached from far out at sea. I extinguished my cigarette, moved into the shadows hugging a support beam, and quietly watched as two large open Panga Boats made a high-speed bee-line for the shore and ran the boats up onto the beach. Within minutes twenty to thirty people emerged from each boat and quickly crossed the beach into the shadows of the creek bed under the train trestles. As soon as the boats were empty the two man boat crews pushed the boats back into the surf and were gone at high-speed and out of sight within minutes. The herd of human cargo made their way up the creek bed and gathered in the shadows under the trestle of the northbound track.

I hear the train a coming, coming round the bend. (Somebody get Johnny Cash on the hot line) Far in the distance to the south came the bright light of the northbound train. The engineer sounded the horn as the big black locomotive approached and slowed to a crawl as it crossed the trestle. The handlers in the creek bed whispered orders, in Chinese, to the human cargo that I noticed all had nap sacks, back packs, or saddle bags slung over their shoulders, and they all cued quickly in preparation to board the slow moving train. Once the locomotive rounded a slight curve to the right and momentarily out of sight of this location, the handlers quickly loaded their human mules into the cattle cars designated by a day-glow paint swatch on the cars undercarriage. They were smuggler's mules forced to carry contraband into the country they were illegally entering. The smugglers were utilizing the captive manpower available to transport their illegal contraband literally on the backs of their human cargo. Now that's what I call minimizing your overhead and shipping costs, while maximizing your profit margins and bottom line. (Hmm? Must have taken a business course somewhere)

I sat on the cross-member and re-fired the cigarette I had extinguished earlier, and wondered where the smugglers and their human mule cargo would go from here. It made logical sense that some would go to China Town in downtown L.A. and the rest would go to the large Chinese community in San Francisco. The nap sacks, back packs and saddle bags they carried would, know doubt, be stuffed with opium, China White and Black Tar heroin. With the small fortune each smuggled human pays to the smugglers combined with the vast wealth realized through the distribution of contraband narcotics, the process would net millions annually. Each cattle car was worth hundreds of thousands of dollars.

The moon moved a little farther away to the west, I smoked a few more cigarettes, and then, right on schedule, two Panga boats roared ashore from somewhere beyond the horizon. Within minutes the human cargo was off-loaded onto the beach and then quickly hustled into the shadows within the creek bed. The two boat crews pushed the boats back into the surf, just as they had done before, and then they were gone.

The handlers drove the herd of mostly female cargo to a staging area across the creek bed from where I sat high in the trestle structure.

This load of human cargo was different from the first however; besides being mostly female and not Chinese, these were young blonde girls that were chained around the waist and strung approximately three feet apart in a line, five or six at a time.

This particular cattle car load of white slave trade was destined for Sheiks and Sultans of Dubai, Brunei, or any one of the oil rich tribal fiefdoms springing up, along with their endless sea of oil wells, throughout the parched deserts of the Middle East.

The rumble of the southbound train could be felt on the trestle, followed by the bright light of the approaching locomotive far in the distance to the north. The horn sounded and the locomotive slowed to a crawl as it approached the crossing, just as the northbound train had done only minutes earlier.

The train crossed the trestle and made a slow curve to the right following the rugged shoreline. When the locomotive was out of sight the handlers quickly and efficiently loaded their white slave cargo aboard the cattle car designated by a swatch of fluorescent paint on the undercarriage.

I waited until the last cattle car passed under where I stood, then jumped the short distance to the roof of the slow moving car just ahead of the long line of empty oil tankers. It took a few uneasy steps to get my train-legs under me but by the time I reached the rear of the car I was practically sprinting. I climbed down the ladder at the back of the car to a small landing where the cars where coupled. I waited a few moments then slowly opened the sliding metal door and entered the rear of the car. This cattle car like all other cattle cars was enclosed by horizontal wood-slat sides, solid metal bulkheads with sliding metal man doors at each end, and wide sliding cattle gates on both sides to, on and off-load livestock. There was a small metal inspection hatch in the center of the roof of each car.

After a long boring ride and somewhere I guessed to be near National City, east of San Diego, the train began to slow. I stood and peered through the slats on both sides of the car, but saw nothing but darkness.

The train finally came to a dead stop at an unmarked road crossing in the middle of nowhere. Suddenly the headlights of a dark sedan parked on the road illuminated the side of the cattle car loaded with white slave cargo. The rear door of the sedan opened and there was some commotion as whoever was being removed from the back of the sedan seemed to be resisting. The side livestock gate slid open on the cattle car and the people from the rear of the sedan were being manhandled toward it. As they crossed in front of the headlights, they appeared to be two females handcuffed together being loaded onto the cattle car with the others. As soon as they were aboard the gate slammed shut and the train began to move slowly forward.

It occurred to me that the train crew had already been compromised in some manner; how else would a pre-arranged halt to the train in the middle of "TimBuk-Three" be accomplished? So far during this trip I have yet to hear or see a brakeman either. (Makes you wanna' go hmmm? I don't have a good feeling about this.)

We rolled through the cold desert night for hours and then somewhere around Nogales Arizona the train began to slow. The moon was near the horizon and cast long shadows across the sparse desert landscape of fine white sand, sorrel cactus, horny toads, Gila monsters and sidewinders. The train gradually came to a halt on a non-descript piece of moonscape, under brilliant canopy of starry night's summer sky.

I watched through the slats as the side gate slid open on the cargo laden car and several of the handlers climbed from the train and crossed a short distance to a small pile of rock boulders amid a sparse outcropping of scrub brush. They bent down and removed the pile of rocks then picked up a large canvas tarp covered with sand. Hidden under the tarp was a set of small wooden barn doors that appeared to be the entrance to a tunnel.

I would have to do something now, before they got their cargo off-loaded and into the tunnel; that would be the point of no return. Once they reached the end of the tunnel on the other side of the border there would be no possibility of a rescue; they would simply disappear and for all intent would cease to exist. I eased my 'snubby' from under my arm and quietly crept to the rear door, out to the small platform and climbed down to the rail bed on the opposite side of the train from the open side gate and the tunnel entrance. I crawled under the train car between the tracks and took cover behind a heavy steel wheel and suspension carriage.

Several handlers began to move the females out of the cattle car, down the loading ramp and herd them toward the tunnel doors. I took careful aim. I would have to take out as many handlers as I could when they gathered to open the tunnel doors. Two handlers bent down and opened the heavy wooden doors. Suddenly two shots rang out and the two handers snapped back and hit the ground. I began firing on the other handlers as they scrambled for cover and returned fire. There was total chaos; the captives began screaming hysterically and frantically running in terror. The barrage of gunfire from all directions continued for several minutes with rounds ricocheting off the heavy metal and impacting the sides of the train cars splintering the wood slats and spattering into the lunar landscape like small comets........then there was dead silence. The air was thick with acrid blue smoke and the familiar smell of spent gunpowder. A bright flashlight beam from the tunnel entrance illuminated the steel wheel and heavy suspension system where I hid. "F.B.I., throw out your weapon and come out with your hands where I can see them!" I recognized that voice. "Randi, it's me Travis. Hold your fire." I holstered my .38 and crawled out from under the cattle car. Randi emerged from the tunnel entrance and seemed genuinely glad to see me. She threw her arms around my neck and we kissed long and hard.

The train began to move once again; slowly at first but gained speed rapidly. It was the railroad version of the 'quick get-away'. "Oh Travis you don't know how happy I am to see you. Seems like I've been riding these god damn trains for an eternity, but I do have a pretty good handle on what's going down; at least partially anyway. I don't have a complete picture yet, but I'm getting a grasp of it. There are other players in the game besides the ones involved in the white slave trade and the smuggling of illegals. There appears to be a convergence of conspiracies working in conjunction with one another for totally different objectives." (Sounds like de je' vu all over again doesn't it?)

Chapter Nine

Day 9

("Hey kids, all you Romper Room and Ding Dong School graduates, this is Pinky Lee inviting you to join me and all my friends this Saturday morning on my new T.V. Show; 'Pinky's Playhouse.' We'll have songs, games and cartoons. Then you can wake-up your big brothers or sisters for Dick Clark's American Bandstand on ABC channel 7. Now let's return to Casey Kasem and America's Top 40 Billboard Countdown on Armed Forces Radio, and remember as Casey always says; keep your feet on the ground but keep reaching for the stars".)

("Welcome back to Billboards Top 40 Countdown, I'm Casey Kasem. I image some of you parents are probably scratching your heads when you hear the names or the lyrics for many of today's top 40. Lyrics such as; he wore tan shoes and pink shoelaces, a polka dot vest and man oh man. He wore tan shoes and pink shoelaces, a Panama hat with purple hatband. Or how about song titles like; Itsy bitsy teeny weeny yellow polka dot bikini. Or my personal favorite; one eyed one horned flying purple people eater. We're not in Cole Porter or Henry Mancini land anymore are we mom and dad. But listen-up folks, debuting this week at number 37, Henry Mancini with The Days of Wine and Roses.")

I reached across Fia's beautiful brown body, firm young breasts and perky nipples that pointed the way to heaven, to push the correct button on the first try and create silence from my newly discovered transistorized Japanese clock radio. I gazed upon her smooth dark body and the soft silkiness of firm thigh and pouty girl parts. She acknowledged my blossoming admiration with a sigh and a sweet smile.

I rolled over to where Precarious lay slumbering on her back with her long blonde hair scattered helter-skelter over her stunning Norwegian features and proud puppies that seemed happy to be exposed to another sunny morning. I was the cream filled center in a duplex Oreo cookie. Who's the lucky boy?

We arrived just before dawn back at my apartment at Mona's after I spent the late night and early morning hours with Randi Andretti rounding –up the scattered groups of blonde captives who fled in terror during the ambush and shootout only hours earlier. All were eventually found thanks to a squad of Customs and Border Patrol agents, with eyes in the air and boots on the ground. Precarious, Precocious' gorgeous twin sister, and Fia were located with a group of five or six others still chained together. I was thankful and relieved to have found them before it was too late, and for the most part safe and sound. They had a few bumps and bruises, and a couple of scrapes and scratches. Until we had recovered them I wasn't even aware that Precarious was missing. I was looking for Jamie Ervine and Fia. I still don't know where Jamie is; neither do Fia or Precarious.

During the pre-dawn darkness and while the manhunt for the scattered blonde cargo ensued, Randi told me what she had discovered during her extended marathon tour aboard the *Western Pacific* rail service. "It appears that the white slave traders, the coyotes that smuggle illegals from Latin America, and the Chinese Cartel that smuggles Chinese immigrants and imports Chinese heroine, are organized under an umbrella group that coordinates their endeavors; separate groups working in conjunction with one another, with their own means and motivations to their own separate ends and rewards."

"The Chinese illegals, the white slave cargo, and the heroine are most likely brought ashore from a mother-ship by way of Panga Boat. A Panga Boat is similar to a large open Dory Boat equipped with powerful outboard engines fueled by numerous five gallon jerry cans. The white slave cargo is transported on the southbound trains, the Chinese mules carrying Chinese heroine and the Latin American illegals are transported on the northbound trains, not on any specific schedule. The train crews have obviously already been compromised by whatever means, but the operation would run more efficiently and without threat of discovery or oversight if control could be wrested from Mr. Stanton."

"However, there still remains a missing piece to the puzzle; that is the pressure being forced upon Mr. James Ervine regarding his property on the coast near San Clemente. Granted, the Panga Boat crews find the secluded beach near the creek bed, and the slowing of the train crossing the trestle a perfect spot for an amphibious landing, but there are many other locations along the coast that are equally well suited. No, there is something else there that we're not getting; something big of which we're not yet aware. If we discover what, perhaps we can figure who benefits and why. It's an enigma, wrapped within a mystery, surrounded by a conspiracy." (I hate when that happens.)

The phone began to ring incessantly, the girls exclaimed disgruntled expletives and rolled over covering their heads under their pillows, and I once again reached across the beautiful naked young Samoan body to answer the phone and cease the annoyance. It was Precious and she was on the verge of tears. I don't think I'd ever seen that from her before. She began to spew, both scolding me for not being able to be reached, and imploring me to do something because Precarious has disappeared and no one has been able to contact her in days. I immediately reassured her that I had Precarious and Fia with me as we speak and they both were sleeping soundly. There was an audible sigh of relief and she seemed to calm immediately. "Oh Travis, I wish you had passed on this assignment. I realize you were just helping an old friend, but I knew you couldn't just stand on the sidelines and provide moral support; you always take control, you're the Alpha Dog."

She was right of course; I had no argument with her thesis and provided no defense. Instead I asked her about Rita. She told me that Rita was holding-up and performing like a trooper, but that she missed me terribly and longed for my return. The Casino operation was running smoothly, but Rita was becoming weary of managing it herself. It was becoming a chore instead of a joy. "You need to come home Travis."

The girls and I showered together in my cozy walk-in with the skylight high above that bathed the enclosure in soft moon light at night and defused glow of golden sun light in the early morning. We stopped for a quick breakfast at *'the Shack'*, and were waiting on the seaplane tarmac in Pedro for the first morning flight to the island.

Precious informed me during our phone conversation that she had run a check on Mohammar Kadjetski and Tobey Juan Cannole'. She came up with a blank on Mohammar until she contacted her connection within Interpol. They are aware of the name that pops-up here and there in connection with the international white slave trade, but Mohammar is very elusive, extremely difficult to track, and there is very little hard evidence available. He functions as a logistics expert, transporting human cargo, large quantities of narcotics, and black market military ordinance. He's a Libyan contractor operating out of Lebanon and Syria. With regard to Toby Juan however, she came up with nothing, nada, het, zilch the big goose egg. Nobody ever heard of Toby Juan; he was a big zero.

Kamikaze's little red Grumman made a picture perfect splash down in the calm channel and taxied up the tarmac ramp. The side hatch opened from the top and lowered to the ground functioning as steps into and out-of the plane. At the top of the stairs stood former L.A.P.D. detective, and current Avalon Police Constable, Inspector Frank Lugar. Lugar was an old friend who pulled my bedraggled butt from the smoldering ruins of my own destruction on several occasions in the past and I owed him my life. I was surprised to see him.

He came down the stairs with a big smile and a big hug for the girls, followed by Kamikaze Steve. They were all genuinely happy to see one another; it's a small family back on the island and we all tend to watch-out for one another. I received the same treatment from them both. It looked like a family reunion.

I mentioned to Lugar that I was surprised to see him, that I expected to see Kato here to escort his sister back to the island, and was informed that Kato took off half-cocked when he heard about Fia and Jamie Ervine's abduction and hasn't been heard from since. Nobody knows where he is or what he's doing.

We loaded the girls and a cute elderly couple, on their anniversary pilgrimage to their original honeymoon island paradise, onto the plane for the morning flight to Avalon. Kamikaze came to me and suggested that I accompany the girls back to the island. Rita would love to see me even for a short while, and Kamikaze had something he thought I would want to see for myself.

I strapped into the co-pilot's seat and after a quick run-up and smooth takeoff we were airborne into a clear blue sky, smooth seas below, and the spectacularly beautiful island that is Santa Catalina dead ahead. A topaz and jade gemstone set in a glistening azure sea. An unfamiliar feeling began to slowly engulf me. The warm comfort of coming home; coming home, it had been a long time since I experienced that feeling.

Kamikaze brought-her-in low and slow from the north cresting the waves like a lone pelican and allowing me a long lingering look at the island off our starboard side. We flew by Emerald Bay, Cherry Cove and Fisherman's Cove where the local Chinese and Korean fishing fleet that ply the shallow waters around the island for shell fish, eel and octopus, moor their small boats.

As we approached Ah Louie and Yung He's two story bungalow on the shores of Cooley Town that serves as living quarters and local apothecary, I could see 'Sensei' and the beautiful Yung He sitting at an umbrella table at the water's edge enjoying morning tea, assorted fruit, and chillum of opium. I slid the window open and waved as we passed. They recognized me, Sensei waved and Yung He blew kisses. Kamikaze gave them a wing-wag as we departed, pushed the throttles forward gaining altitude and banked left as we swept past Twin Harbors at the Isthmus crossing and headed south; destination Avalon.

We flew by the beautiful and majestic Casino, the quaint fishing and resort village of Avalon, and the pale blue harbor filled with private boats in all shapes and sizes, from small fishing skiffs to immense, gleaming mega yachts and world class Regatta sailing craft. The commercial shipping docks, warehouse facilities and the seaplane tarmac went by on our starboard side and the Commodore's private dock where *'The Lucky Dutchman'*, my current abode, is tied.

Kamikaze made another steep turn to port and lined up for the landing approach. After a few goony bird bounces across the wave tops she settled in and we taxied up the tarmac ramp and were directed to a secluded area of the tarmac where a fairly sizable contingent of security personnel awaited our arrival.

It looked like a family reunion when we reached the bottom of the stairs and stepped onto the tarmac. To my wonderful surprise Rita was the first to greet me with breathless embrace and lingering kisses. We held each other close for a long while. She felt wonderful in my arms once again. I began to realize just how much I missed this girl. Like the lyrics; *you don't know what you've got 'til it's gone.* I never want to leave her again. (Did *I* say that?)

Precious and Precocious were there to welcome Precarious and Fia home to the security and comfort of family and friends on the island. Everyone had tears of joy and there were group hugs all around. It felt good to be home. (***Who*** said that?)

Precious, always the logistics manager began to arrange occupants, their respective security detail and their transportation, including the cute and crusty honeymooners, with their immediate destinations and clear the area as soon as possible; she was anxious to get the girls back to the security of the Rigney estate.

She took me aside while the security caravan got their ducks in a row and informed me that the registration numbers on the shiny black *Bell* helicopter that I asked her to trace belonged to a somewhat sketchy shipping conglomerate out of Yemen called *'Petro-Con'* that operates a global fleet of super tankers transporting millions of barrels of crude from the middle east to refineries on California's west coast and refined product on the return routes. (Makes you wanna' go hmmm).

Once the security caravan had departed Kamikaze and I climbed back into the cockpit of his little red Grumman, fired her-up, taxied down the ramp and into the water. We waited for the *Catalina Steamer* to clear our take-off path and tie-up to the pier, then throttled up to full speed and after a few soft bounces we were airborne and gradually gaining altitude. Kamikaze throttled back to cruising speed and made a slight course adjustment that would take us north past Arrow Point and out to the commercial shipping lanes.

Kamikaze Steve glanced in my direction with that same devilish grin that has gotten us in trouble on several occasions; the last of which resulted in his Catalina PBY being impaled upon the immense barrel of Gerald Bull and Dr. Con's Super Gun; thus the name Kamikaze. "You ask me before about where that shiny black helicopter may be coming from, remember Bombardier? Well I think I may have found the answer to that question, and maybe something more. I thought you would want to see this for yourself and we'll see what you think."

He throttled up, pushed forward on the yoke and brought her down until the altimeter read one hundred feet above the surface of the water. It seemed like the skip-bombing water balloon attack runs that he used to unleash upon Max von-Jekyle's converted P.T. boat with his PBY. I noticed that Kamikaze had installed identical aluminum balloon chutes on either side of this cockpit as well in order to continue his juvenile onslaught of water balloon bombletts on other unsuspecting recipients.

A huge, shiny black Magnum Raptor Mega yacht appeared on the horizon off our starboard side. It was at anchor, the British Union Jack flying from the jack staff, and as we approached along the port side stern to bow, the name on the stern read; *'DARK STAR'* Hong Kong. Kamikaze pointed to the flight deck over the fantail and the small hangar with roll-up door. I experienced a momentary war time flashback when I looked at the markings painted on the flight deck landing pad; it was an X within a circle, the same designation we flew on the tail of our B-29 while incinerating the shit out of Japan from twenty-nine thousand feet a decade earlier. We were the *'Crosstown Boys'*.

As we swept by off its port side I could see the spiffy Chinese boat crew in their summer whites busily swabbing the teak decks, polishing the brass and the bright work. I also noticed a Chinese in natty western business suit standing on the flying bridge intently watching us through powerful binoculars. The short- hairs on the back of my neck began to bristle. Kinda' like de je vu' all over again. I glanced over to Kamikaze who still wore that silly-ass grin on his face. "That's not all Bombardier I have something else to show you that I think you'll find quite interesting."

With a slight course adjustment due west and an increase in altitude we flew out toward the busy commercial shipping lanes bustling with traffic coming and going to and from ports in Los Angeles, San Pedro and Long Beach; the busiest shipping ports on the west coast that on and off-load cargo to and from the emerging markets throughout the Orient and the Middle East.

I began to get a real bad feeling about the whole situation. The more I began to connect the dots the bleaker the picture that began to emerge. Precious had informed me just prior to take-off that the helicopter with NE1410S registration numbers originated from a shipping company out of Yemen and was the same aircraft I saw on Ervine's property just off our surfing spot at Surf Beach near San Clemente. The logical 'connect-the-dot' trajectory would be a line leading to a dot related to Super Tankers and oil shipping; perhaps storage and pumping facilities ashore with underwater lines on the seafloor to an anchored platform for off-loading of crude from tankers off-shore. That particular location also would facilitate the use of the railroad that runs along the inland perimeter. We already know that someone is willing to go to drastic measures in order to take control of Mr. Stanton's railroad, for what Randi Andretti and the F.B.I. are currently investigating as a white slave, illegal immigrant and drug smuggling operation. If the super tanker operation and the organization behind the immigrant and smuggling trade are two separate entities, then there will be an inevitable conflict between the two interests and it will be vicious, bloody and nasty. However, if the two interests are working in conjunction with each other, with each having their own separate motivations, agendas and rewards, as Randi had suspected, then there must be a third party coordinating their efforts, and with an agenda of which we are not yet aware, as Randi had also suggested. (Like I need this shit.)(I think I'm getting a head ache....maybe it's a tumor.)

Kamikaze reached over and slapped me on the shoulder and out of my tumor stupor, and pointed to the immense super tanker coming up on our starboard side. We zoomed down the starboard side of the giant ship bow to stern. The name on the bow read; *'Aga-Con'* Singapore. Kamikaze continued the low pass around the stern and up the side of the monster on its port side. "Do you notice anything unusual?" he asked. Upon closer inspection I saw to what he was referring; the lifeboats under the canvas tarps were large Panga Boats. I also noticed the landing pad with the signature X within a circle. I realize lots of helicopter landing pads have X's within circles, but somehow this time it seemed like a sign or an omen.....a bad omen...... more like a curse.

The little red Grumman gained altitude and speed as we winged our way toward Avalon. Kamikaze switched on AM radio, turned the dial to XERB exes e' de a lea, Tijuana Mexico, The Wolfman Jack show, that was in the middle of uninterrupted hour of The Drifters, The Coasters, The Penguins, and the soulful sounds of the great Sam Cook, which allowed me to settle back and regurgitate and assimilate recent information input overload. I've got to get ahead of this situation before it's too late for Jamie Ervine. I'm afraid she won't be returned unharmed even if Mr. Ervine signs-over the property. I've got to find out who is behind this and is running the show, and I've got to find out fast.

We flew past the casino and out past the harbor directly over the big white steamer on her twelve o' clock noon return trip across the channel to Long Beach. Kamikaze made a wide turn to starboard, came in slow and smooth from the south, performed a picture perfect landing upon a calm sea, taxied up the ramp onto the tarmac and came to a stop next to an impressive black sedan with my old friend Roscoe standing stoically beside in sharp, gray tailored chauffer's uniform and his ever present wide smile.

As I lowered the steps and started down the gangway, Roscoe opened the rear door of the sedan and out stepped lovely Rita in bright flower print sundress and matching opened toed pumps. Her big brown eyes sparkled with delight and her beautiful smile was a welcome and exciting vision. Rita's long raven hair blew gently with the afternoon breeze as I rushed to her and swept her into my arms. We kissed passionately and held each other close. Tears began to fill my eyes. I couldn't believe how I missed this girl and never wanted to leave her again. I looked into her eyes and she had tears as well. It seemed like an eternity even though we've been apart for little more than a week.

Roscoe whisked us from the seaplane tarmac followed by a security detail and within minutes delivered us to *'The Lucky Dutchman'*, the Commodore's private yacht and my current abode. Spaulding, the Commodore's butler and manservant, prepared and served a scrumptious gourmet meal of oysters, Crab Florentine, passion fruit and of course a lightly chilled bottle of *Dom Perignon '55*.

Rita and I spent the afternoon together making up for lost time, holding each other, kissing each other, loving each other. It was a thrilling reunion of savage passion, breathless wanton desire, and primitive, relentless and insatiable torrents of lust and love, culminating in endless waves of torrid, breathtaking convulsions. The more we loved each other, the more we wanted each other.

At dusk we showered and dressed, then strolled along the soft beach next to a calm and serene harbor bathed in warm glow of a fading sunset. Avalon was bathed in purple shadow of Mount Orizaba and the lights around the harbor began to magically twinkle to life in unison with the first evening stars.

Antione's is an upscale 'tiki-hut' bar and restaurant that literally sits over the water's edge and commands a breathtaking unobstructed view of the majestic harbor area, the wide blue Pacific, and on clear nights, the twinkle of yon distant mainland skyline.

Rita and I sat at a comfortable, well- worn leather booth in a corner alcove next to the window surrounded by an unobtrusive contingent of Samoan security personnel occupying nearby tables. Our exotically gorgeous Tahitian waitress arrived attired in short sarong, multi layers of flowered leis and a floral tiara crowning a long mane of silky dark hair that flowed down her curvaceous derriere' and past her short sarong. I ordered a Mai Tai for the lady and a vodka martini for me, agitated not propelled.

Conversation over cocktails inevitably turned to business when I casually asked Rita who was minding the store tonight? She informed me with a smile that she had been surreptitiously training our old and trusted friend Inspector Lugar in the fine art of Casino Management. He apparently made mention of the fact, during the course of an evening's inebriation session, that he was not a young man anymore and began to ponder pursuing venues other than law enforcement. The thrill has gone and the enthusiasm for the job is quickly waning. "I gave him the title of assistant manager, his own mezzanine office and a safe in which to record and deposit the night's canister drops. I hope that's ok with you Travis. I needed a break, I couldn't get in touch with you, and it seemed like a logical and sound business decision."

Chapter Ten

Day 10

Precious met me at the sea plane tarmac in the morning before the first flight back to the brown grunge on the horizon that is the mainland. She told me that she had received a pre-dawn phone call from a terrified Bucky Strayhorn and he was shaking in his boots. "He was calling from D.C. where he had claimed his brother's body and was making arrangements to have his casket shipped back to his family in Texas for burial. Only someone tried to kill him. They planted a bomb under his rental car; Lucky for him, the detonator miss-fired producing nothing but a loud bang, a small fire and huge smoke plume. He's currently in hiding and desperately wanting to talk to you." She gave me the pay phone number where he would be at midnight tonight eastern time. "He's afraid to come out of hiding in the daylight. I'll see what else I can find out about his brother and in what kind of nuclear bullshit he was involved. Oh, and by the way Travis, thank you for bringing Precarious and Fia home safe." She put her arms around my neck and kissed me with sweet sincerity. "I love you Travis, and be careful ya' big dick."

We landed back in Pedro shortly before nine a.m. I thanked Kamikaze for his due diligence and the info. He wished me luck and told me to be careful. I found the old Desoto covered in a thin layer of pollutant particles in the parking lot and after performing a thorough undercarriage and engine compartment inspection, had the delta-winged Adventurer burning up the cool early morning highway headed south; destination, *The Golden Bear.*

I pulled into the parking lot and realized it was a bit too early in the morning for anyone to be there, so I parked the car and walked down the alley behind Mona's then turned north at Walnut Avenue and walked across Main Street to *the Sugar Shack*. All the girls in sailor suits were being brash and slinging hash. It was a typical busy early morning rush of local surfers, fishermen, shop keepers and municipal workers. The floor was perpetually covered in a layer of beach sand and there were various modes of transportation parked at the curb in front. I found an empty stool at the far end of the counter next to the swinging café doors into the kitchen. Pammie- babe whizzed by and dropped off a fresh cup of coffee, a set-up and the morning newspaper, without skipping a beat on her way through the café doors into the kitchen with a bouncy buxom "Aloha Baby", and an arm load of bussed dishes. With the in-coming swing of the café doors came Stephanie, the young blonde surfer girl who the other girls at the *Shack* call Steffie, and the local surfer boys call 'Stiffy,' for obvious reasons; besides being a beautiful blonde haired, blue eyed, peaches and cream, tanned and toned young shiny surf babe, the horizontal stripes on the thin knit under-sized sailor shirt she wore, were stretched to their limits by her oversized sweater puppets and pubescent protrusions dancing the dance of youth with each bouncy step.

I followed Stephanie's mesmerizing progress, with her arm-load of breakfast plates and a pot of coffee for the bushy-haired surf punks in the corner who were covered with a thin layer of dried sea salt, until I suddenly realized that seated next to me was Nita Menage'. She had her dark hair pulled back into a long flowing pony tail and her big brown eyes were as bright and sparkling as her beautiful smile. She wore a bright yellow canvas jump-suit with the zipper in front pulled far enough south to expose most of her impressive and pouty puppies as well.

"Wow you horny turd, what does a girl have to do to get noticed around here?" she asked, pulling her jumper zipper partially north, but still providing an inviting view. "By the way, that girl is young enough to be your daughter?" "I thought she looked familiar," I responded. "Maybe she is."

"You know Macho Man, you must be losing it; in the old days I could never have sneaked up on you like this, especially in this outfit. Are you sure you're up to the task?" "Funny, that's what she said," I laughed.

She turned toward me and spoke in hush-hush conspiratorial tones. "Mullins and Mc Burney came in last night for their usual Irish coffee break and told me that Papa and Mona should be prepared for an impending vice raid, as the scuttle-butt around headquarters is that Inspector Golly anticipates receiving the search warrants for which he has been feverishly gathering evidence as of late. There have been a series of closed-door, multi-agency meetings including ATF, narcotics and vice squad special tactics units. Apparently there also have been several deliveries of those *Kevlar* vests you made so stylish, as well as an armory full of assault weapons, helmets and repelling equipment."

Pammie-babe returned with order pad at the ready, a cup of coffee for Nita and a refill for me. I ordered a breakfast that I hadn't been able to swallow for years after the wars; I had consumed so much corned beef hash in the service that I literally had it coming out the wazoo. Poached eggs and corned beef hash is a weekly staple in the armed forces; that, and 'shit-on-a-shingle'. About halfway through my tour of duty in the Korean conflict, those became corn flakes mornings for me. Two eggs over medium, corn beef hash and toast kept it simple. Nita made it ditto.

Nita continued when Pam disappeared through the café doors. "I told Papa what the boys in blue had divulged and he and the guys working the bookie operation upstairs and the gambling people downstairs have folded the operations and stashed the gaming tables, slot machines, bank of phones, wire service ticker-tape machines, betting slips and anything else incriminating, in the tunnel under the vacant lot between the *Bear* and the Truck service on the corner. I called Mona after I closed the box office and I believe she plans to take the girls and go on a spontaneous sabbatical. Papa and Mona are getting plenty of bang-for-their-buck with our two favorite flat foots aren't they? They're definitely getting their monies-worth of heads-up info and personal insurance."

"Don't forget that they saved my butt in the back alley shoot-out and backed me up with Inspector 'Ass-breath' during the inquisition afterword. Did they say what evidence Golly has gathered to satisfy the requirements of a search warrant?" I asked. "No, and I didn't think to ask. But they did make it clear that I should advise Mona to secure her 'little black book' in another location if she hadn't already done so."

Pammie-babe arrived with our breakfast, a refill on our coffees, and all the accoutrements one could wish for, including Tabasco which magically emerged from the sorceress's apron. During the course of our meal I asked Nita how Papa was holding up. She said that he was holding up pretty well and as always was more concerned for the safety and wellbeing of his family and employees.

At the conclusion of breakfast Nita and I walked down a bustling early morning Main Street past Mona's to *the Bear*. The marque out front read; the velvet tones of Mel Torme'; should be a well- mannered and well behaved audience tonight. Nita said they had almost sold out both shows already.

The cleaning crew was busily scrubbing restrooms and backstage dressing rooms, disinfecting, sanitizing and deodorizing. I stayed with Nita while she collected her cash drawer and got the ticket office open and ready to sell out the remaining seats to tonight's shows.

I kissed Nita adieu then made my way through the sidewalk throng of pubescent newbies eagerly anticipating their first season of exciting beach adventures arriving daily by the bus loads all giggly, bouncy and enthusiastic. I turned the key in the lock, climbed the stairs to the foyer and found Mona and the two resident sisters Alana and Swallow seated at the chrome deco dinette in their soft, transparent nighties. It was after smiles, kisses and soft squeezes all around before I noticed that besides having a coffee klatch, the girls were cleaning several hand guns and loading clips for their impressive and formidable personal arsenal. "I see you've gotten the heads-up on the impending, unannounced visit from our intrepid Inspector Golly and friends," I said while pouring myself a cup of java and pulling-up a seat at the sensual and provocatively attired assembly line; (Kudos to the Personnel Department.) "Yes, our tax dollars at waste," Mona declared while re-assembling her Browning ten-shot semi- automatic 22, then snapping back the slide and squeezing-off an imaginary round in an empty chamber, with the distinctive 'click.' She then jammed a full clip into the grip, snapped back the slide loading a live round into the firing chamber and set the safety. She took a long pull from her cigarette, blew a series of smoke rings into the air and slammed the weapon down on the table like a veteran 'gun moll.'

"It looks like you plan on going to the mats and shooting it out," I said while perusing the assemblage of weaponry. "No," Mona replied. "We're bugging- out Travis. I'm taking the girls to visit their mother in Pomona, and then I'm taking the last ferry out of Balboa to Avalon. I've already reserved the penthouse suite at *the Glenmore Hotel* under an assumed name."

The phone began to ring as I entered my apartment; it was Precious. "Travis, I just got a call from Mr. Ervine and he wanted me to inform you that a representative from the individuals behind the extortion and kidnapping is due to arrive at the estate today at three p.m. with a 'Quit Claim Deed' for him to sign-over the property on the coast. Mr. Ervine also wanted me to remind you that he is fulfilling your request, as he agreed to do, to inform you when contact with the perpetrators had occurred. Now he has a request of you; do not interfere with this transaction until his daughter Jamie is released unharmed." I asked Precious to contact Kamikaze Steve and our own intrepid Chief Constable Lugar to see if they could arrange their schedule in order to be available as air-cover to track the courier by air in-case I lose contact on the ground. "We need to know where that courier goes." There was a long poignant pause. "Travis, remember I told you that I was going to look into what type of projects Bucky Strayhorn's brother was into and for what agency he was working? Well, through my contacts at the *National Security Agency*, and surprisingly through my cousin at Interpol, I think I can make a fairly accurate, educated guess-timation as to what he was doing."

At two p.m. I sat in the Adventurer, off a well maintained fire-break, high up on Saddleback Mountain across Ortega Highway from the Ervine Ranch, overlooking the Guard shack entrance at the gates and the Ponderosa high on the top of a hill at the end of the long-winded and winding sentence,.................... I mean road.

I had an *'In-n-out'* burger and a soda on my lap and a high powered set of binoculars on the seat next to me. The long wait gave me plenty of time to contemplate the information that Precious had divulged before my hasty departure. According to her highly placed sources which also happen to be her relatives, William Strayhorn was a member of *the' Manhattan Project'*, but not as a nuclear or atomic scientist per say, his university degrees and his fields of expertise are in geology; he's a dirt person. As an original member of the project his initial assignment was to find the best location in which to carry out their experiments in complete isolation and secrecy far from any population center, but more importantly his specialty was in the effects of the intended experiments on the geologic substrata with regard to fracturing and the topographic ability to contain highly radioactive atomic explosions. It was all theory at the time of course as to what would happen when a nuclear explosion occurred, both above ground and deep below the surface as well; was there a possible danger of creating a catastrophic earthquake, would the surface at ground zero be instantly fused into glass for miles all around? Later after the war, he was the guy who chose *Bikini Island* in the middle of the South Pacific for a series of Atomic Bomb blasts, and later the nuclear test range in Nevada and the *CIA's Groom Lake and Area 51*.

His recent endeavors are shadowed in secrecy and he has apparently contracted his experience and expertise to every acronym in the federal government's telephone directory. According to several deep-cover operatives, Strayhorn's current project is with the *Nuclear Regulatory Commission* and is on special assignment with the *Atomic Energy Commission*. His department is in charge of locating, geologically testing and analyzing, including the location and assessment of damage probabilities from the nearest earthquake faults, and approving suitable sites throughout the country for the purpose of constructing nuclear generated electric power stations........ (No shit? Talk about an ah-ha moment)

He was fished out of the Potomac and the Coroner's autopsy report concluded that he had drowned. There were no signs of foul play; no contusions, ligament marks, no scrapes or scratches. His clothes were intact, and his I.D. and wallet were found in his unlocked car with the keys in the ignition in a parking lot upstream from where his body was located. The Coroner classified the 'cause of death' to be 'accidental drowning.' "The investigation found no evidence of suicide; no suicide notes, or known bouts of depression or alcoholism, no family, gambling or financial problems, however suicide is a possibility." Seems to me that all those possibilities would have been thoroughly investigated and Strayhorn would have been extensively vetted before he would be approved for the security clearances required for the extremely sensitive and secret projects in which he was involved. No, I believe foul play is the only obvious answer. William Strayhorn was compromised by whatever means to divulge classified information, then discarded when he protested, threatened to expose, or was no longer useful. The raw onion in my burger was creating gastric disorder............maybe it's an ulcer.

The drone of Kamikaze's Grumman Goose could be heard high over Saddleback Mountain as the little white Studebaker Commander, Sunbeam Alpine, or Nash-Metropolitan turned off Ortega Highway coming from the east into the ranch entrance and up to the guard shack and intimidating iron gates. I watched through immense ornithologist's, or perhaps astrologer's set of oversized binoculars as the compact tin-can coffin was smartly greeted by the red coated Mounty on duty, then struggled up the incline to the' log palace in the sky' spitting and sputtering all the way with wisps of high-miler smoke.

175

A guy wearing a white short- sleeve dress shirt, dark tie and slacks, a close-cropped crew cut and an official clip board emerged from the little white death trap and strolled efficiently to the door and rang the bell. He was either a courier service schmuck or a highly motivated Jehovah's Witness. After a few moments Gregory answered the door and showed him in. He emerged from the mansion after a short time and began the return trip down the long drive. I fired-up the Adventurer and made my way down the mountain to the highway before the courier cleared the gates. I waited at a distance until he went by headed west toward the coast. I followed at a discreet distance as the little white courier car made a left at the end of Ortega Highway onto PCH headed south.

I honked and waved to Laguna's unofficial greeter as I passed through town with the courier car on the immediate horizon. We continued south through Corona Del Mar with the sun beginning to dip toward the Pacific in the west and the distant drone of Kamikaze's subsonic, low altitude U2 Spy plane high overhead.

As the courier car approached the Ervine property that is at the center of this situation, I could see the shiny black helicopter approaching from the west over the bright blue Pacific. I passed by as the courier car turned off the highway and down the bumpy set of ruts through the yellow field of mustard weed to where the chopper had landed and was waiting for the courier's arrival. I parked the Adventurer at a small vista point area approximately one hundred yards farther down the highway and watched through the binoculars on steroids, (whatever that is?), as the courier delivered the package to the occupants of the shiny black overhead rotary aircraft.

A few brief moments later the courier returned to his car with official clipboard in hand and drove back across the yellow meadow and onto Coast highway headed north. I watched as the chopper flew out over the ocean from the direction in which it had come, and disappeared over the horizon. I looked skyward and saw Kamikaze's Grumman as a small dot high overhead in a clear blue sky.

I turned the Desoto around returning to the highway and to follow the courier to his point of origin, when suddenly the Adventurer was lit-up with automatic weapon fire. In-coming rounds shattered the rear windshield, side windows and peppered the winged tank with penetrating rounds that sparked and ricocheted throughout cab, blasting large hunks of mohair interior and blowing out big chunks of metal exterior upon exit.

I caught a glimpse of a muzzle-flash coming from across the highway. It was coming from a Zebra striped jeep parked on a cattle trail above the creek bed on the Ervine ranch.

I stomped the go pedal, turned hard left and ducked below the dash board. High velocity automatic rounds continued to rip and puncture the thick metal skin of the Desoto and explode throughout the interior like grenade shrapnel. The roaring Adventurer made several dirt-spewing donuts then careened through the meadow churning-up great clouds of dust and mustard weed, attempting to get on the opposite side of the hill from the shooter and out of the line of fire.

The big bad Desoto rolled over the barbed wire fence like Rommel's tanks over Ethiopians on horseback and bounced out onto Coast Highway in a tornado of dust and yellow flowers dragging a short section of wire fence and a thick wooden fence post heading south. An abrupt high-speed, tire screeching U-turn flung the post and attached fencing off the side of the road and down a steep cliff as the 'winged wonder' roared down the highway now heading north.

I flew the delta winged Desoto off the road and over the cattle guard before smashing through a wood gate and blasting it into a chaotic cloud of splintered kindling as I bounced the Desoto down the cattle trail that Randi and I had ridden to the train trestle and onto the beach when I first arrived. Clearly the big heavy 'D' wasn't designed to race the Baja 1000, but she was quickly gaining on the billowing cloud of dust just ahead. When I got within range I pulled my Moms O'Malley .45, and with my left hand out the window blasted several shots into the fleeing striped jeep. He was scrambling across the bumpy terrain like a scared Zebra. He tried to loose me by going off road and blazing a trail up the side of a grassy hill, over the top and down into a narrow valley. Heavy 'D' roared up the hill and along the crest at the top claiming the high ground.

Ahead, I could see the jeep was quickly approaching the end of a shallow box canyon; he had no other option but to try and beat me to the top of the hill at the end of the canyon. I slammed down the go peddle and the Adventurer hit the after burners. We flew through the air then slammed to the ground plowing-up wide furrows of the terra firma while screaming toward the inevitable train wreck at the end of the canyon. It was like trying to beat the train to the crossing. The runaway jeep driver must have realized what was about to happen because he slammed down the gas pedal and the jeep screamed into a rip-roaring, out of control flight up the embankment at the end of the canyon. When he reached the top of the hill a flash of zebra flew into the air directly across the path of the massive chrome cattle crusher that is the grill of 'Heavy D's' four-hundred Hemi-horsepower; the Clydesdales of V-8 pony power. The Desoto slammed into the flying Zebra's left rear quarter-panel as it streaked by sending the jeep into a wicked twisting multi-revolution barrel roll across the trail and down the shallow embankment on the other side culminating in several bone-crushing end to end flips landing upside down in a huge cloud of dust. Luckily for the driver, he was ejected on the first revolution and tossed clear of the ensuing heap of twisted and disintegrating metal. He lay like a rag-doll crumpled and lifeless in a meadow of short grass. I didn't care if the son-of-a-bitch was dead or alive; I was going to kick his ass anyway. I slammed on the binders and turned hard left. 'Heavy D' swept off the ridge and made a long dust-choked slide down into the meadow, coming to an ugly stop not far from where the jeep driver was beginning to catch his breath and gather his scattered marbles. I leaped from the car and came storming out of the dust cloud like a rabid jackal, a rampaging Tasmanian devil out for blood.

He struggled to his hands and knees facing toward me spitting mouthfuls of dirt, blood, and a couple of his teeth. He never saw me coming and didn't know what hit him. I stormed down the shallow slope and kicked him in the face like I was attempting to boot a fifty yard field goal. He turned two back flips and landed flat on his back. I was on him like a pack of wild dogs. I slammed his head into the ground and pummeled his pulping face with a barrage of continuous rights and lefts until I began to run out of steam, and his face became almost unrecognizable... I recognized him; it was Harden Johnson Boehner.

I rolled off of him, sat up and lit a cigarette, contemplating why this big smiling ass hole had gotten involved. I watched as he struggled for each breath, making nasty gurgling noises with each attempt. I wondered what he had to gain by assassinating me. How does this big dip-shit figure in this thing?

I rolled him over onto his stomach before he drowned in his own blood. I removed his dump-ass want-to-be cowboy string tie with its big turquois slide, and tied his wrists together with a half-turn and two half-hitches; good luck struggling out of that laughing boy. I removed his stupid-ass want-to-be cowboy belt with the ten gallon buckle and tied it around his ankles. I picked him up by the back of his collar and dragged him the short distance to the terminally wounded metal Zebra lying smoldering on its back, wheels in the air. I sat the severely injured and bleeding Boehner against the side of the jeep and went to retrieve the jerry can of potable water and the military canteen that are standard issue equipment on all ranch vehicles that had been strewn about and widely dispersed during the violent rollover.

I returned just as Boehner was beginning to come around and attempt to stir about grimacing in pain. I had no sympathy for him and gave him a vicious, high-velocity face-douche with water from the jerry can making sure the majority splashed up his broken nose with great persuasion and intended pain. (Water-boarding on steroids; whatever any of that is.)

He screamed in pain gushing massive amounts of blood from his nose and mouth. I gave him another douching with less velocity, more to wash-off his breathing holes. I took a long drink from the cool canteen while he struggled to regain his breath. Once he had, labored as it was, I mercifully gave him a sip of water from the canteen. He coughed most of it up as a pink sludge, but managed to swallow the next with little effort. I sat back and lit another cigarette watching Boehner to determine what type of injuries he had sustained and if he was going to live long enough to answer a few questions burning within; the first three of which would be," what the fuck do you think you're doing, who are you working for and why?

Judging by the continues flow of blood from his mouth, labored breathing and distention of his abdomen, it was obvious that he had suffered major internal injuries like broken ribs or sternum, punctured lung, or ruptured spleen. He probably wouldn't survive long without immediate medical attention before he bled to death internally. Immediate medical attention wasn't going to happen, but instead, just like the guy that got snake-bit on his pecker and asked his friend to save him by sucking out the venom, and his friend replied; " I'm afraid you're probably gonna' die!"

I gave him another drink from the canteen and watched his eyes closely. He looked dazed and confused and the nasty gash and big lump on his forehead, as well as the blood seeping from his ears was a good indication of a concussion and possible skull fracture. He had a broken nose, a big welt on his cheek bone under his severely blood-shot eye and looks like he bit-off the end of his tongue, which I can only hope was the result of my fifty-yard field goal attempt.

"What's your story Boehner? Why did you try to kill me?" He looked at me with an expression of pure terror. He stared at me like he didn't know who I was or what was happening. He had the blank stare of an advanced Alzheimer patient. (Whatever that is?)

I waited a few moments then grabbed him up by his neck and slapped the living crap out of him several times. "Wake-up Boehner or I'm going to leave you out here to die!" I slammed him back against the dead Zebra and gave him another splash from the jerry can. He came up coughing and gagging, but he was also talking. He was hard to understand without the end of his tongue and he was talking so fast that he was hard to decipher, but what I think I heard was that Boehner got seriously in arrears with the Chicago 'Outfit' on several occasions when he was there for the buying and selling of cattle futures at the commodities market. Instead of crushing his knees the 'Outfit' sold his gambling debts to a group of individuals who wanted to have leverage over him. They wanted Boehner to help orchestrate from within, the take-over of the Ervine property on the coast. At the successful conclusion of the transaction Boehner would receive a very generous finder's fee and would be relieved of his gambling debts; if he refused they threatened prolonged agonizing torture and death. They even planted a bomb and blew-up his rental car to make their point. Of course the sixty-four thousand dollar question is; who is THEY? Boehner didn't know who THEY were. He was always contacted by phone or by a big scary representative of theirs who would step from the shadows out of nowhere and frighten the crap out of him. Boehner didn't know who or why. He took his last labored breath, and passed-away with a final death shudder. I've witnessed that last dying convulsion on too many occasions. It's not the kind of thing you forget. Try as you might to stuff those memories into a cubby-hole way in the recesses of your subconscious, it only takes a sound or a smell to bring all those unpleasant experiences rushing back in torrents of anxiety, sleeplessness, outbursts of rage, or the dark depths of depression. I suffered re-occurring wartime nightmares for several years after the war. Only recently have the nightmares and cold sweats subsided.

I backtracked along the ridge-crest down to the creek bed and through the gaping hole where, the now splintered, cattle gate once stood. The golden radiance of setting-sun behind purple shadow of Santa Catalina Island shown on the horizon as I pulled onto Coast Highway heading north. I stopped in Corona del Mar, called the ranch and spoke with Mr. Ervine. I informed him of the attempt on my life and the recent demise of Harden Johnson Boehner in the unfortunate rollover accident, omitting the gambling debt confession and his dying last words, or why I was in the vicinity in the first place. The less he knew, the easier it would be to contact the authorities. It was simply an unfortunate accident. Although now I remember that I forgot to remove Boehner's automatic assault rifle from the scene after replacing his tie and belt, which could complicate things. Maybe the Sheriff's Department will surmise that he was hunting. At this point in the game I don't think I give a shit anyway. I told Ervine to leave my part of the story out of it or a whole new investigation will be launched at a crucial time and he didn't need any more interference in a very delicate situation. "Just tell the cops that you found him like that. Let them figure it out. Oh yeah, you better send a ranch hand out there to repair that gate or you're gonna' have cattle roaming out onto Pacific Coast Highway at night, in the dark." That seemed to light a fire under his ass. He abruptly said 'sayonara' and that he would take care of it from here. He hung- up the phone and went to mount-up, round-up a posse, ten-feet of hog-wire and a roll of baling wire.

I arrived back at my apartment after dark. The building was empty. I quickly showered and changed, lit a cigarette, and sat on the couch with a vodka bottle and the telephone. I sat in the dark, smoked my cigarette, drank straight from the bottle and stared at the phone.

At nine p.m. I dialed the number that Precious had given me. Following a few clicks and several high-pitched buzz-tones the phone in D.C began to ring. Bucky Strayhorn answered on the first ring and spoke in hushed tones. "Dugan, I wanted you to know that I was contacted by these people a long time ago and pressured into providing inside information that I might discover or over-hear at the ranch regarding the property on the coast." "Take a breath Bucky, I said. Slow down. You're talking so fast I can barely understand you." "I don't think I have much time, Dugan. These people compromised my brother in some manner to divulge classified top secret information, and then when they were done with him they killed him. They tried to persuade me to do the same. I agreed Dugan, because I'm afraid of these guys, but I never really passed on any information that was of any use. I played along to keep from getting killed. I don't think that matters anymore. They're just covering their tracks now and eliminating anybody with any knowledge of the conspiracy. They're cleaning up loose ends."

After a long pause he continued, though even more hushed and rushed. "Dugan, my brother worked for *the NRC* and was responsible for choosing the most acceptable sites throughout the U.S for the construction of nuclear power plants. The Ervine property is at the top of a short list of the most desirable and advantages sites."

"It's located on the ocean from which to utilize an endless, un-interrupted supply of sea-water- induction for cooling of the reactors and fuel cells. An established rail line runs along the eastern perimeter on which to transport radioactive waste, like spent fuel cells, to a secured location, to be determined later, for immediate storage and future deep- burial. The rail line and nearby access to a major highway is a distinct advantage for that location during the construction phase of the project as well, for the transportation of construction materials and supplies. Following the construction phase the easy access to PCH will benefit the hundreds of employees the generating station will employ twenty-four seven, three hundred and sixty-five days a year. Dugan, you must realize that a ninety-nine year lease on the property with Pacific Gas and Electric, Southern California Edison, or whoever is the operator, will be worth millions of dollars well into the next century."

Suddenly there was an explosion of automatic gun fire and shattering glass on the other end of the line, and then it went dead...... Another loose-end cleaned-up. I sat in the dark staring at the dead phone and eventually killed the bottle of vodka as well.

Chapter Eleven

Day 11

I was jolted awake sometime in the pre-dawn darkness by the sound of smashing glass, the stomping of many heavy boots and doors being kicked in. My apartment door exploded into the room followed by a bunch of angry yelling vice cops attired in snazzy new *Kevlar* vests. "Police, get on the floor, face-down hands-up!" They didn't wait for me to comply but instead yanked me off the couch and body-slammed me to the floor with much aggression. They then proceeded to ransack my room, as I heard them doing throughout the building. It seemed more like an excuse to trash the place; which they did with exuberance and enthusiasm.

After the initial excitement had calmed somewhat and they had discovered my Moms O'Malley .45 semi- auto, my venerable snub-nose .38, and my personal weapon of mass destruction; my B.A.R. 30- caliber assault rifle and a dozen thirty–round fully loaded banana clips, then Chief Inspector Sven Golly made his grand entrance attired in the latest fashion trend for official police-raid chic. He wore steel-toed spit-shined paratrooper boots, black multi-zippered jump-suit with the words;' Special Weapons Assault Team' emblazoned across the back, gloves, helmet, and goggles. Of course he wore a *Kevlar* vest, was armed to the teeth and with camouflage paint on his face, looked like he just amphibiously assaulted the beach with *Seal Team Six*. (Whoever they are?) Or he's auditioning for *KISS* or the *Village People*. (Again, whoever they are?) Or perhaps he's on his way to '*Comic-con*'. (You know the drill.)

He sauntered around the room fingering through my personal papers, I.D. and wallet. He acted like an arrogant *'Playhouse 90'* asshole cop in his best *Dragnet's* Joe Friday 'Just the facts ma'am' persona. He asked the predictable, dumb-ass official police questions regarding my recent whereabouts and the whereabouts of Mona Loud and the two wayward women that reside here. I told Sven-cop Robo-Golly to bite me, until he was able to produce an official, signed search warrant authorizing this blatant act of destructive vandalism and for what specific evidentiary purpose. After ten minutes of searching the numerous fucking zippers in his god damn storm trooper uniform, Robo-Gort finally retrieved the requested document. I half expected it to read;' GORT-NIKTOS- BARADA'.

The warrant authorized a search for unspecified evidence related to the homicide of the young adult Asian female discovered in the alley, and who was known to be associated with the alleged escort service and prostitution ring suspected to be operating out of Mona's private social club. He was looking for Mona's little black book. I told him that I didn't know where Mona or the girls were. When I returned last night the place was dark and there was nobody home. When he asked the predictable question as to from where I had come when returning last night, I gave him the predictable answer as to bite me. I wasn't named in his search warrant and it was none of his business from where I had come.

It was obvious that Commando Golly was getting hot under his *Kevlar* collar. His eyes bulged within bubbled- goggles, his face reddened like a ripe Baboon's ass and began to develop a slight twitch on one side. The commandos from the other agencies involved were anxious to wrap this operation and call it a day; a day of fun and an exercise in futility. I think they could smell a fresh batch of donuts somewhere in their vicinity; it's a finely honed sense, a gift really.

Eventually Special Weapons Assault Team Commando Golly became disgruntled after all the preparation and effort expended produced nothing to further along his investigation. He gathered his band of merry mercenaries took all their toys and went home.

Nita arrived shortly after their departure carrying a vacuum cleaner, dust pan and broom. She told me that they had just finished cleaning-up the huge mess left by Gung ho Golly and his mincing munchkins after they had pulled the same stunt at *the Bear* shortly after closing. She said that they found nothing and simply took the opportunity to trash the place. Nita suggested that the motto;" to protect and serve" on the side of their squad cars instead should read; "To harass and Intimidate." But she's not bitter.

We spent the remaining pre-dawn twilight cleaning and repairing the extensive damage the' mod squad' created in their exuberance to seek and destroy. They smashed through the glass in the front door down stairs and crashed through the windows in the foyer upstairs after repelling from the roof. At daybreak Nita called Armando, the resident downtown handyman, to replace the broken glass and repair or replace the interior apartment doors that had been demolished.

At the conclusion of our sanitization session we sat down with a fresh cup of coffee that Nita had prepared. I lit a cigarette and was preparing to call Precious, back on the island, to inform her of recent events and to inquire about Mona's safe arrival on last night's ferry, when the phone began to ring incessantly and seemingly more urgent than usual. It was Precious and she sounded more anxious and more immediate than ever before. "Oh Travis, I'm so relieved that you answered. Yung He's cousin Long just contacted me by ship to shore radio from his Skipjack located approximately two miles due west of Land's End. He said that he had received a short radio signal that simply said; Kato-Jamie-*Aga Con.* That was all he got, the signal never repeated, and he got no response when he attempted to raise them on a return signal. Kamikaze Steve is on his way to pick you up at *Meadowlark Airport* off Warner Avenue, e.t.a. approximately thirty minutes. Grab all the fire power you can muster and go get' em Travis. I love you, be careful, and bring'em back alive baby."

***

As I sped north on PCH with the wind whistling through the blown-out glass, numerous holes in the cab, and various pieces and parts dangling from what now looked like Bonnie and Clyde's last ride, I couldn't help thinking what Crooks and Straight's expressions would be when I returned to *Aloha Family Motors* with the second totaled vehicle within a week, or how tickled Jerome Bailey would be as well. I see another pink donut box in my immediate future.

I pulled the Adventurer into *Meadowlark Airport* just as Kamikaze Steve and his little red Grumman touched-down and taxied over to where we could on-load my impressive stash of weaponry. To my surprise Inspector Lugar was riding co-pilot and had his venerable Smith and Wesson .44 police special strapped under his armpit.

Once we had on-loaded my personal arsenal, we climbed aboard and taxied out to the end of the runway. I smiled when I saw that Kamikaze had removed most of the twelve seats in his amphibious flying machine, save for two that were bolted to the deck back to back facing outboard just inside the openings on either side of the fuselage where the doors had been removed as well. Secured to the cockpit bulkhead was a wooden crate full of mortar rounds to send down the makeshift water balloon chutes on either side of the cockpit during Kamikaze's death defying dive bombing or skip bombing runs. I'm almost sorry that I showed him how it's done. I've flown with him on several occasions and half-the-time we've crashed into whatever we were attacking; thus the nickname Kamikaze. The last flight ended with Kamikaze's PBY pig-boat, with a five hundred pound bomb in the bomb bay, impaled nose to tail upon Dr. Con's Super Gun, which ultimately blew the shit out of the gun, the plane, and the bat cave back on the island in Smuggler's Cove. He had a lot of 'splaining' to do when the Eleventh Coast Guard District opened an investigation regarding the bombing and strafing of civilian and foreign-flagged vessels in international waters. There was an inflatable rubber raft packed into the rear of the plane that brought back quick flashbacks of me bailing-out of a rampaging 'balls to the wall' full-throttle PBY, in a rubber zodiac just after the plane bounced off the surface of the water and just prior to impact upon Con's 'Super Gun' in Smuggler's Cove.

I buckled into the starboard side seat in front of the open doorway as Kamikaze revved the engines preparing for the run-up and take-off. He released the brakes and we began to lumber down the runway gaining speed until we reached critical velocity then he pushed the throttles to the instrument panel, pulled back on the yoke and we lifted off into a clear blue sky with the morning sun rising behind us as we climbed directly over *Warner Drive-in* and the estuary wet lands at Tin Can Beach: Destination, Catalina Island, dead ahead where sea and sky meld into muted blue horizon.

Once we had reached cruising speed and altitude I unbuckled and went forward and sat on a fold-down jump-seat between the pilots at the cockpit bulkhead. I asked what the plan was, somewhat apprehensive of what Kamikaze's agenda might include. He told me that the plan thus far was to fly out and intercept the *'Aga-Con'*, find some way to board her and find Kato and Jamie Ervine. He looked at me with that same crazed grin I have come to know all too well; "We're flying this mission by the seat of our pants Bombardier, it's a spur of the moment situation. You've got about twenty minutes to educate Lugar here in the fine art of deploying bombs down the balloon chute during a screaming dive, and getting you and your personal Gatlin Gun buckled in, locked and loaded, and ready for Captain Kamikaze's wild ride; have your 'E' tickets at the ready and don't forget to keep your arms and legs inside until the ride comes to a complete stop. Thanks for flying with *Kamikaze Air Adventures*."

Lugar and I spent the next several minutes intensely concentrating on the process of loading mortar rounds down the chute during a dive bomb and low-level skip-bombing run. I doubted that we were going to attempt skip-bombing mortar shells on this mission, but with Kamikaze at the helm anything is possible.

Catalina Island beckoned like a long-forsaken lover, far off our port side, lying in the coolness of an azure satin sea. When we reached the location where the *'Dark Star'* had been at anchor, it was no longer there. Far in the distance, almost to the horizon, was a tell-tale wisp of smoke from a ship's stack disappearing in the gentle trade winds out toward the busy commercial shipping lanes, along with the last vestiges of smooth water between a ships wake slowly being consumed be the oceans relentless currents.

Kamikaze reached into an overhead compartment and withdrew a pair of military binoculars and handed them to our co-pilot, the intrepid Inspector Lugar who adjusted the focus, then set his sights on the 'straight-as-an-arrow 'boat wake and the billowing exhaust trail ahead. "It's the *Dark Star* all right, running full-throttle due west. She's crossing the shipping lanes and headed full-steam out to open ocean."

We eventually caught the *Dark Star* and made a slow pass down the port side, stern to bow. The shiny black *Bell* helicopter had been rolled out onto the pad and the rotors were beginning to turn in preparation for take-off. Kamikaze made a shallow banking turn to starboard and across the bow of the behemoth mega yacht. Several well-dressed Chinese stood stoic out on the flying bridge as we passed overhead. We flew down the starboard side and made a wide turn to starboard around the stern and prepared to make another 'look-see' fly-by as before. This time however, Lugar handed me the binoculars and said that I should take a look. I peered through the lens at the flying bridge and couldn't believe my eyes; it was like a bad dream, a reoccurring nightmare. I blinked my eyes and took a good close look at one individual on the bridge exclusively. "Well I'll be go-to-hell, no shit," I muttered under my breath as I looked over to Kamikaze Steve. He sensed something was wrong, perhaps it was the color draining from my face. "What is it, Bombardier?" he asked. "It's Dr. Con." I answered expressionless.

As we flew across the bow and prepared to bank right and sweep down the starboard side I gazed through the binoculars at the other individuals on the bridge. One of the well-dressed Chinese stood in a firing position and had a bazooka poised on his shoulder and pointed directly at us.

"In-coming RPG starboard!" I yelled. Kamikaze stomped the right rudder-peddle, turned hard right, and pushed the yoke to the dash. The right wing dropped and we went into a critical bank to the right as the RPG streaked through the open hatch on the starboard side, straight through the fuselage and out the open hatch on the port side. "Whoa! No shit!" I yelled. "Un-freaking-believable!"

Kamikaze pushed the throttles forward and pulled back hard on the controls; we gained speed and altitude surprisingly quick. I unbuckled from my jump seat and folded it back into the bulkhead, then opened the crate and handed Lugar a half dozen mortar rounds which he gently placed in the padded milk crate between his knees to be deployed down the balloon chute. I then grabbed my B.A.R and the bag of ammo clips and assumed my position buckling into the seat at the starboard hatch opening with my feet braced against either side of the opening. Banzai!

Kamikaze eased back on the throttle and let the nose dip toward the sea as we began a long steep dive toward the stern of the fleeing 'Dark Star'. The silent, high speed dive reminded me of flying A-26's over Korea in the dark of night, screaming down into the deep canyons and valleys to ignite troop trains and truck convoys with napalm wing pods, 50-calibers blazing away from the nose, and an assortment of ordinance in the bomb-bay.

"Bombs away!" yelled Lugar as he carefully slid three mortars down the balloon chute as Kamikaze pulled back hard on the yoke and pushed the throttles hard forward and the little red attack Grumman lurched into a steep climb. The helicopter lifted of the pad as the first mortar struck the fantail over the stern. The second mortar scored a direct hit smack-dab in the middle of the 'Crosstown Boys' bulls-eye on the helipad. Had we arrived a few seconds sooner we would have obliterated the helicopter while still sitting on the pad. Instead, the chopper made a wide sweeping turn and quickly gained altitude as it swung around the stern of the fleeing mega yacht. The third mortar hit on the bow and the '*Dark Star* began to billow a large smoke plume as it continued due west under full power; it began to look like a runaway.

Kamikaze made a hard banking turn to starboard and followed the same tract that the helicopter had taken. "Light'em-up Bombardier!" yelled Kamikaze as he brought us around and up the port side of the '*Dark Star*'. I opened up with my B.A.R. spraying the entire length of the boat with blistering rounds that ripped through the superstructure and shredded the bridge windows as we came across the bow and down the starboard side.

Suddenly the slash of shiny black came streaking out of the sun dead ahead, blasting rounds through our fuselage as it screamed by, dropped below us and came around in a tight right turn preparing to make another pass along our port side. Kamikaze dropped to the surface of the waves and made a hard right turn around the stern of the *Dark Star*, attempting to use it as a shield from the faster, more maneuverable helicopter. As we cleared the bow full-throttle and barely above the waves, the helicopter cleared the bow on our starboard side and flew along pacing our airspeed. I could see the whites of the Chinese gunzel's eyes who braced in the open door of the chopper and was sporting a Kalashnikov automatic assault rifle. My fire breathing B.A.R. ripped that little bastard to shreds and created a large hole in the helicopter's fuselage opposite the open door where the smiling gunzel once sat.

"Yahoo Bombardier, that's what I call shooting!" yelled Kamikaze; "that's why he gets the big money!" The helicopter began to trail black smoke from the exhaust. It quickly gained altitude and headed at full speed due west out to the open ocean, but not before rotating around above us and riddling the Grumman with ripping and shredding rounds that began to grenade the props and the tail rudder. We began to trail smoke from the engine as we slowly began to climb above the waves before the small flames within the engine cowling ignite the wing. Kamikaze feathered the engine and the flames went out. We were still trailing plume of smoke but there were no flames. "Good job Kamikaze!" I yelled. He looked back at me and seemed concerned. "We've got worse problems Bombardier, we have no rudder control."

I unbuckled and went forward. I unfolded the jump seat from the bulkhead and took a quick look at all the gauges; fuel and hydraulic pressure, engine temperature and oil pressure. All looked operable except we will need to get the port engine re-started in order to gain altitude and more importantly, to enable us to steer the plane utilizing engine thrust; not an easy operation even under the best of conditions.

The little plane began to yaw side to side like a kite that had lost its tail. It wouldn't be long before we begin to flat-spin, falling from the sky out of control and eventually wing-over in a succession of violent snap-rolls and nose dive into an inevitable high-speed fiery crash.

After several attempts Kamikaze finally coaxed the port engine to life, even though there was a lot of resistance, back-talk and grumbling before she did so. There was still a small fire and smoke trail from within the engine cowling, but engine performance wasn't effected yet, and the oil pressure while low and getting lower, would hold-out long enough; probably a ricocheted round punctured an oil fitting or line, but didn't seem to penetrate the engine housing itself.

We quickly gained altitude and ground speed. We followed the tell-tale wisp of trailing smoke on the horizon and leveled off at three thousand feet; the ideal altitude from which to begin a dive bombing attack. Kamikaze worked the yoke, wing flaps and still functioning rear ailerons, while I adjusted thrust on the engines to affect rudder control and direction or flight path.

The 'Aga-Con' appeared on the horizon heading due west at full speed billowing dark clouds of diesel exhaust. As we approached, Lugar peered through the binoculars at the immense supertanker steaming high in the water. The shiny black helicopter was sitting on the helipad rotor blades still spinning. Kamikaze smiled that familiar grin that always results in some kind of horrendous crash landing……

and I use the term 'landing' loosely; on both occasions we had to bail just before impact and total destruction of the aircraft and whatever it crashed into. (I hate that grin.) But as Kamikaze reminds me; any landing you can walk, or in our case swim away from is considered a successful landing. (I hate that analogy)

"We're only gonna' have one shot at this Lugar," yelled Kamikaze," so make sure you shove all of those mortars down the chute before the nose comes up,........or, if it doesn't come-up, we smash full-throttle into the big–ass ship." Lugar looked slightly apprehensive about the whole plan; with good reason, as the port side engine burst into flames and threatened to burn through the wing.

We lined-up following the ship's wake, and as I pulled back gently on the throttles we nosed-over and began a long swift glide out of a cloudless sky diving ever faster toward the fleeing supertanker. As the little red attack Goose screamed from the heavens the wind velocity blew out the flames in the port engine. The closing rate increased as we dove on the ship from the rear; I prayed that we were able to pull-up and climb-out, as opposed to nose-diving into an explosive fiery conclusion.

Lugar yelled "Bombs Away" and quickly slid the remaining three mortars down the chute. I slammed the throttles forward and Kamikaze pulled back hard on the controls. We slowly and laboriously leveled out just above the bridge at the stern of the huge ship as the first mortar impacted into the wide main deck of the super tanker followed in succession by the other two. They caused little more than cosmetic damage, igniting small superficial fires that had the ship's crew scrambling to extinguish in short order.

As Kamikaze pulled back on the yoke and I pushed the throttles forward once more, the plane began to shudder and began a slow barrel roll to starboard as we gained altitude. Kamikaze fought hard to counteract the roll but to little affect. Finally, I rammed starboard throttle forward and yanked port full back. The little Grumman slowly began to correct the roll but in the process performed an aerobatic loop that instead, at the top of the loop, turned into a climbing stall and nose-over free fall; a stunt it was not designed to perform and one that we were not likely to survive. We streaked from the sky nose-down and out of control. Kamikaze was standing straight up at the controls and had the yoke pulled-up under his chin. Lugar was braced against the floorboards, had the yoke pulled to his chest and was screaming like a flaming banshee. To add insult to injury we were about to impact into the sea directly in the path of the big ship to be run over and smashed to smithereens then sliced and diced into mince-meat and spewed-out by the gigantic twin screws churning full-speed at the stern.

I slammed both throttles 'balls to the wall', then I unstrapped the wooden case from the bulkhead and as the lumbering, shuddering' little plane that could' gradually nosed-up and slowly began climb from the wave tops, I kicked the crate toward the rear and as it slid down the length of the fuselage and slammed into the rubber life raft in the stern the plane lurched upward just in the nick-of-time. When I turned and looked out of the cockpit windshield the bow of the big ship was dead ahead and the closing rate was heart-stopping. We all held our breath as the windshield filled with the big black hull of the steaming behemoth. "Whoooooa Shiiiiiit!" we screamed in unison like little choir girls in falsetto three part harmony, as we barely cleared the bow then clipped the jack staff and ripped the tail section off the plane slamming the fuselage down hard and at high-speed onto the wide deck of the tanker. We pancaked in hot and skidded the entire length of the immense wide deck out of control amidst a rooster tail plume of blinding sparks and red hot disintegrating plane parts, then began a slow spin to the right until we finally impacted backward into the superstructure below the bridge. Luckily there was no explosion or fire.

After the initial impact it seemed still and silent. Didn't last long; we began receiving heavy automatic weapons fire that ripped and shredded the crumpled metal of the valiant little fighter plane. I scrambled to the demolished rear of the terminally injured plane and grabbed my fire-breathing B.A.R. and ammo bag. I began returning fire from a gaping slash in the fuselage and spraying the flying bridge and quarter decks scattering the well- dressed mercenary army of Asian miscreants and' want-to-be' Tong turds in all directions. I lay-down a continuous burst of cover-fire while Kamikaze and Lugar dislodged themselves from the aircraft carcass and prepared to storm the parapets.

Suddenly the starboard side vestibule hatch swung open with a loud bang against the superstructure bulkhead. It was Kato, with a commandeered Kalashnikov waving us in. I shoved a fresh clip into my Browning Personalized Gatlin Gun and sprayed the entire clip as cover-fire across the quarterdecks and bridge while Kamikaze and Lugar scrambled the short distance into the vestibule hatch, with me following close behind.

Once inside the superstructure of the fast moving ship I asked Kato if he knew where Jamie Ervine was being confined. "Yeah Brudha, follow me." We followed the goliath-sized Samoan as he sprinted through a labyrinth of passageways like a gazelle on steroids, (whatever those are?), and slid down ladder after ladder to the very bowels of the beast. I was surprised that we didn't encounter any resistance along the way. "Where's the rest of the crew?" I asked as we made our way from deck-to- deck. "One by one I find 'dem last night in da dark." He clasp his mammoth sized hands together across his chest, then yanked them apart while making the sound of a neck snapping violently. "I 'trow 'dem overboard; chum for sharks," he laughed. "The only crew left in 'da engine room, 'da boiler room and 'da bridge, Brah; all 'da rest sleep with 'da fishes; shark bait." I asked about the cadre of well-dressed Chinese Tongs that were firing RPG's at us from the flying bridge. "Not see 'dem. 'Dey come in 'da chopper." Then I asked if he had seen Dr. Con. That brought him to an immediate halt, which caught everybody else up short and we all banged into each other like *Max Sennett's Keystone Cops.* All the color momentarily drained from his massive cranium, and quickly rushed back as his jaw muscles tightened. "No shit Brah? We should kill him this time."

We finally came to the compartment where Kato said Jamie was being held captive. He produced a ring of keys he had commandeered and eventually found the one that unlocked the heavy metal hatch. When we opened the hatch we were astonished to discover that the compartment, used as a rag locker, also contained about twenty-five young blonde girls, no doubt destined for 'a midnight train going a-n-y-w-h-e-r-e.' (Get Steven Perry on the phone.) They all appeared to have been beaten and abused. They had been completely broken down physically and mentally; they stared with a hollow gaze and they seemed without hope. They had that living dead, dull-stare of someone who had just 'main-lined' a crystal ship full of smack into their vein.

"Jamie, we're here to take you home. Jamie Ervine, are you in here?" I announced. Slowly, a bedraggled, beautiful young blonde girl turned around in the middle of the crowd, moved a length of hair from her vision and looked up at me like a pound puppy whose time was up and was about to get *'the big sleep'*. "Did my dad send you to take me home?" she asked in a timid whisper. "Yes Jamie, we're here to take you home." I answered softly with a smile.

We gently gathered the girls and with Kato on point and Kamikaze at our six, Lugar and I slowly moved the lethargic and confused group through the passages and up the ladders to the main deck and our only option for escape, the Panga Boats.

When we reached the main deck I heard the helicopter fire-up out on the pad aft in preparation for lift-off. I motioned for Kato and the girls to continue through the vestibule out onto the forward deck and load everybody into one of the Panga boats attached to the lifeboat davits suspended over the side. Lugar and Kamikaze helped guide the boatload of blonde girls forward and I went aft to the helipad.

I put a fresh banana clip in my B.A.R. and crept toward the open hatch that led out onto the pad. The chopper was gaining rpms and rotor blade momentum as Dr. Con and the rest of his well-dressed entourage moved toward the open door. One of the Chinese body guards spotted me crouching in the hatch-opening and began firing. The vestibule exploded with ricocheting rounds zinging in all directions like a volley of roman candles on the fourth of July. I opened up with my Browning automatic scatter-gun splattering body parts and pieces of body guards all over the deck. The helicopter lurched skyward dumping the passengers attempting to board out onto the pad as I emptied the clip into the cockpit shattering the glass bubble and sending the chopper into a right hand auto rotation, spinning out of control. The chopper gained altitude and spun out over the port side and continued to spin ever faster forward around the superstructure in tight circles until it made a steep climb over the main deck and then plummeted out of the sky and spun into the ship's bridge and helm with a fiery explosion of full fuel tanks like the incineration of a napalm inferno.

Dr. Con and two of his stunned minions pulled themselves off the pad and started toward the open vestibule on the port side into the superstructure behind a barrage of automatic weapons fire. I pulled my Moms O'Malley .45 auto and retraced my steps back through the starboard side passageways and out onto the open main deck of the immense supertanker. Con and his cronies were about to open fire on Kato and the boat full of blonde girls being lowered in the lifeboat when I took two of them down with my hand cannon. Con moved quickly and escaped being splattered against the gunnels. He crawled forward hugging the deck like a cockroach attempting to hide behind the slight rise of the below-deck tank hatches.

We continued exchanging repeated shots at each other until both weapons ceased functioning with the distinctive 'click' of firing pin striking empty chamber. We played peek-a-boo for a few moments until we had come to the conclusion that we were both indeed out of ammo.

Finally, Con rose to his feet and let his weapon fall to the deck. He looked at me with a confident smirk. "Mr. Dugan you have interfered with my plans for some time now, and I have contracted numerous assassins to eliminate your interference to no avail. I propose that you and I bring this unfortunate situation to a satisfactory conclusion, at least for one of us. What do you say Mr. Dugan? You and me, man to man, once and for all. I can assure you that I will take great pleasure in killing you myself. I can think of nothing that would bring me more pleasure or satisfaction than to eliminate you and inflict much pain and suffering while doing so. This will be the final solution, Mr. Dugan." I stepped out onto the deck with a smile. "I look forward to ripping your guts out Con. I'm here to exact my personal revenge and execute my own brand of justice. You are going to die, and die hard motherfucker." (Somebody call Bruce Willis. Whoever he is?)

Con moved out from behind the pile of scrap, that used to be Kamikaze's Grumman, to an open area in the middle of the immense deck between the oil tank hatches that we had used like an aircraft carrier for our crash landing earlier. He motioned for me to bring it and when I got within range the up-tight, button-down, wiry little shit unleashed a relentless attack that included lightening quick punches and an impressive array of spinning back kicks, back-flips and pirouettes that would earn him an audition with the Bolshevik Ballet. I managed to block most of the more powerful and potentially damaging blows, but I was moved steadily in retreat until I backed into the superstructure with no escape; I either land some heavy break-out punches or stand my ground and get my ass kicked.

As with Toby Juan Cannoli earlier in this adventure during our cattle car encounter, I covered my vital parts and pulled a 'rope-a-dope' on the unsuspecting, over-exerting, slicked-back little rice burner and let him have his way with me, so to speak, until he began to fatigue and his breathing became labored; he began to huff and puff. I dropped to the deck, performed a 'crouching Tiger' spinning back kick that swept his feet out from under him, slamming him to the deck flat on his back and bouncing the back of his head off the boards like a basketball, momentarily double-dribbling his brain cells. I should have stomped his throat and finished him off then and there, but I didn't. I wanted to inflict excruciating pain and lots of it.

I leapt to my feet and backed-off toward the bow onto the wide open deck, allowing Dr. Con to gather his marbles and regain his feet. I motioned for him to bring it, and when he got within range the feisty little bastard unleashed another offensive onslaught; a barrage of relentless blows that threatened to stream-roller over me. I began to suffer some vicious hits and was forced to retreat, farther toward the bow of the runaway supertanker. I went as far as I could go, the end of the line, the jagged remnants of the jack-staff that we sheared –off during the afore-mentioned crash landing.

Con stopped several yards away and smiled. He had me cornered, virtually trapped like the proverbial rat. He slowly and deliberately reached in his pocket and withdrew several shiny Chinese star darts. "Well Mr. Dugan, it appears as though we have reached the end of the trail, as they say in your maudlin western movies." His smile slowly grew into a smirk as he assumed the stance of a Kung Fu Grand Poobah and quickly delivered the star darts in rapid succession. All three hit me in the chest and imbedded themselves deep into my Professor Peabody *Kevlar* vest. I was momentarily stunned by the ferocity of the impacts; Con was perplexed by the in-effectiveness of his deadly little toys; didn't last long.

He charged at me like a raging bull, when suddenly he was knocked off his feet by a huge explosion at the stern of the runaway ship. The tanker began to sway from side to side as it rampaged through the open ocean. As Con began to raise himself from the deck, I charged him and delivered a vicious kick to his face that flipped him over flat on his back. I grabbed him by the neck, dragged him to the bow of the ship, lifted him over my head and slammed him down onto the shattered jack staff impaling him from stem to stern. I stepped back and watched as he squirmed upon the jagged lance protruding from his chest, struggling like a freshly gigged frog.

Suddenly the stern of the immense supertanker began to quickly sink into the briny deep. The waves began to swallow the superstructure, the top of which at the bridge was still furiously burning with the remains of the helicopter firmly entangled within. The sea began to wash over the wreckage of Kamikaze's valiant and crumpled little red

Grumman spreading debris and interior contents over the wide deck only to be ultimately consumed by the relentless ocean.

The superstructure slowly sank into the deep, extinguishing the rampaging flames with a loud hiss and an immense white steam cloud as the wide deck began to surrender to the onrushing sea. Con kicking and screaming, attempting to dislodge himself and calling me every vile name in the Chinese dictionary and a few in the English one as well. He squirmed and screamed in agony……..just as he should.

The bow on which Con was impaled began to raise high into the sky as the stern began its long cold journey to the bottom of the deep dark sea. "Come on you egotistic little shit, stretch your arms out, throw your head back and scream at the top of your lungs; *I'm the King of the world*!"

I began a long slide down the now vertical deck and consumed within the dark swirling vortex of the massive sinking ship. The last thing I would see as I sank into the darkness was Con being consumed by the cruel unforgiving sea. Then there was darkness, all consuming darkness within a tornado of cold rushing bubbles, pulling you down, ever deeper into the cold dark silence…..

Soft sound of gentle wave rushing smooth upon white beach, breathless whisper of goodbye, last farewell upon retreat. Muted shades of vibrant colors float on blusterous breeze, to gently fall on fresh- mown lawn and warmth of summer's ease. The soar of gentle shadows, gliding high on dappled field, the flicker of playing card swept by spoke within vibrant whirl of children's wheel, and breathless wonder upon first site, green expanse of baseball field.

Innocent whispers of budding love, intimate nights of passion, love and loss then heartbreak and sadness, depression in painful fashion. Conflict, death and killing far away from home, terrifying nights of cold- sweat fear, in the dark and all alone.

Summer nights, bareback-rides, white sands and starry skies, moonlight's shine on balmy sea, soft fire and lover's sigh. Island dreams that bloom like spring, warm nights of sweet romance. Then music fades, lights go dark, the conclusion of the dance.

Suddenly there was an all-consuming rush of uplifting bubbles that gently carried me as if upon the wings of angels to the warmth of bright light. I emerged from the depths of the sea within cocoon of Kamikaze's rubber raft that had been mashed into the rear of his crumpled little plane. I lay on my back staring at the sky as the raft continued to swirl in the dwindling vortex of what was *'Aga-Con'*.

The great black beast rose up before me with seething white ferocity and swallowed me down like Jonah and the biblical whale.

Chapter Twelve

Day Twelve

At last the soothing sounds of Etta James, the fragrance of fresh lilacs, and the annoying consistency of a beeping monitor of some kind. I became aware of the warmth of a soft caress and a gentle kiss upon the cheek. I opened my eyes and gazed upon the stunningly gorgeous Claire Voyent; C.I.A. agent extraordinaire and the only qualified female U2 spy plane pilot. Claire nailed a starring role in my last Catalina adventure. Perhaps 'pile-drive' would be a more apropos depiction.

"Well, well Monkey Man, it looks like you're going to make it after all," she whispered close in sensual breathy tones. "Is that my hand under your sheet or am I just happy to see you?" she giggled.

Another voice from my past chimed in from somewhere beyond my immediate field of vision. (I began to wonder if before you meet St. Peter at the pearly gates perhaps you must serve as guest of honor on a strange and other worldly cosmic version of "This Is Your Life.") "Glad to see that you survived without destroying too many brain cells, old chap, you don't possess enough to be sacrificing even one." Yes, I recognized that pansy-ass English accent; it was none other than the handsome and debonair British Secret Service agent, and another surprise guest from past adventures, Pond, Blaine Pond.

"We poured about a gallon of sea water out of you when we hauled your bedraggled, water-logged ass out of the briny deep and brought you aboard, old chap." "Aboard what", I asked with great discomfort through salt water aggravated esophagus. "My friend you are in the sick bay aboard the *U.S.S. Nautilus*, the flagship of America's Nuclear Submarine Service. We put the torpedo up the aft of the '*Aga-Con.* ' We would have launched sooner, but waited until the life boat full of blondes was a safe distance away."

Commander Wilkerson, *Nautilus* sub commander entered followed by the Chief Medical Officer Lieutenant Leonard McCoy. *Claire Voyent held fast with her firm grasp and kept things close at hand. As not to create an embarrassing display, she held staff safely at half-mast.*

The Doctor began to unplug the various medical devises attached to me and thankfully one of which ceased the incessant beeping coming from somewhere behind me. Commander Wilkerson stepped forward and shook my hand. "First of all Mr. Dugan allow me to thank you on behalf of the United States Navy and the American people for your service to your country. Secondly, it's a pleasure to welcome you aboard *the Nautilus*. The officers and crew are honored to have you with us. "You're a very lucky man Mr. Dugan, that massive burst of bubbles that brought you back to the surface was the result of the boiler explosion as the *Aga-Con* sank to the bottom. Had that explosion not occurred precisely when it did, it's unlikely that we would have recovered your body."

"Fortunately for you, the *Nautilus* and its crew just happen to be conducting sea trials in the area on our way to Seattle when we received a communication from the American C.I.A and British Intelligence MI-5 requesting that we surface, bring aboard Mr. Pond and Miss Voyent', and render assistance in the rescue of those aboard the tanker '*Aga-Con*'. Pond and the lady were transported to a rendezvous with the *Nautilus* by Marine helicopter out of Camp Pendleton. *The Nautilus* is in transit to Seattle in preparation for the world's first undersea circumnavigation of the North Pole."

The Commander looked at his watch. "The U.S. Coast Guard Cutter' *Ponchatrane*' should be on scene about now extracting the rescued passengers from the life boat and bringing them aboard. That makes the E.T.A. for a rendezvous with the *Nautilus* in approximately thirty minutes, at which time we will transfer you to the *'Ponchatrane'* as well for transport back to the mainland."

The Commander gave me a prim and proper salute, tipped his cap to Pond and the lady, wished us good luck and a pleasant voyage, and returned to his duties on the bridge. The medical officer requested that I sit on the side of the bed for the obligatory two-fingered thump search up and down my back, the rubber mallet tap to below the knee-cap reflex check and of course the pen light across the pupil dilation stimulation. Having found things ship-shape he packed his bag and excused himself.

Claire looked at Pond and gave him a 'scram-ola' head- nod toward the door. "Well yes, of course," he said. "I believe I'll go top-side and see if the smoking lamp is lit and leave you two to express a proper welcome or farewell." With that he clicked his heels together, a curt bow, turned and departed. Claire turned to me with a twinkle in her eye and a sly smile on her face. She hiked up her shirt and removed her black lace panties. She unbuttoned her blouse exposing her proud and pouty sweater puppies then gave me a motor boating opportunity. She began by kissing me gently on my lips then worked her way down slowly. She magically transformed my *Little Oscar Meyer wiener whistle* into *Big Bad Voodoo Daddy* and indulged her lollipop fetish, demonstrating that her uvula also functioned as her clitoris. Before a premature happy ending could occur, she climbed aboard and requested that I remind her why I was known as the vagina-cologist for the C.I.A. After a lot of heavy breathing, sweating and screaming, she told me to shut-up and slowly slithered down to give the farewell Bone voyage' that I won't soon forget. She told me that she wanted me to remember her fondlingly; and I shall.

At the conclusion of our interlude, and I do mean lewd, and while we were showering within the tight quarters of a shipboard sickbay shower stall, Claire told me that she and Pond had been on Con's trail since we last saw each other on the island at the conclusion of the last installment of this serial adventure. She said that Dr. Con and cannon trajectory expert Gerald Bull were still pursuing their plan to build the 'Super Gun.' "We lost track of Con in San Francisco's China Town, and the next thing we knew he turns-up in Hong Kong buying oil and petroleum super tankers. Don't think that didn't send up a few red flags around the globe," she giggled while polishing the hardware; always the perfectionist.

"You're F.B.I. girlfriend Randi Andretti uncovered the immigrant, drug smuggling and white slave trade angle, but we knew there must be something else driving this conspiracy; something more lucrative, more profitable and above all, to further- along the ultimate quest to build the super gun."

"You recall Travis, that Dr. Con the petro chemical engineer merged his 'perpetual propulsion' formula with Gerald Bull's expertise in long range cannon trajectory to successfully build and test fire their 'super gun' on Catalina Island. Their goal was to provide the technology or a working model to any dictatorial despot or military junta around the world that could afford the price tag. With that long range weaponry and any number of biological warheads attached to the projectiles being fired, any turban-headed camel jockey, terrorist organization, or fledgling rebel militia would be in parody with their nuclear neighbors or capable of annihilating their hapless adversaries. And that, Monkey Man is what ultimately brings the conspiracy to Mr. James Ervine's front door, or perhaps more accurately, to his coastal property on the sunny shores of southern California."

"Through extortion, blackmail, or threat of bodily harm to a family member or whatever, Dr. Con's organization compromised Bucky Strayhorn's, a.k.a. Robert Youngblood Strayhorn, brother Billy, a.k.a. William Bonner Strayhorn to divulge the results of the *NRC* and *AEC's* geologic study and eventual short list of suitable property for the construction of a nuclear powered electric generating facility. Short-sighted as it seems, for whatever reason, once they got the information they killed him and tossed him in the Potomac."

"That's when Con and his cronies began focusing their attention on Mr. Ervine for his chosen shoreline property and Mr. Stanton for the extreme convenience of his railroad line running along Ervine's property. Apparently getting little response from standard threats, Con's boys killed China Lei, a girl intimate with both men, and left her in a place where both have been known to frequent. The purpose of course was to get their attention and get both men to take Con's threats seriously, and it succeeded; enter *Travis Dugan Private Investigations*. From that point we simply followed you around knowing that you would somehow lead us to Con and his conspirators; and you did."

I contemplated the information while we dressed and prepared to go topside. "Seems like a lot of trouble just to gain access to a long-term federally funded lease or private contract lease with one of the major power companies, much less to futz around with a railroad that they seem to have compromised already anyway," I queried.

Claire smiled at me while she searched the area for her wayward black lace panties. "C'mon Travis think a few steps ahead. And remember Con's ultimate goal is to successfully build and distribute his 'Super Gun'. What better way to make it more lethal at virtually no extra cost, and make a complete system available for sale to the highest bidder, than to supply the radioactive materials to produce what's known as a 'dirty bomb.' Aha! She said retrieving her panties from the rotation of the overhead ceiling fan; how they got there I haven't a clue? "What's a dirty bomb?" I asked. "It's a nasty, prolonged and gruesome way to contaminate a large population, their water supply or food source and doom them to an ultimate grisly painful death."

The shrill melody of a boatswain's pipe sounded over the p.a. system with high-pitched ear- splitting decibels just shy of that of a dog whistle. "Attention all hands, attention all hands, deck force personal report topside to receive small boat port side. All deck force hands on deck immediately."

On our way through the narrow passage ways and up a couple of ladders to topside Claire explained in layman's terms, that with access to the nuclear facility's spent radioactive fuel rods periodically replaced from within the cooling pools and stored on site for the foreseeable future, Con would have easily attainable radioactive waste with which to produce a poor man's atomic device; a dirty bomb.

We climbed out on deck in bright sunshine and a deep blue sea. The Coast Guard Cutter *'Ponchatrane'* sat off our port side a couple of hundred yards away. A rubber zodiac boat came alongside and onto the sub's rounded lower hull. The afore-mentioned and mustered efficient deck crew grabbed the boat, brought it aboard and secured it to the top-side deck.

Claire turned to me surprisingly with tears in her eyes. She smiled and threw her arms around my neck. "Well Monkey Man I guess this is where we say goodbye......again. Remember when we first met I told you that I was psychic and that I had a feeling that we were going to become very special friends? Well I'm sure glad that we have Travis. You're a wonderful guy and I sure hope that our paths cross again sometime." She held me close and kissed me long and hard, just the way she likes it.

"Aren't you and Pond Coming with me?" I asked. "No, he and I still have business to attend. We need to catch the *'Dark Star'* and board her. I want to process the evidence on board and gain as much intel as possible on the rest of Con's organization, how it functions and location of its operatives. We also must locate and interdict Con's petroleum tanker the *'Aqua-Con"* somewhere in the Pacific steaming toward 'Sandy Beach' on Ervine's San Onofre seaside property crammed with illegal Chinese immigrants and China White and black tar heroin."

The Commander looked at his watch and said that if Pond and Miss Voyent' wanted to catch the *'Dark Star'* before sunset then the *Nautilus* needs to get underway immediately. He gave me a smart salute, about faced and barked-out orders for the crew to prepare to get underway. Blaine Pond shook my hand and gave me a sincere hug. "Good show Mate, it's always an adventure. I looked forward to our next. In the meantime keep your chins-up Old Man."

I climbed into the zodiac, the deck crew lowered it to the surface of the water, the Coxswain fired-up the outboard and we were underway back to the '*Ponchatrane*' where Jamie Ervine and the other rescued girls waited along with Randi Andretti and were anxious to get back to their families and loved ones. Kato, Lugar and Kamikaze Steve were weary of the adventure and perfectly satisfied to return to their humdrum everyday existence. Our little section of the world is safe once again and life is restored to the beauty we once knew. And me, I can't wait to get back to lovely Rita and resume our lives aboard the '*Lucky Dutchman*' and my role as Casino Manager extraordinaire'.

THE END

EPILOG

So there you have it Precious, my extended nightmare of a busman's holiday right down to the minutia of details. I don't know why you insist that I submit a summarized report, including my thoughts and feelings at the conclusion of each case? What, are you writing a book or something? Do you have a literary agent and a contract with '*True Detective*', or perhaps more apropos Alfred E. Newman and '*MAD*' *magazine*?

I feel bad for China Lei and the way in which her life ended. She was nothing more than an exclamation point, a way to get Stanton and Ervine's attention. That just proves what ruthless bastards Dr. Con and his associates were, as if we weren't already well aware of that. I'm glad I was the one that finally killed him and watch him sink into the deep. There are plenty of bad people that I was glad to eliminate but none deserved it more than Con and I've never experienced the satisfaction of pure, raging revenge like I have in killing Dr. Con.

Papa Nikos and daughter Caroline have *the Golden Bear* up and humming along in a full- tilt-boogie and rumor has it that Caroline has fallen for a music promoter named Rick, with whom Papa is thrilled and is anxious for them to marry and with Rick's brother Chuck, take-over the day-to-day operation of *the Bear.*

Mona Loud and the girls are happily busy and their social club has gained popularity with the Nuevo Riche' designers, engineers and high-wage assembly workers that have migrated in mass, V.A. loans in hand, to the acres of flat bean fields that are being transformed into endless cookie-cutter *Levittown* tracts of split-level ranch-style houses with detached two-car garages and roofs covered with crushed white rocks. *Lockeed Aircraft* completed a *'skunk-works'* type research, development and assembly facility on the outskirts of town in the middle of an enormous eucalyptus grove, that is rumored to be developing next generation satellite spy technology or something called the *SR 71 Blackbird* supersonic high-altitude spy plane with super-secret radar-cloaking design and coating composition called *'Stealth.'* Within the same classified high-security complex *General Dynamics Corporation* designs and develops America's future nuclear submarine fleet and clandestine ground-hugging *'Cruise missile'* technology. Those endeavors have attracted thousands of pent-up, stressed-out, pencil-protected horny nerd-balls that have plenty of disposable income burning holes in their lab coats and free weekends of drunken debauchery in which to blow it all on cheap liquor and expensive women.

Mona and the girls have embarked on a new venture in partnership with Deacon Yeager and his brothers. It seems that the abortion Doctor with the cartel of clandestine Inland Empire clinics staffed by illegal Filipino nurses was raided by agents from Customs, FBI and U.S. Marshalls. The good Doctor is now cooling his heels in a federal holding facility in the isolated high-desert community of Boron California. Subsequently, the Yeager-meisters have acquired the luxury mega yacht once belonging to afore mentioned Doctor who's dozen-or-so naughty nurses of the month, Deacon would entertain with a tropical debauchery cruise to Catalina one weekend a month; now, with Mona booking her high-end clientele for weekend fishing 'charters-with-benefits' cruises; they all do very well.

Nita Menage' is engaged to her high-priced 'boob-job' Doctor/boss and has moved into his exclusive Brentwood estate on Bundy Drive. Lola married a Casino owner in Vegas and is the resident choreographer for the *'Folies' Bergere'*, and *'the 'Ziegfeld Follies'* can-can musical revues at *the Stardust* and *Tropicana Hotels*. In her spare time she competes on the International Formula One racing series currently at *'The Grand Prix of Monaco'*.

Here are some interesting tidbit factoids that you may or may not be aware; unfortunately our happy little *'Haberdasher to the Hollywood Stars'* and resident Jewish mobster Mickey Cohen is about to be convicted of tax evasion for the second time, and this trip to the slam will incarcerate him on *Alcatraz Island* in the Frisco Bay where he'll probably get himself piped into a coma; And not in a good way.

Aryan Kraut-head Commando Sven Golly got internally investigated, and not in a good way, and now serves as sheriff in the rough-and-tumbleweed border town of Bizby Arizona, where he and his indigenous Mayor girlfriend Sara Phalin 'can see Mexico from their house'.

As you may have heard, former beat cops Mullins and Mc Burney have accepted the positions offered by the Avalon town council to replace the retiring Inspector Lugar who has become the new assistant manager of the *Avalon Casino*.

The Double-mint twins, Precarious and Precocious have embarked upon their national whirl-wind tour to promote their advertising campaign and having the time of their lives. Here's the part you didn't know about; the night before the twins embarked on their tour we celebrated with dinner and drinks at the world famous iconic Hollywood eatery the *'Brown Derby'*, where they met none-other than funny-man entertainer Jimmy Durante seated in a booth under the two caricature portraits of him; one portrait for his face and one for is nose. The twins had a great time viewing the celebrity portraits and squealed with delight when the real-life inspirations entered the intimate derby-shaped restaurant.

Not so coincidently, Mr. Stanton and Mr. Ervine rendezvoused with the twins and me at the *'Derby'* and presented *'Travis Dugan Private Investigations'* with a couple of extremely generous donations toward our retirement fund. As a matter of fact there are plenty of funds for you to purchase that Mediterranean-inspired condo in Hamilton Cove once the Commodore completes the project.

I saved the best for last Precious, hold onto your hat; I think I've enjoyed about as much of this private investigator bullshit as I can stand. *The thrill has gone. The thrill has gone away from me.* After all, as you have previously pointed out, we aren't getting any younger and I don't have the stamina I once had. I also don't have the enthusiasm for the chase or the thrill of the kill. I really don't give a shit about anybody else's problems that they probably got themselves into in the first place. Besides, the bad guys already blew the office of *Travis Dugan Private Investigations* into oblivion and yesterday's news. Let the young-bloods run '*Blackwater Personal Security*' while we back-off, collect our percentage each month, and enjoy our golden years lying in the noonday sun.

And finally Precious, I'm going to ask lovely Rita to be my bride. Rita loves me unconditionally in spite of my faults or my sordid past. She brightens each day and is totally committed to our relationship together. I don't have to worry that she will ever hurt me. I can allow her within my fortress protecting my inter-most feelings and thoughts. I can trust that she will not break my heart. Yes, I have fallen in love. I have arrived at a place in my life where I feel completely comfortable and totally content. After all the impossible adventures, miles and miles of terrifying darkness and lonely despair, I have finally arrived in *Shangri-La, Nirvana and Paradise* all rolled into one, and with a gorgeous island princess who loves me free of jealousy, judgment or rejection ....You know Precious, I believe this could be the beginning of a beautiful relationship.

Aloha Baby.

"A Nostalgic, Noir' Romp through another ***TRAVIS DUGAN*** Mystery Thriller.

Destined for ***THE NEW YORK TIMES BEST SELLER LIST"***

Aynsley Quagmyre's "Readers Weekly"

From the Author of

THE BIG CASINO

and

REVENGE OF THE GOLDEN DRAGON

MURDER

at the

GOLDEN BEAR

Nightclub